D1118842

THE WARSAW DOCUMENT

ADAM HALL

THE WARSAW
DOCUMENT

DOUBLEDAY & COMPANY, INC.
GARDEN CITY, NEW YORK
1971

Library of Congress Catalog Card Number 77–139027
Copyright © 1971 by Elleston Trevor
All Rights Reserved
Printed in the United States of America
First Edition

CONTENTS

THE WARSAW DOCUMENT

1
LONDON

There would be no warning, I knew that.

In the total darkness I thought I could see things: the glint of his eyes, his bared teeth; and in the silence I thought I could hear his breath and the soft tentative padding of his feet as he looked for me; but all I saw and heard was in my imagination and I knew that soon my nerves were going to start playing up because of the worry: the worry that there'd be no warning when he came at me. He'd come the instant he found me.

Breathing was difficult because this place wasn't very big and we were so close that one drawn breath would be a giveaway; also it would have to be expelled before the next inhalation and I was afraid of being caught with empty lungs. I breathed tidally, right near the top, part of my conscious mind registering the smell of hemp and coconut.

It was worse than I'd thought, the waiting. There was nothing to go on: no means of orientation. He was only a man but he was invisible and inaudible and these were the attributes of a phantom and my scalp was raised. It needn't be true that he was where I thought he was: somewhere in front of me where my hands could get at him. Even in the dark there's comfort if the enemy can be faced: the real dread is of being taken from behind.

That was where he came for me: from behind. We hadn't touched; we had simply come so close that the instincts were triggered and the nerves galvanised and I was already in a throat lock with my knees buckling to a flat kick before I could hook at him, but my hands were free and I caught him and reached his thumb as we pitched down, breaking the hold while he used his foot again and missed and tried again and connected a fraction too late, his breath grunting as I forced him over. We fought close, neither wanting to lose the other in the unnerving dark. My shoulder hit the wall and I used the chance, going down low and recoiling against him, but the momentum wasn't enough, and he deadened the spring and forced me into a spine-bending *yoshida* that paralysed the arms. Then some fool came in and switched the light on.

Kimura helped me up with his usual courtesy and we touched palms and looked for our towels.

"It was good," he said.

"No," I said, "it wasn't." I wiped at the sweat, trying not to worry. I shouldn't have let him throw that deadly yoshida so soon, when he was fresh enough to follow it through; it had left the plexus exposed and he could have killed me within the next five seconds if he'd wanted to, a straight chop to the heart from under the ribs. It was all right here in the gym but it wouldn't be all right one day in some back street in Buenos Aires or wherever the hell I'd be when it happened again. "Can't you," I asked Stevens, "shut that bloody door?"

"Interrupted, did I?" He turned and shut the fog out, pushing his face into his handkerchief again. He'd come up to Norfolk for a routine dose of what they call Refresher 5 and then caught a streaming cold before they could start work on him. He was better off anyway because Refresher 5 is the course where the instructors break every bone in your body unless you can giggle them out of it.

"It was only the wall," Kimura told me. He knew I was worried. "I heard you go into it, and assumed you would make use of it, you see." He nodded his reassuring smiles at me, towelling the sweat off his small ivory-coloured body; under the wire-meshed lamps the sword scar looked deep mauve, running from one shoulder to the top of his shorts like a zip fastener. "You can not execute such a move, you see, without ending up with the abdomen unprotected. But of course you would have extricated yourself from my yoshida if this gentleman had not appeared."

I didn't think so.

"London, old boy." Stevens stood like a forlorn penguin, mopping at his beak.

Kim was pretending to kick one of the coconut mats straight where we'd been milling about. I said: "Don't worry, you made your point. The next time I get near a wall I shan't leave myself open to a yoshida. That do you?"

He nodded quickly, pleased. He took his job seriously and if a report came in that somebody'd been found with his neck at the wrong angle in the chain locker of a Reykjavik-bound banana boat he liked to feel it wasn't his fault. He went across to the showers, walking like an independently sprung tiger.

"What?" I asked Stevens. A bruise was developing on the upper right arm and I'd taken care Kimura shouldn't notice it because his chief conceit is that whatever he does to you he never leaves a mark; the other instructors aren't so proud and we always look like a bunch of bitten-eared alley cats while we're at Norfolk.

"London wants you." He was putting in his time as a duty runner till he was fit enough for beating up.

"On the phone?"

"In the flesh."

"Stuff London."

"Message understood." He drifted dismally away in a nimbus of Vick's Vapour Rub.

In the showers, Kim said: "Also one must narrow the eyes, you see, in the dark, and not stare about like that. With the eyes half-closed, vision is only a little reduced, but the shine on the eyeballs is much less easy to discern." It was civil of him not to point out that this was how he'd come up from behind me: he knew I was worried about that as well.

"All right, I'll remember."

"Ah-ha-ha," he sang through the steam in approval, much as Mum does when Wee Willie hits the potty first time. I was getting fed-up. He'd pulled off a first at the Tokyo Games and we weren't expected to reach that standard but we weren't expected to be shown up as amateurs either. I span the taps to full cold and he noted the change in the noise. "Also one must finish off with warm water, you see, following a training bout, since the muscles require to relax."

In London the fog was worse and even the pigeons were feeling the cold, huddling in rows along the window sills. Below me a long stain of light crept through Whitehall, the traffic nose-to-tail.

"I'll take you in now."

So it wasn't Parkis. He always keeps you hanging about to stop you getting ideas above your station. You never know who you're going to see when you're "wanted in London" because the Bureau doesn't officially exist and if there's ever been a door here marked *Information* it's been wall-papered over.

She led me upstairs, her snagged heels ricketing on the rubber strips that were peeling away from the treads. On a landing I saw Fyson going into *Reports*, still looking a bit nervy about the eyes: someone's bright little op. had come unstuck in Israel, so we'd all heard, and they were being flown home, those who were left.

This wasn't the room with the Lowry and the smell of polish. It was originally a dormer, I suppose, right under the mansard roof, the kind of place where the little frilled domestics had hacked at their lung spots through the winters of the nineteenth century. There hadn't been much progress; Egerton was rubbing chilblain ointment into his raw blue hands when I came in, and looked up rather guiltily as if discovered in the enactment of a mystic rite.

"Ah yes," he said vaguely, and fitted the lid back onto the tin.

An opaque grey panel showed where the window was, its grime and the fog outside filtering whatever daylight was still in the sky; a single bulb in a white porcelain shade dangled from a flex looped in paper clips to keep it out of the way: we might have been at the bottom of a mine shaft instead of the top of a building.

Egerton gestured to the only chair for visitors, an incongruous Louis Quinze with little yellow puffs of stuffing exposed to the wan light. I'd only seen Egerton twice before, on any kind of real business, and each time it had been in this room. He was a thin and tired-looking man, his eyes weathered by too many winters of inclement thought, his mouth still slightly twisted from the shock of his first disillusionment, whenever that had come; it was said his wife had committed suicide during one of their seaside holidays at Frinton, and that the smell of a certain suntan oil made him physically sick; but then he might have always looked like this, a vessel of despair, and that might be why she'd done it. And anyway facts are short at the Bureau, where nobody's meant to exist, so rumours are a prime necessity of the resident staff.

"How was Norfolk?"

"Foggy."

He smiled thinly. "We always consider we have a monopoly, here. Sorry to have fetched you away." His voice was beautifully modulated, an actor's voice. "I expect you've heard what happened in Gaza."

"A wheel came off."

Of course he hadn't got a hope. They were still flying them in, what was left of them, and if they meant to send a second wave to mop up the mess they could count me out. I was strictly a shadow executive under contract for solo missions and these paramilitary stunts weren't in my field.

"Nobody's fault," he shrugged. "Policy is changing from day to day. There was time, once, to plan things properly, but now there seems so much need for hurry, so instead of picking quietly at the lock we just hurl a brick at the window and grab at whatever happens to be in reach."

He was talking about intelligence. Even when Parkis or Mildmay threw in a scratch hit-and-run unit with clearance on explosives, it was still purely an intelligence operation or the Bureau wouldn't be handling it at all.

Egerton said with a note of concession: "Of course that kind of exercise isn't in your area."

"No."

"But policy affects everyone, really."

It didn't sound very good and I began digging my heels in, but the trouble was that Egerton was already softening up the ground I was digging them into. He was Control, not Bureau: a mission director, not admin. But if he'd fetched me down from Norfolk to give me a job, it looked as if I'd have been better off up there as a daily breakfast for Kimura.

You can always refuse a mission: it's in the contract. But you can't ever judge the odds because when they send you in it's in the dark. We don't mind that. We know we'd be scared stiff by the size and scope of a big operation if we could see the overall picture, and all we want is our own little box of matches to play with in the corner while the boys at the top work out how to stop the whole house going up if we make a mistake. But it means you can't assess a mission at the outset, so you don't know whether you're accepting a job that's going to blow up in your hands because of someone else's incompetence or refusing one that could turn out a real classic. Last year Dewhurst nearly refused a dull routine investigation of a hijack attempt on

board a Pakistan International Airlines Boeing 727 and
finished up three weeks later jumping the Roumanian frontier at Orsova with short-range shots of the heavy-water
installations north of Piatra that everyone had thought were
a sugar-beet processing complex. You can never tell. All I
could tell at the moment was that if Egerton had a mission
for me he was quite certain I wouldn't like it and all
I could hope was that he'd be wrong. Because I wanted one.

"It affects training," he said, "particularly." He meant
policy did. "People are being hustled into sensitive areas
without preliminary experience even in minor operations.
I'm not talking"—he looked at me quickly—"about this un-
fortunate debacle in Gaza."

"No." He was.

In his dead eyes I could see two red sparks, the reflections
of the little electric fire with its cracked insulators that was
perched on a pile of split-spined encyclopaedias near my
chair. "To a limited degree we can resist these dangerous
changes in policy—or at least avert some of their dangerous
results."

When the telephone rang he didn't look at it for a moment, as if deciding not to answer it. Then he picked up
the receiver, the ointment gleaming on his knuckles.

"Yes?" All I could hear was a name—Gilchrist—from the
speaker, but Egerton was saying sharply: "Couldn't they?"
He tilted his narrow head back as he listened, his eyes cast
down. "I'll go and talk to his wife. Don't let her get the news
from anyone else. Warn Matthews particularly; they were
close friends." He put the receiver down and said with
slight irritation: "They shouldn't get married; it's inconsiderate. Where was I?"

A small cracked 250-watt heater like this would never get the chill out of Egerton's room. I thought they must have been after something pretty serious to throw in a man like Gilchrist. I'd never liked him but he'd been first-class. So had Lovett, only last year in Hannover. I'd liked Lovett. We seemed to be getting a bit too cheap.

"Changes in policy," I said. "Averting dangerous results."

"Yes." He studied his shiny hands. "We've just taken on someone new."

"Long live the king," I said.

He looked at me sharply but there was no reproof in his tone. "He's not replacing Gilchrist. He's too young. And he's been given his first mission before he's had time to feel his way." Carefully he said: "That is my opinion. Unfortunately it's for me to send him out. The exercise isn't inherently dangerous but you know better than I do how easily things can turn awkward."

No, I thought, I won't bloody well play.

He was hunched over his clasped hands, as if without any heat of their own they could warm each other. "His name is Merrick. Good background in the Foreign Office; he was in Prague as an assistant attaché during August 1968 and was deeply affected by events there; he is now with a different embassy and is at present here in London on sick leave, following a slight accident. His father is Sir Walford Merrick, an equerry of the Queen's Household. Would you like some tea?"

"Not really." I got out of the chair, not wanting to sit there while he tried to truss me up. In the raw chill here I felt suffocated by the deadness of his eyes and the beautifully modulated innuendoes and the way he'd thrown the epitaph across the wreath: *It's inconsiderate.* "Look," I asked him, "have you got a mission for me?"

"No."

"Well it's time somebody had. I've been out for nearly three months and I'm going to seed."

"That's why I thought you might like a little trip abroad."

"Where to?" Durban would be all right, or Mexico. Anywhere out of this freezing hole.

"Warsaw."

"Christ, in winter?"

"It would be convenient, I know, if we could choose—"

"It's all I'd get out of it, a bit of sunshine. Send him far enough south and I'll do what you want. I'll go with him and hold his hand."

He didn't say anything. Maybe I was raising my voice too much; you don't do that till you start feeling you're on a loser. Among all the stuff on his desk I could see my dossier and among all the things it said in there was the fact that I spoke a bit of Polish. Not many of us did; it was like stuffing your tongue in a jar of used razor blades.

I quietened down, so that he'd know I wasn't worried, that I wasn't going. "You'll have to find someone else."

He waited five seconds and then said:

"You needn't decide immediately. Not for a few hours yet."

"*Hours?* You called me in a bit late, didn't you?"

"Everyone else has refused."

I looked away.

It wasn't in my dossier. Or if it was, it was written between the lines. That was where he'd been busily reading. It said if you want to find Quiller look for the man who stands facing the wrong way in the bus queue just to show the world he can do without a bus, look for the man who wants the window open when everyone else wants it shut. The awkward bastard who's going to kill himself one day trying to prove he's bulletproof. And if you want him for a job that he'd normally throw back in your face, tell him that everyone else has refused it.

I was looking at the little electric fire. The coiled filament had broken in two or three places and someone—probably Egerton—had twisted the ends together; the splices were glowing brightly, absorbing so much of the current that the rest of the filament wasn't more than cherry red. I knew he wouldn't speak next.

"What sort of mission have you given him?"

"Nothing complicated." The phone rang again and he said 'yes' to someone and hung up. "I haven't met him yet, myself. He was rather wished onto me." He sat back now, his donnish head tilted to watch me. The chilblains made red cobbles on the blue skin of his hands and I thought vaguely that as soon as I'd gone he would get up and hold them near the fire again. "That's why I'm really most grateful to you for helping me out. Really most grateful."

"You haven't met him yet?"

"Not yet. I want you to go and see him first and size him up. He's been fully screened, of course, and given general briefing on security. Then I'll arrange for the three of us to talk before you fly out."

"Where do I find him?"

"Personnel Section, Foreign Office." He got up as I took

my gloves off the arm of the chair. "You don't want this little chore, I know, but don't blame Merrick. You're a veteran and he's only a raw recruit. Don't break the poor little devil up."

2

MERRICK

I filled in the green card.

P. K. Longstreet. To see G. R. Merrick. By appointment.

"Thank you, Mr. Longstreet."

The hall had the dusty acoustics of a cathedral. The security doorkeeper at the desk by the stairs watched me, nibbling on a fingernail.

"Mr. Merrick, please." The two other girls stared disinterestedly at the doors. "Will you try and find him? He's got a visitor."

I went to the doors and came back.

"I'm sorry to keep you waiting, but he doesn't seem to be in. Are you sure there was—"

"He's in. I'll go on up."

"I'm afraid you can't go up without an escort. We have to—"

The doorkeeper was out of his desk as I reached the stairs and I showed him my pass. It took him a couple of seconds to register because this one wasn't seen too often: this was the one that could get you into the Houses of Parliament

with a barrel under your arm even if the green card said
G. Fawkes.

"That's all right, sir."

I went up the stairs and turned left. Merrick must have
been in the lav when she'd rung because he was back in
Personnel when I got there. *Twenty-four, medium height,
brown hair, blue eyes, heavy spectacle frames, recent scar
left hand.* "A slight accident," Egerton had told me. There
were a few other people in the room and Merrick's desk was
near the door. A girl in a lemon blouse looked in and said:

"Oh, *there* you are. Visitor for you in the hall."

He'd seen me and said: "Yes, he's here, thank you."

She gave me a pert blink. "Well *that* was quick."

Someone on a phone was saying: "If I were you I'd put
Mrs. Pymm onto it—she'll sort it out if anyone can."

"Where do we talk?" I asked Merrick.

"I'm not quite sure." He was standing behind the desk, his
long fingers shifting some papers to no purpose, his slightly
magnified eyes watching me nervously.

"Come on, then."

"Yes." He followed me out, catching his foot against something. "I think there's one of the undersecretaries at a conference this afternoon, so I suppose we could use his room."
Trying hard to please. "It's just along here."

I sensed him watching me obliquely so I said: "Worst
bloody winter since '47."

He worked it out as fast as he could and then took it
straight from the book. "In my paper it said since 1939."

"You mean '39."

"Oh. Yes." By the tone of his voice he was kicking himself.
It wasn't important, here and now; but as the years go by

you learn to worry less about the mistakes you've made and more about what would have happened if the circumstances had made them important. The code-introduction for fifth to twelfth was to throw in a random two-digit number and listen for one below and two above, the same thing in London, Rio or Hong Kong, wherever you were and whatever you were doing, it made the whole thing simple. He'd put in the circumspect "19" from sheer nerves.

He tapped on a door and there was no answer, so we went in. Very lush carpet and solicitor's-office furniture and a portrait of the Queen and a small photograph suitably half-concealed by a filing cabinet, an overexposed long shot with plenty of camera shake, girl on a horse. Egerton should have a room like this, but what would he do with it? Plug in a beat-up 250-watt heater and crouch over it with his miseries.

"How long have you been in Warsaw?"

"Six months." It was said quickly. He was going to get everything right from now on. He sat forward in the other chair, watching me very directly and breathing on his nerves. "I went out in—"

"How long's your tour?"

"A year."

"Where were you before?"

"In Prague. Then there was a home posting before I—"

"You were there during the Prague spring?"

"Yes."

"Isn't it unusual to get posted to another Moscow-controlled country the next time out?"

"I asked for the post."

"Why?"

"I was very affected by what happened in Prague. I liked the people there—I made a lot of friends." He took something out of his pocket. "It looks like happening all over again, this time in Warsaw." It was an atomiser and he pumped it into his mouth. "Excuse me," he said.

"So you want to be there, all over again."

"Well, yes, I—"

"No wonder you've got asthma."

He stopped pumping and put the thing away. "If the Poles can win their freedom I'd like to be there. It'd be something to remember, wouldn't it, a thing like that?"

"Were you born in England?"

"Yes. You can't enter the Diplomatic Service unless—"

"Englishmen don't think much about freedom."

"Well, no. But that's because they've got it, isn't it?"

I wondered what sort of freedom Merrick hadn't got. It was no good asking him: he wouldn't know; it'd be below the conscious level. But he'd tell me, if I listened. I said: "You've made friends there too?"

"In Warsaw?"

"Yes."

"A few. A few friends."

"They in the underground?"

"Well, I mean almost everyone's in the underground, people of that age. My age."

"Students?"

"Oh no. Well, a few. But they're mostly engineers or shop assistants, people like that. You have to work, you see, if you want to eat. Some of them have more than one job, doing night shifts as well, just to get enough money for food and clothes, especially in winter—"

"What's the general drift of things out there, Merrick?"

He leaned forward, his long hands chopping at the air. "There's been tension ever since the Prague spring—there was a lot of sympathy for the Czechs of course—and now the underground forces are becoming quite organised. This is known, and a few months ago the authorities started trying to soften up the workers by leniency all round—less checking of sickness reports at the factories, smaller fines for indiscipline, lighter sentences for stealing state property, that kind of thing." A shade triumphantly he said with a chop of his hands: "Well, it didn't work."

"What's the aim of these candlelight crusaders you've been running with? Wreck the talks?"

He drew back into his chair. "They're not just a lot of irresponsible students. Their aim is to bring Russia to the brink. That's quite a—a serious intention, don't you think?"

"Could be serious, yes. For them. The other side of any brink is a long drop and if Russia goes down she'll take Poland with her, don't they know that?"

"Their aim," he said slowly, reading from the dog-eared manifesto they'd been waving at him in the cellars out there, "is to overthrow the present régime and set up a truly national government in time for the East-West talks to take place in a free Poland."

"They're cutting it fine." The West German delegates were due in Warsaw on the twenty-third. Today was the sixth.

"I'd put it a different way. They're completing their preparations."

"You said it was 'known.' So what chance have they got?"

On the defensive again he said quickly—"It's one thing for the authorities to know of widespread dissension, and another thing to stop it exploding in their face. They've withdrawn the lenient measures designed to keep people calm while the talks are on—they're trying the other tack now. Stronger discipline, heavy sentences, suppressive control of private life." In the clear eyes behind the glasses burned the zeal of the convert. "And that won't work either."

I got up and looked at the Queen's rather Mona Lisa smile as a change from looking at Merrick's face shining with its secondhand ideals. Correction: they weren't secondhand, no. They were superimposed on someone else's. If the Poles ever got free, something was going to get free inside Merrick.

"If it *doesn't* work," I told him over my shoulder, "then Moscow will find something that will. Didn't you say you were in Prague, for God's sake?"

"This is different." I heard him get up and start wandering about. "There are the talks, this time. Moscow wants them to succeed. I expect you've read—"

"It doesn't matter what I've read."

I could hear him pumping the damned thing again. Then he swallowed and said: "Well, that's why there's a brink. The action's been planned for three days before the opening of the talks, and if Moscow orders tanks into the city there won't be any talks. Russia's been trying to make the world forget Prague ever since it happened, and she'll remind us in a big way if she does it again; but if she *doesn't* resort to armed force this time, it'll mean a new government, overnight. Whichever way she moves, she'll lose."

When I turned away from the portrait, he was staring at me so I told him what he wanted to hear. "Hurrah. Poland is saved."

"Well, they've got to do *something*, haven't—"

"Christ, they're not expecting a wave of arrests are they by any chance? How many brave little soldiers of freedom d'you think there'll be left to start this 'action' of theirs? A week before the talks half the population of Warsaw's going to be in a strict-régime camp in the Urals, don't they realise? What's it called, this 'action,' got a name?"

Numbly he said: "Just 'the action.' *Czyn.*"

His long scrubbed schoolboy's hands hung by his sides, sticking from his sleeves as if he'd not finished growing out of his suit; but the defiance was still there behind the shine on his glasses and I knew that whatever I said it wouldn't knock the bright god Czyn off his pedestal.

"How did you get into this game, Merrick?"

"I'm not really in it. They're just friends I've made—"

"I don't mean their game. Ours."

I was watching him and he wasn't bad: they couldn't have had time in a crash-course to train him to this pitch of instant-reaction concealment and 90 per cent of it must have been in his makeup. Perhaps this was one of the things that had appealed to whoever had wished this boy onto Egerton. There'd been the slightest flicker across the eyes, gone now, and it was only experience that had let me sense that my question had opened a wound. I went on watching.

"I'm not sure," he said. The tone was all right too, almost steady. But this was why Egerton had told me not to 'break the poor little devil up.' Because it was easy and you could do it without even trying. "I suppose it's a chance for me to help them, in secret." Then he was saying quickly as the thought surfaced from below the conscious level—"Even my father doesn't know."

This was the freedom that Merrick hadn't got.

I said: "Of course not."

"But you don't expect to have—"

"Yes," I said, "you do."

He nodded. "Then that's all right."

I turned away. "What are your orders for this trip?"

"Don't you know?"

"It doesn't matter what I know."

"I'm to find out everything I can about Czyn and pass it to London. Surely you're meant to be helping me, aren't you?" He sounded uneasy.

"How much training did they give you?"

"Two weeks, if you include—"

"All right."

I turned and looked through the window at the trees in the park. Their black lacework of branches between the fog-yellowed lamps half-masked the pale reflected face that stared at me and waited. Two weeks. *There was time, once, to plan things properly.* It's no go, Egerton, you can't do it, you can't send this kid out there in the dark without even a candle, or if you want to do it then I won't bloody well help you.

"I suppose," he said as cheerfully as he could, "that doesn't sound very long. But I took it all in, and they told me I'd done rather well." His lips moved on the glass. His voice came from the trees out there, the dark trees. "I won't let you down."

Above the haze of the skyline there were vast clouds gathered, coming in from the north. Some people said it could snow tonight.

"There are a few things," I said, "they won't have told you." I didn't turn round. His eyes had shifted from me to my reflection. "They probably told you that just as a war is an extension of politics, espionage is an extension of diplomacy. The idea is to find out the things you can't find out by asking someone at a conference table: the things nobody will ever tell you, the things everybody badly needs to know. It's a means of keeping the peace, like the bomb is. No one can chuck the bomb without getting it back on his head, and no one can start a conventional war because the enemy's already within his gates, ferreting around and exposing all his plans before he can put them into action. It doesn't always work, the pressure gets too high now and then, but it works more often than people ever know. The balance has got to be kept between one half of the world and the other, East and West, so that the whole thing doesn't blow up. That's what we're for. We're the angels of peace, see how we shine. That what they told you?"

He watched me from the dark.

I said: "It doesn't matter. What they didn't tell you is that once you're in this game you're on your own. You don't do what you do for the sake of your country or for peace, though you can kid yourself. You do it to scratch an itch, that's all. I'm not talking about the ones who do it for the money—they're just whores. Most of us do it because we don't get a kick out of watching the telly and pushing a pen and washing the Mini on Sunday mornings; we want to get outside of all that, be on our own so we can work off our scabby neuroses without getting arrested for it. We want to scratch that itch till it bleeds."

As I turned away from the window his face opened in surprise. He looked more vulnerable at this moment than I'd ever seen a man, perhaps because in my trade the men I meet have long since grown a shell, the years and the deceits and the betrayals adding to it layer by layer until they want to get out and know they can't, because it's themselves they've been deceiving and betraying over all those years; the shell grows from the inside outwards, like fingernails.

"The thing is, Merrick, I don't think you're the type. You make friends too easily; you like people too much; you don't want to cross the line and live your life outside society because society's made of people and you'd have to shut yourself away, cut yourself off. Values are different out there; let a man show friendship for you and you've got to deny him, mistrust him, suspect him, and nine times out of ten you'll be wrong, but it's the tenth time that'll save you from a dirty death in a cheap hotel because you'd opened the door to a man you thought was a friend. Out there you'll be alone and you'll have no one you can trust, not even the people who are running you, not even me, because if you make the wrong kind of mistake at the wrong time in the wrong place and look like fouling up the mission and exposing the network then they'll throw you to the dogs. And so will I."

His hand had moved twice to his pocket while I'd been talking, and twice had stopped; but his breathing was painful now and he swung away and jerked the thing out and squeezed it, his back to me.

It was almost silent, the improved model designed exclusively for people of discretion who prefer not to embarrass their friends.

"Excuse me," he said.

On my way out I told him: "Think it well over. There's just enough time. We've got a rendezvous in the morning, eight o'clock at Clive Steps. I hope you won't turn up."

3
WARSAW

They looked like this when there'd been a military *coup
d'état* and they'd been hustled out of the cells and stood
against a wall, the only concession a handkerchief across
their eyes if they wanted one. This was how I remembered
him on Clive Steps, standing perfectly still and perfectly
straight in his neat dark coat, the first light seeping from a
leaky sky and striking across his glasses.

How long had he been here? His face was white with
cold, with nerves. Long enough to make sure I didn't turn
up a minute early and go away again in the hope of getting
rid of him by saying look, first he bungled the code-intro
and then he missed the rendezvous so I'm not taking him
out there, he's inefficient.

"Well, it's your funeral," I said.

We didn't talk much along the Mall except when I asked
him what his Polish was like.

"I took the advanced exams before I was posted there."

I suppose he wanted me to throw him a biscuit for that.
We walked quickly because of the cold and I took him

into Piccadilly to use up some of the time. The mist clung to our coats. Just after Park Lane a bus went by, pulling away from the kerb, and I nipped onto it, giving him room to follow.

"Are we late?"

"Not really."

The conductor was still on the upper deck when we got off, and I took him north and went left along Curzon Street, crossing into the Park. I heard the taxi slowing from behind us before we'd reached Marble Arch; the door came open and I got in first so that he'd have to use the tip-up seat and face the rear, which was what Egerton had wanted.

"You realise," he said to Merrick in slow modulated tones, "that you are first and foremost a second secretary at the Embassy, just as you were before. This is very important." He had dark glasses on, which was why he wanted Merrick to face him the whole time. "We've no concessions on the part of the Embassy enabling you to behave as anyone other than a member of Her Majesty's foreign service, careful in conduct and unimpeachable in character. Let me put it this way: we would rather go short of the information you'll be seeking than risk upsetting the Ambassador by exposing yourself to criticism on his part or to suspicion on the part of the local authorities."

The taxi was keeping in the slow lane, rounding towards Lancaster Gate. Egerton's hands were folded on his lap, the ointment leaving dark patches on his gloves, and Merrick watched him steadily, a little disturbed at not being able to see his eyes.

"You should also bear it well in mind that there must be no exchange of confidence between yourself and the people you'll be dealing with. Confidence will be entirely on their side. Nor must you lead them to feel that the United Kingdom is in any way prepared to assist them in whatever projects they have in mind, morally, physically, officially or unofficially. You must not even let them infer that such is the case, from anything you say; and if you think that despite your caution they have so inferred, then you must negate it." He studied Merrick in silence for a bit. "Is that perfectly understood?"

"Yes, sir."

We went down towards the Serpentine and got snarled up twice in a pack of traffic while I listened to Egerton briefing him: paramount importance of security, limited and circumspect use of protected communications, attitude if apprehended, so forth.

"Their methods of interrogation, as you know, are less charitable than in the West. You must therefore avoid any risk of their taking you into custody, as far as is possible. You will have Mr. Longstreet in support, of course, but don't allow your benefit of his greater experience to minimise, in your mind, the very real hazards you'll be exposed to."

Merrick was quite good, sitting to attention on the tip-up and never looking away from the dark glasses even when the taxi gave a lurch. He'd heard all this from the instructors and Egerton knew that, but he wanted to tell the boy himself, frighten him with the soft-gloved phrases that would bring his imagination into play instead of blunting it with overexplicitness. The slightly magnified blue eyes held steady as he listened.

Northwards from Hyde Park Corner we found a clear

run and got up speed for fifty yards before a double-decker blocked us off again. *Baronet—with the Tip that Filters Everything but the Flavour.*

"No aftereffects?" Egerton was asking.

"No, sir."

I spoke for the first time. "What was it, exactly?"

Merrick looked at me and then quickly away. "I slipped on the snow, and a tram nearly got me."

"Warsaw."

"Yes."

"You weren't," I said, "pushed or anything?"

"Oh no. I slipped."

Egerton didn't turn his head. "Why did you ask him that?"

"I don't know how deep he's got into things out there. He could have found out a bit too much."

Merrick said prissily: "Those people are my friends."

"Don't trust them. Don't walk too near the kerb. And the next time you keep a rendezvous with me make sure you're clean, is that a lot to ask?"

Gratuitous of course, telling him in front of his director, but I was suddenly fed-up with his harping on people being his friends. One fine day he'd trust a friend too many and next time they'd make sure his head went right under the wheel.

Egerton asked: "When did this happen?"

"This morning. We had to jump on a bus."

Merrick was leaning forward. "You mean we were being followed?"

"Just watch it, in Warsaw."

Egerton said: "You're quite certain, Longstreet?"

"Am I what?" He folded his gloved hands, accepting the

rebuke. I said, "The F.O.'s lousy with tags, always has been, they hang about like tarts."

"Yes. Never mind, Merrick, you're only just out of training, after all."

The bus in front got moving again and at Marble Arch we dropped him off, Egerton just saying he'd be kept informed. The poor little tick started looking behind him as soon as he'd got out.

"You mustn't expect too much, at this stage."

"I don't expect anything. Now that you've seen him d'you still want me to take him out there?"

"They didn't have time to give him more than a token training, as I'm sure you—"

"It's not only that. He's the worst agent material I've ever set eyes on: idealistic, unstable and a bag of nerves. I suppose you know he's got asthma, do you?"

"It's in his report," he said rather tartly. "But there's no pollen out there in the winter months."

"There's none in this clammy hole; the origin's nervous, anyone can see that." We were into the faster lane now and getting a move on; he'd told the driver to make for the Cenotaph. "How much does he know about the Bureau?"

"Nothing, of course. He's never been there; he was trained by Special Branch instructors, not by us. He's seen me only this once and without any chance of recognition, as you note. All he knows about you—apart from anything you've told him—are your features and your cover-name. I've no intention of saddling you with a potential risk, Quiller."

"Accident, was it?"

He took off his smoked glasses and shifted into the corner, facing me obliquely. "You accepted this little chore," he said patiently, "and I'm most grateful. It's only for a few days and you're not going into a sensitive area, so—"

"Apart from an imminent revolution, or is that just a romantic fancy of his?"

He looked past me through the window. "I doubt if there'll be a revolution; we don't think Moscow will let it get that far." By "we" he meant the Bureau's pet department: the political analysts. Meeting my eyes again he got a measure of coy reassurance into his tone: "But the situation out there could well become interesting, and while it's not really our cup of tea we thought we might just give it a stir to see if it's sugared."

Merrick's clearance didn't amount to more than an air ticket, which he got from the Foreign Office anyway. A second secretary was resuming his post at the British Embassy in Warsaw following sick leave and that was all; he didn't need a cover because he was already established and in place.

The Bureau doesn't normally use hired labour, but it was clear enough that he was going out on a special-situation mission and if he survived it I didn't expect to see him again. Egerton hadn't told me this and I hadn't asked. Merrick's long-term future was one part of the overall background picture that I wasn't going to be shown; my job was to check and confirm the information he'd be sending in to London and try to keep him out of trouble while he was getting it. The one thing I'd have liked to know was the extent of his value to the Bureau. At first glance it didn't look too high: he spoke a bit of Polish and had established organisational cover and unofficial access to the underground cell of an

East-bloc republic simmering with dissension. But someone in the Bureau had recruited him and appointed Egerton to direct him despite the fact that they knew he'd need looking after from the minute he left the U.K. According to the rules it shouldn't have worried me but the rules don't mean a thing.

"That one do you?"

I looked at it. Third series, fifth-digit duplications with recurring blanks, normal contractions and all numerals reversed. The alert-key was general, not integrated: you just put a contraction in full.

"Can they recode this for radio?" It looked as if I'd be sending my stuff through the Embassy, diplomatic telegram.

"We've made sure," he said.

"Oh really?"

Codes and Cyphers don't normally go into little points like that; they just select one that nobody's using and try it on for size. This was Egerton, steering me through clearance as smoothly as if he were at my elbow. The same thing had happened in Firearms; they know I never use anything but they usually try a bit of persuasion so they can feel they're still in business, but today they'd just said nothing for you, that right? *Nil* under *Weapons Drawn*. Egerton again, taking care of me, hunched in front of the little fire up there in the other building with his every thought devoted to my welfare. I could have done without that. I didn't like being taken care of so smoothly by a man who'd done his best to pass this thing off as a 'little chore,' 'only for a few days,' 'not really our cup of tea.' Maybe it was just because he was most grateful, most grateful. I didn't think so.

Accounts. Travel. Field briefing. Credentials.

She opened the folder. "Is this all you need?"

I hadn't asked for deep cover and Egerton hadn't insisted because this wasn't a full-scale mission. It was only light stuff: passport with two-year-old border-guard frankings at Danzig and Krzeszow, visa background, C.P.S. membership card and a few letters carrying fairly recent dates; a nice touch was that although their subject matter was in obvious sequence, the latest one was headed January 2 of the previous year, a thing a lot of people do from force of habit.

"These real?" Credentials is mostly a forgers' den.

"The two top ones are," she said. "We had enough time."

To *M. Stasiak, 17 Chalubinskiego, Warsaw. December 20.*

Oh, you bastard, I thought, you bastard.

On Tuesday there was a LOT flight via East Berlin and I'd told them to book me on that. Egerton must have known but he didn't question it.

There wasn't anything about Jan Ludwiczak in the paper the stewardess gave me, but I didn't expect there would be— they always throw a blackout after the first run. It didn't matter because I'd seen the story in a copy of *Zycie Warsawy* I'd picked up on the off-chance at the shop near Cambridge Circus. Jan Ludwiczak, 21—there was no address— had been arrested for subversive acts against the Republic, chiefly the operation of a clandestine printing press with three other men and a woman—none of whom were named— for the publication and distribution of violently seditious material among the bourgeois elements of the universities. The arrest of Ludwiczak's confederates was said to be imminent.

I hadn't been looking for this particular story when I'd bought the copy of *Zycie Warsawy* but it was the kind of information I needed. As a by-product it told me quite a lot about the situation out there because in the paper the stewardess had given me there wasn't a hint of subversive acts or even mild unrest. This wasn't so much an example of typical Russian split-mindedness as a pointer to indecision on the part of the authorities: first they'd tried to 'soften up the workers by leniency'—according to Merrick—and then they'd gone onto 'the other tack,' and they obviously still weren't sure whether to clean up dissident factions by secret arrests or scream their misdeeds from the housetops as a deterrent. On a personal level Jan Ludwiczak was of course cooked and the arrest of his friends was indeed 'imminent'; under the glare the rubber truncheons would work through the routine and their names would come out one by one.

The sky was brilliant, and below us lay an ocean of sludge. After East Berlin I put my watch forward an hour and thought: *you bastard*. He'd known I wouldn't ask for deep cover because the pitch he'd decided to sell me on was the 'only for a few days' ploy. So he'd told Credentials to fix me up with these few letters ostensibly exchanged between me and the people in Warsaw, arranging to meet. That was all right. The meetings weren't important ones: a meal somewhere, a little business, the sort of thing I could cancel or postpone or leave in the blue if it suited my plans. The letters were typed and the ones from P. K. Longstreet were signed in a perfect imitation of my own handwriting so that nothing would look odd if some bright spark thought of checking with the signatures of my passport and visa.

That was all right too. But the first letter had gone off on December 20. So 'everyone else' hadn't refused. They'd never been asked. He hadn't roped me in at the last minute; he'd lined me up for this job nearly three weeks ago.

He wasn't a bastard for doing that. He was Control, not Bureau, and a director puts his ferret to work in the way he chooses, shows him the hole and shoves him down it and stands back and crosses his fingers. No, he was a bastard for knowing I'd pick up the date on that letter when I was going through clearance and was therefore committed, too late to change my mind without actually getting slung out.

"Will you please fasten your seat belt?"

If I must but I'd rather put it round Egerton's neck.

We started a long slow dip towards the sludge.

Query: Why had he wanted *me*? There were several who wouldn't have refused a short trip like this to keep out of Norfolk between missions or break up the dreary round of the girls who were always in bed with someone else when you needed them most, because once a job came up there wouldn't be time for anything except getting in and getting out alive. Waring was in London now and he'd have done it like a shot just to get into their good books after cocking up the Copenhagen lark, but they hadn't asked Waring. They'd wanted a particular *type* of agent to work with Merrick and the one they'd selected with great care was the one who'd proved time and again that he always worked best *alone*.

They weren't fools. It'd be dangerous to settle for that.

The windows went grey.

But I'd done it on their doorstep too. I'd keep to the bargain and look after their new recruit for them but I'd do it in my own way, working alone. Egerton would have known

I'd asked them for the Tuesday flight but he hadn't questioned it. Merrick was due out tomorrow, BEA direct.

The tension had gone out of the airframe and we'd lost weight. Plastic fittings creaked. The 134 was floating at a slant through the muck.

Query: Is it even worse than you think? Have they palmed you off with the worst job of all? *That* one?

I thought about it again because if I didn't I wouldn't sleep tonight. The kid had said no, they hadn't told him to deliver anything to anyone. He'd seemed surprised when I'd asked that. Two weeks in training, how would he know? But I'd believed him and it should have consoled me; it'd be all right so long as they hadn't given him any kind of document to carry, to deliver. But it wasn't easy to get rid of the chill. Because this whole thing made a pattern and it was the only one that could accommodate all the facts. They don't do it often and no one talks about it afterwards. Correction: Heppinstall talked about it, once, to me. It's not that they're squeamish—you can't fight a full-sized cold war without someone sometimes getting pushed off his perch— it's just that there's not often the need to do it because the other ways round are more efficient. But now and then it's the only setup that'll fill the bill and that's when they sign up a new recruit and make a pretence of training him and give him the bait. The bait's not for him—he's already hooked— it's for the opposition, usually a file or a brief breakdown on a spurious operation, some form of written intelligence either encyphered or straight and specifically designed to fox the opposition and send them at a tangent while the real party goes in. In military terms it's the feint attack and the principle's the same.

The mechanics vary. The technique doesn't. You send your man in and he delivers the goods by letter drop and he's caught doing it because he's meant to be caught doing it, that's what he's for. After that it's just dull routine; he's beaten up till he breaks and tells them all he knows but all he knows isn't much, oh, a few titbits here and there to give them something to chew on, the odd bit of info they've had on their books since God told Moses to spy out the land of Canaan, it looks quite good, they know he's telling the truth. And while they're busy dashing off in all directions on the strength of the stuff they caught him with, the real operative goes in. Sometimes he's not told what the setup is; he's simply sent as far as the edge of the area and ordered to wait for a signal. He might not know what the mission is or even that he's got one, then they throw him the works and tell him the field's clear: get in there.

Or sometimes they send him out with the new recruit and ask him to hold his hand.

"I've done mine," I said and she smiled and passed on. Customs Declaration Form to be completed by passengers prior to landing. I hadn't actually done it myself, of course; it's delivered with the visa and the Bureau takes pride in relieving its valued servants of these annoying little details. It's the things it doesn't do for you that sometimes chills your nerves. The things you've got to do yourself.

Heppinstall had been drunk that night and I hustled him round to my place before he could break into Control and knock Loman for six. Loman was his director at the time. 'I didn't have a clue, ol' boy, not a single rotten stinkin' bloody clue . . . an' you know—you know what? There was nothing for me, in the end. No mission . . . nothing. It was

for someone else, you get it?' A white face and the tumbler
shaking in his fingers, his voice thinned with rage. 'Some
other bastard went in . . . got it all lined up, you see, an' all
—all I did was come on home like goo'—good little boy. An'
Christ, they shot that poor little squirt, know that, eh? Put
him—put him 'gainst a wall. Keep me 'way from Lo'—Loman,
will you? Oh, God, 'gainst a *wall.* . . .'

Normally they don't talk about it afterwards but Heppinstall had got deliberately drunk. Also he was unlucky because the U.K. had just sent Sharawi Hassan down for the
maximum stretch of fourteen years for the missile programme filch and the United Arab Republic was smarting a
bit and a decoy's no good as exchange material so they'd
shot him.

No Smoking.

The murk thinned off and I saw lights below and the
twisting course of the Vistula, which looked frozen over.
The runway beacons tilted across the glass as we got lined
up.

Was that the one they'd palmed off on me? *That* one?
Bounce.

4

SNOW

An Aeroflot Tupolev TU–104 had just come in from Moscow and the building was crowded. The people from the TU were waving their papers, eager to show how uplifted they were by complying with the regulations drawn up by their all-wise comrades to protect the rights of the workers. It always speeds up the formalities though, because there's no time wasted arguing: tell them to shit and they'll shit.

The young Pole at Immigration was very circumspect as if he was being observed by a proficiency inspector or someone like that.

"How long do you intend to stay in Poland?"

"About two weeks." I said it first in halting Polish and repeated it in German, the *lingua franca*, to show him I was happier with that. It was no good making out I couldn't speak Polish at all because of the letters from the dealers.

What is your business, so forth. I showed him the letters, taking them out of the envelope for him. The heavy man next to him didn't say anything.

"You have a special reason for meeting these people?"

"Yes, particularly for meeting Mösjö Hrynkiewicz. I'm hoping to buy the Lewinski Collection for an American." It was respectable thinking on the part of Credentials because the Poles need dollars like the Irish need a drink.

"What is that?"

I looked blank as if he should know. "It's the authenticated series with the 10-korony Mayer engravings of 1860 and the 1918 German Occupation inverted overprints. Look, here's the catalogue with—"

"It is not necessary." But he took the Croydon Philatelic Society membership card because I'd been letting it peep out from among the currency vouchers: they always seize on new colours because anything strange is suspect. While he was making a show of reading it, the heavy man beside him reached out and went through the same motions. He wasn't a Pole, this one; he had the flat bland face of the men you always see on the front page standing close to the Chairman of the Presidium when he's just flown in, and whenever they're actually looking into the camera it's because they think there might be some trinitrotoluene inside it instead of some Perutz Peromnia 27.

He raised his colourless eyes from the card and let them play on my face and I remembered a thousand frontiers and a thousand men with eyes like these and this was the danger: that my own show the indifference to scrutiny that will indicate our trade as clearly as the nails of a mechanic will tell of his. So I looked uneasy, as sometimes a tourist does when despite the comfort of his guidebook and Instamatic and Diners' Club card he senses how suddenly close he is to a world he'd rather not consider, where the iron force of alien authority is vested in a single man with eyes like these and where only the conformity of his papers can give him immunity against the nightmare fates that have over-taken other and less invulnerable voyagers, brought name-lessly to mind by images of dark-windowed saloons slowing along dawn streets, of barbed wire and a silhouetted guard.

I looked at the younger one, the Pole.

"May I have my letters back?"

He tucked them circumspectly into the envelope. The heavy man took the envelope and pulled them out again, comparing the signatures with the one on my passport. Look-ing at no one he said in Russian:

"Ask him why he flew via East Berlin."

"Why did you fly via East Berlin?"

"Because the flight was routed that way." Looking quickly around I lowered my tone, tapping the letters in the big square hand. "The Lewinski Collection has only just come onto the private market, and of course M. Hrynkiewicz would prefer to make a deal in dollars, so he told me to hurry and get in first—you can read what he says."

"Put them back in the envelope," he told the Pole and looked past me to the next in the queue.

Going through Customs I remembered the flash of anger in the young eyes of the Pole as he'd folded the letters for the second time. Merrick hadn't been fooling; there were no tanks in this city yet but it already had the brackish smell of occupation. There was a quietness here, voices and other sounds muffled as if by snow, and everyone—passengers, air-port staff and security officials—did their business with each other deftly, ready neither to give nor make trouble in case somewhere a spark were struck to send the whole lot up.

Waiting for clearance I had time to vet the people off the

TU–104 and picked out a minimum of six 'tourists' straight in from the Soviet State Security Service, getting their luggage chalked at the blink of an eye.

My bag came through, the leather panel at one end flapping from the ragged stitches. They won't bother looking for a hollow bottom when the top's obviously having a job to stay on.

"*To jest wszystko co mam,*" I told him. "*Nie mam nic do oclenia.*"

"*Jak to sie nazywa po polsku?*"

"Stanley Gibbons," I said with a shrug. You can't put that into Polish. He passed it but dropped the *Mail* smartly into the receptacle for seditious literature. I'd never thought Kirby much cop but the rest didn't seem that bad. There were three KGB men just inside the barrier but they didn't look at me when I went through: their eyes work at a distance while you're having your shirts picked over and they've seen all they want to see before you get anywhere near them.

Outside the building the cold hit like a wave and froze on the face. The queue for taxis had already built up, but one or two private cars were nosing in and I took a beat-up Syrena; the owner asked eighteen zlotys, three times the taxi fare and worth it because you didn't have to freeze to death in the queue, just part of the black-market service. He asked which hotel and I said I didn't want a hotel, I wanted a woman.

There was an open stove burning split wooden road blocks with a galvanised pipe running up through a blanked-off window pane. The room smelt of tar and sweat and Russian tobacco; a half-finished bowl of *chlodnik* had been pushed under the fringe of red velvet that hung from one of the shelves, the spoon still in it. Her hands began moving.

"Don't do that," I said. "I'm not staying."

Still young and with carbon-black ringlets above the sharp dark eyes, a leopardskin coat and knee boots, where was the whip, her forebears on the distaff side a-whoring for the Goths. "Come near the stove," she said with little white smiling teeth, "it will warm you."

"What's your name?" I switched to German because I wanted her to get it clear.

"Marie." A lot of them use names like that the world over, perhaps to bring into their dingy rooms a touch of the splendid plush and bronze and mirrored ceilings of *La Belle Époque*. In German: "Come near the stove."

She began again and I said again that I wasn't staying and the black eyes sparked; when you don't want the only thing they've got it hurts their pride. She'd said a hundred and fifty zlotys and I put three fifties on the bottom shelf and her head turned to watch, quick as a bird's. "Jan Ludwiczak," I told her, "got arrested a couple of days ago. I want to know his address and where the U.B. are holding him. Then you make as much again."

Who are you and what gives you the idea I'd know a thing like that, so forth. She added in the Warsaw vernacular and tones like a sabre being sharpened that the U.B. were the original illegitimate sons of putrefaction incarnate and that she had no dealings with them.

"You get the other hundred and fifty if you can find out by ten o'clock tomorrow morning."

Her pride stopped being hurt but she thought up a lot of objections in order to raise the price, trilling the low German r's and throwing out the genders, but I kept on at her because I'd come here knowing she'd have a few of the *Policia Ubespieczenia* among her clients; anywhere east of the Curtain the lower ranks of the secret police could get it for nothing or a girl wouldn't stay in business.

"Finish your stew."

She reached for the bowl and banged it on top of the stove. "It is not enough for so difficult a thing."

It was all she'd get—that bloody woman in Accounts was going to question this anyway when it went in as general expenses and even if I put *1 tart, unused* against *please specify*, she'd only put *unjustified* as soon as she'd come out of the vapours.

"Where do you pick up, Marie? What bar?"

"I tell you it is—"

"Oh come on, the *Komiwojażer?*" We'd passed it in the Syrena, the nearest corner from here. "I'll phone there to-morrow before ten and if you've got what I want I'll tell them to give you the envelope."

Sulkily she said: "I may be lucky this time. Are there other things you will want to know about?" She poked at the *chlodnik.*

"Possibly. But not if you don't get it right this time. Not if you bitch me."

It was their reaction that was interesting.

He'd got as far as the airport; perhaps he'd booked on a plane out and they know that or just suspected it or someone like Marie had sold him out while a U.B. man's trousers were still slung over the chair. Anyway they got him. A Scandi-navian Airlines flight had just come in but most of the peo-

ple in the main hall were Polish, friends or associates or
people with reservations on the SAS plane, and their reaction was interesting because they didn't just stand watching as most crowds do; there was a distinct movement
forward as if they wanted to help, then hesitation.

The Moskwicz hadn't got a heater, so I'd screwed Accounts for a Fiat 1300 because there'd be some surveillance
to do and that meant sitting around at anything down to
twenty-five below zero. I'd left it in the car-park and the
Wolga had come up very fast, two of them piling out as it
slewed in alongside the Departure doors just when I was
going through. He was ahead of me and they'd seen him
because he'd turned his face to look back, perhaps sensing
the danger or hearing the way the car had pulled up. Apparently he was recognizable to them because they seemed
perfectly sure and broke their run and walked in step towards him while he stood there with the dead fixed look of a
rabbit in the headlights.

Perhaps they'd hoped they could do it discreetly; he was a
man of some age with silver hair below the edges of his black
fur képi, an academic face with nothing desperate in it, only
despair; but at the last minute he tried to make a break, nothing sensational, just a kind of token jerk sideways as if he
didn't ever want it said of him that he hadn't resisted; it
worried them and they used more force than was needed,
swinging him round and hustling him back to the doors so
fast that he couldn't keep up and they had to half-lift him
as if they were moving a waxwork. It was then that I noticed
their reaction, the crowd's, the forward motion as if they
wanted to help, then the hesitation when they realised there
was nothing they could do.

The BEA flight was twenty minutes late and I read most of the news section of *Trybuna Ludu* which for double-think motives saw fit to quote some of the problems facing the fourth congress of the Polish Psychiatrists' Union, now convening in the capital: mental breakdowns up by 11 per cent, suicides up by 10, alcohol and tobacco consumption up by 20. On a different page, full coverage was given to the fall from grace of 'several hundred' local civil servants, party workers and journalists accused or suspected of 'anti-socialist leanings' incompatible with those in responsible positions. Additionally a further twenty-seven 'known Zionists' had applied for emigration, specifically to Israel; this report being innocent of any hint that most of them would follow the fifteen hundred who since 1968 had changed planes and turned up in Copenhagen.

No mention of Jan Ludwiczak. I hadn't even looked for it; the last faint ripple would have gone by now and the surface would be smooth.

Across the monochrome tarmac the Trident reversed its thrust and drew out a haze of kerosene.

I kept to my cover near the edge of the group. Others had joined it: they'd moved by casual heel-cooling paces from farther away where they hadn't seen anything clearly.

"What happened?"

"They arrested him."

"Why?"

"I don't know."

"Who was he?"

"I don't know."

They looked away from each other. Across at the tobacco kiosk the sales were going up. What would the Polish Psychiatrists' Union recommend as a solution to the problem? Chewing gum?

He began looking for me as soon as he was through the Customs and I turned away and gave him a few minutes and took the end doorway, watching him from a distance across the freezing forecourt, the grey winter light striking across his glasses, his shoulders hunched inside his coat, his young forlorn face reddening to the bite of the air. He looked for me everywhere. When he joined the group for the Orbis coach I went and sat in the Fiat, running the engine to work the heater.

I was fed-up. Did he think I'd book on a different plane so we shouldn't be seen together and then turn up to meet him when he got in? That was one reason. That was why Egerton hadn't had the nerve to question it; he knew it was routine security. Anyway I hadn't told him I'd meet him, I'd just said I'd get in touch, so what was he gawping around for?

The coach dropped him at the Orbis office in Ulica Krucza and I stayed in the Fiat, letting him get across Mokolowska so that I could take a long look down the narrowing perspective. That was another reason and so far he was clean. When he turned into Aleje Róz I drove past and parked at the far end, looking through the half-misted rear window to watch him go into the Embassy. He was still clean.

I started up and turned right into Wazdowskie and went round the square and came back and parked on the other side of Aleje Róz so that I could watch through the windscreen instead of the rear window. It was a short street and the Fiat was a bit close to the police observation post but they were there to survey people entering and leaving the Embassy and nobody else, and the afternoon dark was coming down so they wouldn't be able to see if there were anyone still in the car.

The thing was that I might just as well have taken the cheapest according to standing orders, the Moskwicz 408, because if I wanted any heat in the Fiat I'd have to keep starting up every half-hour and they'd hear that and wonder why I never got into gear and moved off. But even if it meant freezing to the wheel, I'd wait till he left the Chancery for the Residence. I'd give him till midnight, wherever he went; wherever he went, till midnight, I'd be there and he'd be safe because if those bastards in London had sent him out with a fistful of marked cards to pass to a contact or shove in a letter drop I'd be there before he was caught. It was what they wanted, wasn't it, hold his hand?

They'd done it to Heppinstall and they'd done it to others but they weren't going to do it to me.

Two hours before dawn there was the tail end of a moon lying hooked across the heights of the buildings that stood against the west. In the half-dark they seemed windowless but windows were there and maybe from some of them another attempt would be made, today or tomorrow, and maybe succeed, swelling the numbers of the 10 per cent. The cost of living in captivity was going up and the soul knew a cheap way out.

They brought me hot water and I thought about him while I washed. The worst of the worry was over and I'd slept for nearly five hours. If they'd been going to do it they would have arranged it for some time during his first few hours here; that would be logical, to send him early into the trap as if it were important for him to pass the stuff as soon as he could after landing from London, the implied urgency raising the value of the material in the eyes of the opposition. But his light had gone out behind the shutters in the Residency before midnight and I'd come away.

I didn't know how long it was going to take me to find my way into the Czyn network or how long it would be before Merrick signalled London through the diplomatic radio to say I was missing. London wouldn't take any notice but it was the sort of thing he might do because in only two weeks' training they wouldn't have covered even a précis of the practical experience he lacked. He'd expected me to show up at Okęcie to meet his plane and now he'd expect me to telephone him or call at the Embassy and ask him to infiltrate me into Czyn and help him analyse its potential. That was understandable because he knew those were the orders I'd been given but he didn't know—he couldn't instinctively see—that I had to work alone and make my own infiltration simply because it'd be too dangerous not to. They hadn't checked him from the airport but from now on he'd be under routine surveillance by the observation post across the street from the Embassy. He wouldn't be given an actual shadow like the military attaché, but if he made a mistake and revealed his connections with Czyn, the central monitoring cell of the U.B. would advise the observation post and they'd slap a tag on him every time he left the Embassy.

I'd have to make protected contact with him because my orders were to check and confirm the info he was sending to London and try to make sure his face didn't get trodden on while he was doing it, but he was expecting me to turn

up at the Embassy like a long-lost friend and trot him across
to the Pink Elephant Club for a drink and I wished he'd got
the sense to know that I'd be going as near to him in public
as I'd go to a rabid dog.

So I hadn't unfortunately done it on Egerton's doorstep.
He'd known I'd get the point before long; he'd wanted a
particular *type* of agent to work with Merrick, the type who
could do it best by working alone.

The bit of paper that had been waiting for me in the bar
had told me 29 *Ulica Zawidska*. It was in the Praga district
on the east side of the river and I took up station there in
the Fiat an hour before dawn. It had begun snowing and I
used the wipers at intervals. She came into the street at
half-past eight and turned left, away from me, and for a minute I sat watching the flakes drifting across her dark blue
greatcoat, then got out and locked the car and began following.

5

ALINKA

Her name was in small gold letters on the triangular block but I needed to know more about her than that.

"You speak English?"

"Yes, I do."

She was in uniform, the tunic dark blue like the greatcoat had been, a very white collar below the dense black hair. Clear stone-blue eyes that glanced behind me through the windows and flickered back to my face when I spoke.

"All I'd like are the London schedules."

"BEA?"

"And your own."

A. *Ludwiczak* in small gold letters.

"BEA operate direct flights to London on Mondays, Wednesdays and Fridays . . ."

I'm never good at telling their age. Say between twenty-five and thirty and divorced, too efficient to have lost it through carelessness and quite a few years to leave a mark as deep as that; married too young then and the break quite recent or the mark would have gone; with this straight nose

and decisive mouth she'd probably got it off with one ir-
revocable tug and hurled it as far as she could. Not Jan,
now being worked over in the glare of the lamps in the 5th
Precinct Bureau; he was only twenty-one. He would be her
brother.

"Alinka!"

"Excuse me, please." She turned away, taking the form
from the girl and signing it, swinging her head up as she
turned back, her eyes focussing on someone behind me; ten
seconds ago there'd been the thump of the door and a wave
of cold air from the street. It was a quick questioning glance,
the kind I was getting used to seeing: sometimes there was
defiance in it and sometimes fear; I'd seen it on my way here
in the tram along Jerozolimskie—they'd made a spot-check
on identity cards, the snow on their padded shoulders as
they pushed between the seats, and at Zawiszy Square
they'd taken someone off, his patient Jewish eyes downcast
as he passed me, the blue-veined hand uncertain as it
touched the rail as if doubtful of even this much support.

Apparently it was all right because she looked at me
again, though it was an effort to remember what I'd been
asking. Three other men and a woman, it had said, adding
that their arrest was imminent.

"We operate on Tuesdays, Thursdays, Saturdays and Sundays."

"If I need to know anything else, when do you—"

"We are open until five o'clock."

The main meal, *obiad*, was from four onwards and she
went home for it soon after five. He just kept on past the
house without turning his head and I waited till he'd gone

before I unlocked the Fiat and got in. It was normal routine
surveillance between where she lived and where she
worked—it had been a different man this morning—and I
wasn't worried; I'd have been worried if they *hadn't* put a
tag on a relative of someone they were grilling in the 5th
Precinct because that would have been inconsistent with the
situation and I'd have had to start beating the air for the
answer instead of concentrating on the way in to Czyn. She
was the way in, the threat in my hand, and I didn't want
anything to snap it.

Not long after seven there was a tug on it and I waited
outside the place so that I could go in immediately behind
a group of youths carrying a hollow-ribbed mongrel they'd
found in the snow. It wasn't far from where she lived and
my shoes had covered some of the traces left by her own.

She'd been expected and he'd ordered coffee for them
both; he sat tall in his chair and his wide confident hands
were clasped on the table; now and then he thumped it
gently to emphasise a point and she watched him with
steady attentive eyes as she tore up, with unconscious effi-
ciency, the blue hand-out advertising the Hungarian troupe
at the Cristal-Budapest; the one on my own table was soak-
ing up some coffee the girl had slopped over when she'd
brought it, but Alinka was tearing hers into small neat
squares as she listened to him but refused to accept that it
would be all right, that they wouldn't be too rough with
Jan because he was young and he'd only been printing
the stuff for students anyway and as soon as they could find
out where he was being held they could go there and try
to see him for a few minutes.

I could hear nothing from where I sat—on the dais opposite the bar—and my interpretation of their attitudes could
be wrong because in the past two days I'd already learned
how difficult it was to judge people from their behaviour or
even their expression; in this city the winter was not only in
the streets and they were living on their nerves, the fierce
vitality they'd put into their music and their wars now thrust
inwards on themselves; and it was worse because the surface of their daily lives seemed still intact; they could sit
here and order coffee and complain if it didn't come, and
dance at the Cristal-Budapest and walk with their children
in the park on Sundays. All they couldn't do was call their
country their own and for these people their country was
their soul.

His big confident hands thumped the table again and
anger quickened suddenly on her face as if she needed to
defend her right to feel afraid, but he understood and his
quiet answer softened her eyes and she shut them for a moment, her dark head going down, and only then could he
look away from her, hopelessness dulling his profile, his
clasped hands falling open to rest slackly beside the heap
of torn blue paper. Then suddenly—and, although it was
difficult to judge these people by their behaviour, I sensed
that for him it was an almost violent thing to do—his hand
swept out and the paper whirled like confetti onto the
floor. They didn't speak again until they left. For half a
minute I watched them through the window where the
neon sign flashed, bathing them in its intermittent light. He
wanted to see her home but she shook her head, walking
away alone.

I switched and he took me northwest and then west across the Slasko-Dabrowski Bridge, walking fast and with long strides, the snow heaped thickly along the boughs in the public gardens, the frozen jet of a fountain curving in an arch of ice, bells tolling somewhere along the remote reaches of the skyline. Left and then left again under the deathly blue of the lamps in Krakowskie Przedmiescie, a tram with a snow-plough attachment nosing along the rails, sparks sizzling from the boom. He'd gone.

These were older houses, four-storeyed, one of them with dark smoke creeping in a downdraught like hair across a face. The lift was still moving when I went into the hall and stood listening, watching for the counterweight to come into view. Small yellow lamps burned, shining on the snow that had dropped from his shoes. The weight stopped at the first floor so I took the stairs to the third, Beethoven in my head suddenly, the theme rhythm, a trick of the memory. On the third floor I had to push the time switch. The doors of the lift were narrow panels, swing-opening outwards and with glazed apertures. I couldn't see any snow on the floor of the passage here.

A cable still quivered in the silence, tapping against one of the guide rails. The fanlights of all four apartments were dark. The floor was composition flint with a buffed surface and even after climbing the stairs my shoes had left moisture but his hadn't. I checked the floor above and the one below and came back; he'd left no traces. In the lift was a puddle fringed with slush where he'd been standing.

There was no particular hurry but it shouldn't have taken me so long; you get stale after three months without a mission. The rear panel of the lift was mostly a mirror; damp had got at the silvering over the decades and it looked like scum on a pond, but the frame had been reinforced—they'd seen to that. The catch was above and to one side, a flush-fitted knot in the wood with a medium spring, and I pressed it and swung the mirror towards me. The door in the wall behind wasn't easy to see although I knew I must be looking straight at it; the vertical edges were concealed by the rear pair of guide rails and there was no handle, lock or key-hole. He would have knocked at it to the rhythm my ear had detected when I'd climbed the stairs, my mind failing to register it consciously because from two floors up the sound had been too faint, muffled by the confines of the stair well. Beethoven's Fifth, three short and one long: the V-sign they'd used in the war, just as they'd used this door when the Resistance had gone to ground.

There was no oblique-mirrored Judas hole that I could see; I waited for a minute but there seemed to be no kind of warning device that I could have tripped mechanically or electrically; they didn't know I'd exposed the door.

Then I came away. This was their base and for the moment it was enough that I'd located it. The sensitive area wasn't here; it was in Alinka Ludwiczak's travel pattern be-cause if she were simply a cut-out liaising with two or more of the Czyn units she'd become an immediate danger to them if the secret police decided to pull her in. She looked like a cut-out because she'd made contact tonight in a café instead of coming here; but if she were more than that—if she were the unnamed woman under threat of imminent arrest—they'd pull her in as soon as the time came when the boy in the 5th Precinct Bureau just couldn't take any more.

In either case she could blow half the network and that could expose Merrick.

A new sound had come to the city: the light crunching of chains as they bit into the snow. The sky was clear by mid-day but the streets were still covered and along Grojecka the heavier traffic had packed the surface into ice. The Fiat had been fitted up by Orbis and before dark I found a slot within fifty yards of the airline office and stayed in the car because it didn't matter which end of the tag-route I left it, and for the next forty-five minutes I wouldn't have to freeze to the pavement like the little man with the ear muffs who'd taken up station near the delicatessen soon after I'd parked. It was the same one as last evening; this was his shift.

There was no twilight: the night was suddenly switched on with the lamps. Across the darkened sky an aircraft winked lower on its approach path into Okęcie.

She came onto the pavement at 1707 and began walking north towards the crossing and the tram stop, and he kept pace on the other side of the street. I locked the Fiat and used quick short steps over the cobbled ice to close the gap to fifty yards by the time she crossed to the island and then to the east side. A tram had started moaning behind me, but she wouldn't be taking this one if she were going straight home; last night she'd caught a No. 16 on the direct route as far as the stadium on the far side of the Poniatow-skiego Bridge but I closed the distance again and so did he because we weren't certain. The pattern was the same until a four-door Warszawa with smoked rear windows crunched over the ruts alongside the kerb and halted abreast of the little man with ear muffs. He went up to it and spoke through the open window, turning his head just once towards the tram stop where she was waiting.

It looked like a pickup and I was badly placed but there was a chance, so I started back for the Fiat and got there half a minute after the No. 16 ground its way past going north. With the engine running I watched him through the windscreen at a hundred and fifty yards until a snow-caked Mercedes slid against the kerb and I had to pull out and slow again to keep him in view. He was climbing into the Warszawa and, beyond it, the tram was moving off and they followed, not hurrying. So it was a pickup but they didn't want to do it here in Grojecka because there were too many people about, and there was no need for the rush tactics they'd had to use at Okęcie because she wasn't trying to get on an aeroplane. They'd do it on the far side of the river where the streets were quiet.

Jan Ludwiczak had held out for nearly three days but now they'd got the names and the heat was on. I couldn't do anything about the others but there was a thin chance here, and the Fiat began sliding a bit as I edged out of the rutted shoulder and shaped up to overhaul. Two risks, one of them calculated: I might clout someone if I struck a bad patch and that would leave me blocked while they kept on going; or they might pick her up when she changed trams on the other side of the stadium instead of waiting till she got off near Zabkowska and started walking to the house where she lived. I didn't believe they'd do that because there was no need; her own street was the quietest along the whole of the route and they had her address; they'd follow her there only to make sure she didn't change her direction.

So it was stomach-think, not brain-think, that was playing on my nerves: the fear of leaving her for so long unprotected.

Discount and concentrate.

In Zawiszy Square there was a snarl-up and the civil police were using an M.O. patrol car to drag a buckled Trabant clear of the tramlines and I lost nearly seven minutes and began sweating, because by precise reckoning I had to reach the Poniatowskiego Bridge and leave the Fiat and walk back to the tram stop at the Ulica Solec intersection before the No. 16 arrived there in fifteen minutes from now at 1732.

Add a third risk: if someone else caused a snarl-up worse than this one along the main Jerozolimskie, it would halt the tram and the passengers would get out and walk till they picked up a bus farther on and it was then that the U.B. Warszawa might opt to play safe and take her on board. By now there would be directives in force to mini- mise public scenes because the international spotlight was finding its focus; journalists were already flying in to set up their coverage of the West German talks and the snatch at the airport would have hit all the major European editions and the Polish delegates must be getting sensitive. But there was a limit to what could be done to present this city as the capital of a free people when its citizens were burning to turn it into fact.

Discount the third risk. Somewhere near the Ulica Solec intersection we had a rendezvous, she and I.

The snow had piled drifts along Jerozolimskie where wind had blown from the side streets and their humps were turn- ing black from the city's smoke. The Fiat hit one of them obliquely and was carried across the tramlines before I could bring it back; the traffic was thicker here and the going less easy. When Solec came up, I checked the timing at six minutes behind schedule and kept on towards the bridge because there was still a chance. Just this side of the river a trailer truck out of the rail freight yards had got stuck in the ruts where the shoulder was steep, so I passed it and pulled in and backed up and left the Fiat there with its rear image shielded from the east-bound traffic.

The red blob of the tram was already in sight along the street's perspective, but I couldn't run because in this city a running man was suspect and two uniformed M.O. police were patrolling towards me on this side; I'd passed them in the Fiat and by now they'd be coming up on the tram stop. At thirty yards I saw them beyond the people waiting there, but I walked faster now because it was normal and legitimate to hurry to catch a tram. It had begun slowing and I broke into a trot, slipping on the packed snow and waving to the driver. The people who had been waiting were getting on board. The two policemen were now this side of the stop. I slipped again and found my feet and kept going but they didn't move over to give me room.

"Your papers."

In German I said: "If I miss this tram—" but he wagged a gloved finger.

Passport. Visa. The last of them was getting on board.

"Why do you speak in German?" From inside the tram the buzzer sounded. In thick accents: "You think we not understand English?" He turned aside to study the visa in a better light, the shadow from the cap peak masking his eyes. The other watched me. Beyond them I could see the Warszawa: it had pulled over to halt on the tramlines so that traffic could pass. "Where are you going?"

"To Praga." I shrugged. "If I can get the tram."

None of the three risks had come off but it didn't matter now; the whole thing had become academic. There'd been a chance and it had died on me and it was the last one I'd get because it was no good going back to the Fiat and over-taking the tram again; for one thing there wasn't enough distance left in which to overhaul and establish a lead suf-ficient to let me walk back one stop and try to get on again—we were too near 29 Ulica Zawidska by now—and for an-other thing they'd start wondering why a dove-grey Fiat 1300 kept overhauling them like a pilot fish round a shark. No go.

"Where, in Praga?"

Sparks crackled from the boom and the iron wheels rolled. No go. She was for the labour camps.

"My hotel. The Dubienska Hotel."

A Volkswagen was coming up, not too fast for the condi-tions but steadily, its chains thumping. It would pass be-tween the tram and where we stood.

"Very well." He put the visa inside the passport and gave them to me. In English: "Good night." Then suddenly in his own tongue—"*Uważaj!*"

He may have tried to grab me because of the danger but it would be dangerous only if I slipped; the twin horns of the Volkswagen were blaring and I knew it wouldn't be able to pull up if I fell in front of it. The rear doors of the tram were abreast of me and I ran at an angle to allow for the acceleration; the doors weren't closed yet because they weren't automatic-hydraulic. At the end of my run they be-gan sliding together and then I suppose the conductor saw me because they opened again and someone gave me a hand, pulling me in. I heard the Volkswagen slithering past, a shout coming, yes, if you wish, I am a bloody lunatic, yes, but the point is that I have made some progress.

On the condensation of the rear glass the sidelights of the Warszawa shifted a bit as its wheels were deflected by the tramlines, then it steadied and followed. There wasn't a lot of time left now; the next stop was only three hundred yards from here, just this side of the stuck trailer truck, say forty-five seconds. I couldn't see her uniform; it was the same as the hostesses wore, with a dark blue military-style forage cap, easy to identify among all the black fur képis, but I couldn't see it. People were standing in the gangway, blocking my view of the forward seats, and I started easing my way through them. One of them was the conductor.

Where to?

Ulica Solec.

But that's the next stop, didn't you know?

Yes, never mind.

So forth. A handful of coins, most of them 1-zlotys, take your pick, change can be expensive, cost you ten seconds, twenty, depended.

We'll forget it, he said. It made them feel better, robbing the state, a zloty's worth of revenge, not much but a gesture. You can use the rear doors, there's no need to—

Someone I know, the girl from the airline, I think she's up here somewhere. Edging through the heavy leather coats, not easy, they were helpful but there just wasn't much room, swaying together, say twenty-five seconds now, twenty-four, three. I couldn't see her. Sorry, did I tread on your—? Sorry, *przepraszam*. We all lurched, grabbing at the seat backs, varnish cracked, a lot of it chipped off. The wheels moaned iron on iron. She couldn't have got off earlier because they'd have seen her and taken her slamming the doors but they were still following. I knew that.

She'd do well to be here somewhere because, as I'd told him, half the population of Warsaw's going to be in a strict-régime camp in the Urals. Or the Komi Republic or Murmansk, the schizoheterodoxy political cases in the special mental hospitals of Chita Province, the Potma complex, the sawmills or making heavy boots till your fingers bleed, a bit of barbed wire but no guards because it's too far across the snow, you'd never make it alive. Sorry, *przepraszam. Dziękuje.* Another lurch then I saw her but it was an inside seat, bad luck, have to be very quick now, very quick indeed, because if we overran this stop at Solec, the Fiat wouldn't be there and the whole thing depended on that. Slowing.

We were slowing.

Ulica Solec he called out.

A plump surprised man looking up, a *wieprzowina* sausage in greaseproof paper on his lap, looking up with a jerk and the fear coming at once into the eyes, who was I, what did I want, he had done nothing against the state, as I leaned over him towards the inside seat and spoke close to the dark head as it turned.

"Alinka." To show that I knew her and might therefore know other things, could perhaps be trusted to know them. "We'll speak in English. Police want you. Police. Come with me and you'll be safe. Be quick."

The wheels had stopped rolling.

Her eyes wide, staring into my face, the pupils enlarged. "I understand."

The doors thudded open against the rubber shock-stops.

"Ulica Solec!"

Yes, I called to him, I was getting off here.

The man with the sausage was twisting sideways to let her pass and then she was in the gangway and as we went to the forward doors I told her to take her cap off and she did it with a natural gesture, shaking her hair free. Two other people had left their seats and I took her arm, holding her still so that they could go first, and while we waited I gave her as much as I could; the U.B. car was behind the tram and they'd be watching for her; the grey Fiat was parked in front of the trailer truck and she must get into it without losing time and then crouch low; she should be ready for any word I threw at her and if we had to run she must take care not to slip. All right, she said.

I held her gloved hand so that I could guide her, taking her forward to follow the two people closely; the man got out first and helped the woman down and I drew Alinka past me—"Keep on that side of them and hold your head low." I let her hand go but followed close to make additional cover, trying to judge their angle of view and blocking it, gripping her hand again and forcing her across the packed snow, keeping exact pace with the man and the woman and listening now, listening. We reached the pavement, the four of us, breaking the crests of the ruts, our breath steaming under the tall lamps. Stefan might not be home yet, the man was saying to the woman, and they had no key. Why must he always forget, she asked him, to bring the key?

A red lantern stood on the snow not far from the rear of the truck, to warn traffic. It looked as if they'd decided to abandon it for the night. The tram moved away and I held my head turned so that one ear could hope to catch the sound I was listening for, against the noise of the tram. The air froze against our faces. Then the woman slipped.

Her hand was flung out and the man tried to save her and nearly managed it, at least breaking her fall, but she went down, squealing unnecessarily like a pig. The cover was gone and I said *run* just before the sound came, the click of a door opening but no shout yet, they weren't certain, just alerted by the colour of her coat but fractionally thrown by the altered image, her cap being off. I kept to a steady walk but couldn't hope to judge their angle of view at this distance, an aching temptation to look behind me but not possible, and then a second click and a voice calling a sharp order to the one who'd got out. This was the break-off point and I began running too.

6

ICE

When the colonel comes round you shove some dandelions in a jam tin and kick the crapboard under the bed and the corporal gets good marks for keeping a tidy billet, so tonight the beer's on him and the same principle operates when the capital of any given state receives a foreign delegation: everyone's so busy brushing the worst of it under the rug that you can hardly walk on it for the lumps.

I was in Yugoslavia when Battista Farinelli made a ten-day visit to Belgrade to steer through the U.C.A. Trade Referendum, and although I was between missions I chanced to have access to the security-service directive that was passed to all units a week prior to the visit, and paragraph three stipulated that firearms would not be used unless the life of an officer were 'manifestly in jeopardy' during the execution of his duties. You can put out as many flags as you like, but foreign journalists are going to suspect things are a bit untidy if they can't hear the church bells for bangs.

It's standard practice, otherwise they'd have put one into my legs and although you can keep going if it's lodged in the flesh or the bone, it's no go if it hits a major nerve. Her arm went out once and I thought she was off her balance, but it was all right and by the time I reached there she'd dragged the door open and was hunched on the passenger's seat with her head against the dashboard.

I heard them behind me, the clump of their boots over the snow. She'd left the door hanging wide open and I used it to break my slide, heaving myself in by the wheel column and punching about for the key. Someone shouted and the voice was close; we were cutting it fine but that was all right because the nearer they were to the Fiat the farther they were from the Warszawa unless one of them had stayed behind.

One of them had stayed behind; I heard his starter catch just before mine but it couldn't be helped, and there was a bit of traffic coming through from the lights and that might baulk them because they were on the tramlines and in any case a standing start on tramlines isn't the best pitch, so we still had a chance. The engine of the 1300 was still well into the working-temperature region and fired without any trouble, and I botched in and gave it full gun to get the chains chewing down to the tarmac through the snow; it was the only hope because it would have needed anything up to ten seconds using a sensitive rein and I was aware of him now, very close, nothing visual, just the sixth-sense awareness of a dark milling shape.

The rear end was bedding down and crabbing into the shoulder and there was no certainty of pulling out of here at all; it depended on how the equation worked itself out, weight of the mass, speed of the wheels, friction of the chains against the lubric medium. We could sit here at full throttle and do nothing but make a noise until they came for us, taking their time. I'd missed the armrest twice but got a grip on it now and he finished sideways on to the door as I dragged it towards me but his weight smashed it open again. The chains had found some purchase and the Fiat would have gone forward if he hadn't been clinging to the door, so I used an edge-of-the-hand chop downwards against his wrist and got it right and he fell forwards as his support broke. The whole of the rear was vibrating on the springs as the chains cut at the tarmac and the inertia was killed so fast that we slewed half round as the power took up and sent us away from the shoulder with the door swinging back of its own accord.

"Mind your head."

The acceleration was shifting the loads rearward, but the steering was still wild and we could hit something. She hooked her gloved hands against the edge of the compart-ment and rested her head against them. I would have told her she could sit upright now so that she could watch for a crash situation, but there was just a chance they'd get con-fused and forget the directive about firearms. Something tore at the rear panel and the mirror had movement in it, but it couldn't be the Warszawa because of the distance; the leading car in the traffic coming through from the lights had clouted us and in the mirror its shape swung away.

The driving door had caught at half-lock, so I hit it open and slammed it as we pulled away in second with some-one flashing us from behind and piling up very close because they hadn't left enough time for the braking condi-tions, but this one wasn't a strike and I shaped for a right-angle turn through the Centralny Park and suddenly we were in what seemed forest land, the black trees spectral against the snowscape and the lights of other cars moving like slow lanterns between their trunks.

"You might as well sit upright now. They know you're on board." We were going fast enough to qualify for a high-impact smash if I lost control. "Clip your seat belt." Lights swung into the mirror. "Is Jan your brother?"

"What did you—"

"Is Jan Ludwiczak your brother?"

"Yes."

"They've got him in the 5th Precinct Bureau."

There might not be another chance to tell her.

"The 5th."

"*Piaty.*"

The lights were on full head hoping to dazzle and I tipped the glass a fraction. The surface was much better here: rich-lying snow except for the intersections where the double volume of traffic had packed it harder. Our shadow swerved in front of us most of the time, thrown by the Warszawa.

"Who are you, please?"

Visibility was good because of the albescence and the even spacing of the trees, and to the right and left of the crossroads there was nothing in sight, so I brought the speed up progressively and cleared the harder-packed area with dead-point momentum between acceleration and deceleration, obliquely aware that if we survived this day I would for long remember her calm and rather formal question as we and our shadow flew in whiteness among the winter trees, who are you please.

"There's nothing in a name."

I slowed on the engine for a left-hander at the T-section

and lost everything in the next two seconds because of the ice patch that hadn't showed until we were on it. Full-circle gyration with the wheel slack in my hands and the background slowly spinning, so that for a moment we were sliding backwards and squinting straight into the glare of their lamps and then bucking suddenly with a rear tyre dragging on the buried kerbstone and sending us to the crown before I used the throttle and got some of the traction back and straightened out and kept going.

"Look, I'm trying to make for Sobieski."

"Very well."

At the edge of my vision field, her white face was turned to watch me. Aleje Sobieski was the street of the older four-storeyed houses where the lift had a mirror and they thought they were safe there, that nobody knew.

"If I can lose them or smash them up I'll drop you off there, but I might have to drop you wherever I can if it gets difficult." A wash of light flooded the interior again and the prismatic colours glowed on the bevelling of the mirror. "Operate your belt clip a few times, get used to the release."

We hadn't lost much ground during the spin: the direction and speed had retained most of their values although we'd gyrated through three hundred and sixty degrees, but the Warszawa was closer by thirty yards or so and I didn't like it because if we crashed it ought to happen far enough away from them to give us a chance of getting out on foot. Left into Gwardzislow with a reliable drift across almost virgin snow and we ran now towards Solec again just this side of the Vistula. I didn't know this area so well as the city centre, but we'd be all right as soon as we'd cleared the T-section and crossed left onto the main west-bank highway parallel to the river; I'd studied the street complexes in that area while I'd been hanging about at Heathrow and covered the rest of the central districts since I'd landed here, normal routine orientation. Sobieski wasn't far but some of the one-way streets were going to sticky things up if I didn't watch it.

She was clicking her release, not looking down at it, doing it blind, and it occurred to me that she might have been a hostess on the planes before they grounded her for some reason or she'd got bored with handing out sweets because she was behaving very well considering the odds were that we'd finish up by wiping the Fiat all over a tram. Or worse of course, if they could pick us alive out of a wreck they'd have us under the lamps for what the KGB called implemented interrogation. She knew that.

"You all right, Alinka?"

"Yes, thank you."

She looked behind her sometimes and I asked her what the distance was, and she said about fifty metres and then we couldn't talk any more because the T-section was coming up and a red oblong was sliding across the end of the perspective, bus, not a tram; there'd be no tramlines along the river stretch until we reached General Swierczewskiego and doubled back and tried to get near Sobieski. There was an antenna on their roof and they'd have begun fidgeting with it long before now, but there wasn't much point in their calling on base to deploy support patrols because they didn't know where to send them; if we'd been taking a direct route out of the city they could have set up roadblocks but we'd been doubling some of the time and all they could do was keep us in sight till we smashed.

It wasn't very good at the T-section. We had to cross Ulica Solec to get onto Wybrzeze Kosciuszkowskie along the Vistula and there was some traffic piled up at the major fork; we took the first set of lights on the green but had to run the next on the red and I lost most of the front end trying to clear a pharmaceutical van and not successfully, swinging it half round and hitting a drift that the river wind had swept against the central bollards so that we slewed twice and skinned the long scarlet flank of a bus as the Warszawa closed fast with its lights full on and its klaxon sounding. A couple of M.O. police had a go at waving me in and their whistles were shrilling, but there wasn't anything they could do and I was worried more by some nasty spin from the rear wheels as we crossed the packed ice of a bus stop; the Warszawa couldn't make progress either and we were both shaped up for the long straight haul down the river stretch with the gap drawing open slightly as I flicked into third and settled for the odd chance of piling up enough speed to try slotting some of the slower traffic between us and baulk them before we had to go left towards Sobieski. I didn't think we could lose them now.

It was instinctive to think in terms of overall speed but in these conditions it was traction that counted and I levelled off at fifty kph and even then we were well beyond the hope of slowing in time if anything crossed our bows; the steering kept going slack and for periods we were skating across the surface without any real kind of control and then two things happened in close succession. A black stunted Moskwicz pulled away from the kerb, and ahead of us I saw a truck.

The surface along here was mostly ice ruts with patches

of thin hard snow towards the crown; there was no point in trying to plan anything because action designed to cope with the conditions lying ahead would be right or wrong according to what they turned out to be when we got there. The little Moskwicz wasn't a hazard; we were already in the fast lane and I didn't even have to touch the wheel but I could see that the Warszawa needed to take avoiding action and had started to do it; our shadow, thrown by its lights against the back of the truck, was shifting to the right.

Then something else happened and at first I thought it was gunfire because the effect followed the sound in logical sequence; it was as if they'd shot one of our tyres flat. Chain. One of the chains had gone, its straps half-severed when we'd dragged a rear wheel along the buried kerbstone in the park; it had hammered under the body shell and been flung aside and now the Fiat was in a slow ten-degree pivoting attitude and for the last time the wheel went slack in my hands.

"Good luck."

She answered with something in Polish. Then we heard the Warszawa, metal on metal and the explosive pop of safety glass; the lights swept away from the truck and across to the buildings on the other side and went out. It wasn't important now.

I cut the ignition. There wasn't much noise, just the long hushed skittering of the tyres over the ice as we waited. The pivoting attitude was increasing and periodicy had set in and I knew that nothing could break it; there must come the point where mass dominated momentum and then the Fiat would automatically spin. Left, and right, wider to the left, and wider to the right in a slow swinging action with the brittle whisper of the tyres across the ruts and she spun, breaking wild and closing on the truck in a series of loops that took her down the shoulder to hit the kerb and rebound and spin again and strike it this time front-end-on with the wheels rolling so that she mounted and ran straight for a while with the springs hammering at the limit-blocks, thick snow along the pavement now but the speed too high and the balustrade coming and the swirl of the east-bank lights tiding across the windscreen, and then the balustrade and the impact and the drag on the seat belt and a period of weightlessness as we tilted nose-down and struck and shook and struck again and rolled half-over, the roof sliding, the speed dying, lights in the sky, inverted, reflected in the sheen of the ice, the thought coming, black water below.

Glass shattered.

I kicked at the windscreen. She was already on her feet as I slithered from under the front end; she'd used the side window, breaking it. A faint sound had begun, the crackling strain of the ice crust between here and the bank. She was moving at an angle, loping forward not far from me; the surface was blackish here and we made for the nearest patch of white but the crackling became loud and we couldn't run without slipping and falling. She turned once and I told her to get on. Then the crust shivered and broke in a long crescent and I heard the Fiat strike water, a gigantic bubbling behind us.

Sand, a sandbank, the thin ice breaking as we trod its edges, then stones, the ankles freezing. Quite a long way off, the high alternating notes of an emergency vehicle.

"Keep moving."

There were steps going upwards.

"They'll see us," she said.

"No they won't."

There was snow on the steps and we went up slowly. A freize of icicles along the higher plinth flashed diamond colours as the first lamp showed; I told her to wait, and climbed the last three steps ahead of her, checking the street. Small group round the hole in the balustrade where we'd gone through, well over a hundred yards from here; we'd breached it at an angle and the Fiat had slid quite a long way downriver before we'd got out. Bigger group half a mile distant on the roadway, a lot of people and vehicles where the Warszawa had smashed.

I nodded to her and she came up into the lamplight, dark eyes glowing in a bloodless face, the blue greatcoat ripped at the shoulder, the patent-leather kneeboots neatly together on the snow as she stood with her head turned to look along the street.

"They're too busy," I said, "for us."

She faced me without expression as if she didn't quite understand. It was shock, that was all, shock setting in. It hadn't been much of an impact because we'd hit the iron balustrade obliquely and the stanchions had broken away the edge of the stonework, the thing was only meant for leaning on while you had a sandwich, and the belts had kept us back; it was listening to the crackling of the ice that had worried us most. I put my arm round her shoulders and we started off, crossing over and going down Ulica Lipowa away from the river.

Nobody noticed us: the few people we passed were watching where they put their feet; but we had to turn back twice along Krakowskie to avoid M.O. patrols. I didn't know what the situation was, down by the river; the Warszawa had made a lot of noise but there could be survivors and their radio might not have been bust up.

Sobieski was a quiet narrow street, more like a mews, and we got into the building without needing to check. In the lift I said:

"Have you got a source for papers?"

"What did you say?"

She leaned against the mirror, her dark eyes vague and her gloved hands pressed to her face; she had more to deal with than the physical shock of the Fiat thing; we hadn't talked much on the way here and she'd had time to think, and what she'd probably thought was that if the *Policia Ubespieczenia* had decided to pull her in it was because Jan hadn't managed to hold out.

"Identity papers. Can you get a new one easily?"

The cable tapped against one of the guide rails.

"No. We made some, but they were not good. People were caught with them."

"Give me yours. It's no more use to you."

It was a recent photograph, not much like her, they never are. When I looked up she was watching me, uneasy. They are like that, or they become like that, the people of the police states. They mean so much to them, these dog-eared little cards with their creased folds and their grandiloquent crests. *Polska Rzeczpospolita Ludowa*. Take them away and you take away their identity, leaving them nameless. I knew what was in her mind as she watched me put the card into my pocket—tonight I'd blown my cover and that was just as bad.

The lift stopped, its floor jogging slowly to stillness under-foot.

"Will there be someone here?"

"Yes."

She'd started shivering with nerves and I was suddenly fed-up because I'd mucked it. She wouldn't be spending the next five years stitching boots in the strict-régime camps but it had been a hell of a way to pull her out of a snatch; I might have killed her.

In the passage I said: "Tell them to fix you up with some-thing hot. Rum grog or something."

I took my time going down the stairs because she couldn't be sure that someone was there; you could be there one day and the next day you could be in the 5th Precinct Bureau or some other rotten hole. Three short, one long. When I heard the mirror shut I cleared the rest of the stairs a bit quicker because there was a lot to do.

7

CONTACT

Do you know this woman?

Hotel Pulawska. No go.

I'd been working against a deadline and it was already past because they wouldn't wait till they'd dredged the Fiat out of the river; they'd be on to me before that. We'd started off from the tram stop at Ulica Solec somewhere between 5:30 and 5:40 and as soon as they'd seen I was going to try giving them a run they'd have radioed the number to their base, we are now in pursuit of dove-grey Fiat 1300, Warsaw-registered, so forth.

Do you know this woman?

Hotel Dworzec. No go.

Give them ten minutes to channel the number into Registrations Control and five minutes for Registration to come up with the answer and fifteen minutes for the first patrol to reach Orbis and get the place opened up and find the relevant documentation: yes, we booked this one out on the tenth to a British visitor, P. K. Longstreet, passport number C–5374441. Give them another fifteen minutes to cover the city with a general-alert call by mobile-patrol radios and report-point telephones and that made it a short-limit deadline of 6:15, so at 6:15 the police would have started combing the hotels.

Just as I was doing.

Do you know this woman?

Hotel Francuska. No go.

That was why I'd begun sweating: we were working the same ground. Any time between June and September or anywhere south of latitude 45 I could have holed up in the open, but this was Warsaw in January and if you didn't get under a decent roof you'd freeze. It didn't matter that by now they might have found the bag with the leather panel coming away from the stitches at one end; they were welcome to what they pulled out of it because if I were still a free agent tomorrow I was going to sting that bloody woman in Accounts for a set of new winter woollies. They wouldn't stop looking for me once they knew I'd left the hotel. They knew I'd have to find another one. I had to have somewhere to live.

"Do you know this woman?"

Hotel Alzacka.

I showed him the dog-eared identity card.

He looked at it.

I was relying on his impression of events to cover my accent; there's no precise equivalent for the palatals in English and you've got to do it with the tip of the tongue on the lower teeth and the middle pressed towards the alveolar ridge and it takes practice and I hadn't had much. But events were that a man in a black leather coat and fur képi had come quickly up to the desk and pushed someone's papers in front of his face and shot a terse question, and his impression was predictable and he didn't ask to see my badge. Now I watched for his reaction.

I couldn't hurry him, get it over with and get out if it was no go again. I had to stand there with ice down my spine because if that door opened behind me it could be one of his guests coming in or it could be one of the several hundred police who were now checking the hotels for P. K. Longstreet. The name wasn't here on the books of the Hotel Alzacka, but although they didn't know my face except for a vague description by Orbis, they wouldn't miss checking my papers and they'd see it there instead.

"I've never seen her before."

No reaction.

There was a lot of noise like the building coming down. A brass ashtray crept like a crab across the polished top of the counter. He didn't notice anything. I took her card back and span the register towards me to look at the names but I didn't look at the names yet, I went on looking at him.

Reaction.

Nothing happened to his face. It was big and square with creases weathered into it, a seaman's face that had looked into the eye of the storm and stared it out. Iron-grey Bismarck head and an ear torn at the lobe, boat hook or the dying flick of a shark fin, salt in his soul. Nothing that I could say would change a face like this but the reaction was there all right and it had come when I'd spun the register; he'd drawn a slow breath as he'd straightened up, as a heavy man does when he straightens up, and shifted his feet a bit to redispose his weight, as a man of his weight does. I've never seen her before, shaking his head. It was just a hundredth of a degree too natural and there was another thing: he'd shifted his weight but it had given an odd slant to his attitude and he stood as a one-legged sailor stands but I didn't think he was one-legged.

Of course he'd never seen her before, it was nothing to do with that; it was the number I'd used to open my act that was all, to show I was the hunter and not the hunted. It hadn't worried him but the register had, the way I'd spun it round to have a look. There wouldn't be anything there, I knew that; if you take a man in and put him in a garret with a wardrobe shoved across the door, you don't enter his name in the book. It was just that I was getting warm; a hotel register is a revealing document and the police go for it first and even if there's nothing in it to reveal, it's like when you show your driving licence and wonder for an instant if you've made a mistake and it's out of date, your stomach does a slight skid turn.

The building fell down again but among all the noise I heard a voice from upstairs, and a door banging.

This place would do me.

"I'd like a room."

His heavy lids lifted. The police don't ask for a room. If they want to search a hotel they just bring a bulldozer, they don't have to sleep there.

"You won't mind the noise?"

"They don't run all night."

"What kind of room do you want?" He turned the register with a horny hand. "I'll need your papers."

"I've no papers that I can show anyone. That's the kind of room I want." Nice and high up and out of people's way and with someone down here to press the buzzer with his foot when the police made a visit.

"You can't stay here, without papers."

I didn't expect him to trust me but there was a way.

"At least we can have a drink."

In the back room he poured out some Jasne beer and I mentioned Czyn. It wasn't by luck that I'd only had to try four hotels: almost everyone's in the underground, Merrick had said. I gave my accent a lot more rope now as I talked to him, throwing out the palatals and throwing in some rich Somerset r's.

"Have the police been here yet, looking for an English-man?"

"About fifteen minutes ago."

"He's wanted for helping Czyn. They were trying to make an arrest and he stopped them. What was his name?"

"They're hard for me, English names."

"But they wrote it down for you. He's looking for a hotel, so you were to phone them if he came to yours." I got out my passport. "Is this the name?"

"Yes. That one."

It was a small room on the fifth floor with a decent tem-perature due to a fat black pipe with convector fins that ran from floor to ceiling; he said it was the actual chimney of the boilerhouse feeding the middle room on all floors this side of the building. The window was frosted up and I had to open it to take bearings: platforms 5 and 6 of the Warszawa Glowna with a signal box down towards the shunt yards, the street vertically below and with no canopies or jutting roofs. The fire escape was wrought iron and unob-structed.

I didn't ask, when he left me, who the other man was, the one he'd buzzed. It wasn't my business.

He caught his breath but I said it was all right and he fell into step, quickening his to mine; I'd been hanging about for nearly an hour and I needed some circulation. We walked by the Vistula, along Kosciuzkowskie, because it was mainly for traffic and there wouldn't be so many M.O. patrols.

Shakily he said: "I thought you'd been arrested."

"What for?" It had checked me for an instant because I didn't think his communications could be as fast as that; then I realised what the poor little devil meant.

"Well, I mean I've been expecting you to contact me."

"I have."

The snow was brittle, charcoal-grey from the smoke of the factories, and above us the sodium lamps cast a pallor rather than light; objects and their shadows looked derelict, destroyed, as if we picked our way through the ashen after-glow of the city that not long before had burned under the droning sky. In a different way it was dying now, with less dignity, less rage.

This morning they'd done for Horodecki, a major general at the military academy, not a headline, just a couple of column-inches on page three, a man of honour and high purposes, his brother the chairman of the National Assembly and a leading delegate for the East-West talks. No trial —he was too popular for dangerous publicity—but summary medical certification by a psychiatric board: onset of acute paranoid manifestations with earlier developed symptoms of atherosclerosis. Put him away. No dignity in that, no rage.

And widespread dissension among the proletariat, page six, with absenteeism at the factories up by 30 per cent. Pilfering of state property, minor sabotage and slogans across the walls, the city dying again but in a different way, no mourners but the dead themselves.

"Have you got anything for me?"

He fumbled for an envelope, dropping it because of his stiff gloves, and I stood looking down at him as he picked it off the snow. He never got anything right, tripping on things and dropping things, his hands never steady, his nerves in his eyes. Had he been any better than this before Egerton had reached for him out of the dark and infected him with the spirit of subterfuge and sent him out here to forage for scraps among the dustbins of a sick society? Had he been all right, once, all of a piece and uncontaminated, busy with his own little schoolboy dreams of lighting a candle for the oppressed? Not Egerton's responsibility, of course: 'he was rather wished onto me.' But Egerton could have refused to direct him if he'd chosen, instead of which he'd been party to the decision to use an innocent for their own ends: for the ends of the Bureau, a sacrifice to the sacred bull. So here was their key man in Warsaw, wiping the wet soot off an envelope before holding it out to me, his eyes wide with worry behind the glasses, his face deathly under the sodium lamps.

"I'm sorry," he said.

It had been such a nice clean envelope, his very first report for London, and as I took it I cursed him for uncovering something that I'd thought had been long ago buried under all those years of deceit and betrayal: a sense of compassion.

As my thumb ripped along the fold I wondered by how much Merrick himself had been party to that decision, because he could have refused, too. But like the people of this city he'd been driven to pilfering a bit of freedom for himself, half-frightened and half-defiant, by taking on an enterprise so secret that despite the official sanction of strangers, his own father couldn't be told. That was the only kick he was getting out of this: he was striking a petty blow against tyranny, and the deceit in it was prescribed by others, leaving his conscience clear.

"This all?"

"There's quite a lot. It's closely typed."

I read bits of it as we neared the bridge. Fifteen autonymous units dispersed topographically about the city at what appeared to be strategic points, liaison by cut-outs, fully completed arrangements for street barricades, sniper posts and grenade areas, the three main power stations already rigged for blasting by radio-controlled detonators. Initial stages marked *Sroda* minus 10, *Sroda* minus 9, so forth, final stages just marked *Sroda*. Wednesday. Wednesday the twentieth, three days before the opening of the talks. Seven days from now.

"Sailing a bit near the wind, aren't they?"

"How do you mean?"

"They're giving themselves three days to blow this thing open and clear up all the blood and brick dust before the delegates arrive. If any delegates arrive at all I'd say most of them'll be crouching in doorways counting their rosaries, wouldn't you?"

"The whole idea is to mount a threat, not an action." Excitement came into his tone. "There'll be action all right if they're driven to it, but the aim is to bring off a bloodless coup d'état by showing their strength at a time when it'll be too late for the Warsaw Pact troops to retaliate. The talks are very important to Moscow—you'll find a summary on page five of the public references to the Russian hopes of their success—and no one in Czyn believes they'll risk sending tanks into the city at a time like this. How could they?"

A light wind blew across the bridge and I folded the sheets and put them away and we walked faster again.

"Who's the 'Leader'? Several mentions."

"They never use his name. I think he's a deputy in the Party Committee, quite high up—that's why they're confident that there'll be no tanks sent in, you see, because someone in his position would know what Moscow's intentions would be, at a confrontation."

"Get his name."

In the distance we heard a stationary diesel throbbing, and people shouting. Half a mile upriver there was a ring of floodlights with figures moving about; the boom of a crane stuck out from the bank across the break in the ice, with a dark oblong turning slowly at the end of the cable.

"What's happening down there?" Merrick stopped, looking across the balustrade of the bridge.

Water poured from the oblong shape as it was swung towards the bank. The shouting died away and the figures were still now, watching. It had been a cold job: they must have been hours at it.

"How many copies," I asked him when he'd caught me up, "have you got of this report?"

"I've got the only carbon, and you've got the original."

"In future I want the carbon. I won't be adding any-thing, you're doing this job, not me. How many people at the Embassy know?"

"Only H.E."

I saw them and turned round. "Come on, Merrick." He came trotting after me. "When's bag day?"

"Tomorrow." His breath wheezed. "Eleven-thirty."

"Put this in."

C–5374441 plus visa plus identity card and a short en-coded note that ought to take Egerton's mind off his chil-blains for a bit: *Blown cover. Send new one, West German image. Also new i.c. as per example enclosed for Wanda Rek, 121 Ulica Niska, profession journalist, other details same, same photo. 10 below, you're cushy.*

He took the packet.

"And don't drop the bloody thing."

Third series, fifth-digit duplications. There was no point in using the Telex or dip. radio because all I wanted out of Egerton were some papers to show so that I didn't have to keep spinning round like a ferret when it sees a fox, it was inconvenient. Merrick had a job getting his breath and I didn't think he even knew what the hurry was but he'd cot-ton on, give him a hundred years and he'd cotton on.

"When does the bag come in?"

"Saturday. Will there be something for you?"

It wasn't giving them long but it'd shake the dust up, never a bad thing at the Bureau. I didn't want to turn my head: they'd just started onto the bridge when I'd seen them and we'd been walking faster than they should be, but the trouble was that the pressure was getting higher every day;

unless you looked like a robot they'd pull you in and if there weren't any tanks in this city a week from now it'd be because there was nobody left to shoot at.

"Yes." The wind cut at our faces. "If Customs decide it's a nice day for a snap check try and distract their attention, shut their arse in a door or something."

"Will you call for it?"

"No. Keep it on you."

"All right." Nearing the end of the bridge he said: "Are we—"

"Don't look back."

They'd shut down the diesel. Our feet scuffed over the snow. His breathing was painful and when I finally couldn't stand it and what they were doing to him and what I was doing to him, I left him and went down the steps and along the riverbank where it was dark.

8

CZYN

Everyone's always complaining at Norfolk that in Weapons Recognition they're sketchy about the head-on image. The artist is fond of a certain forget-me-not blue for the shading and we think he's a pouf, but the diagrammatic vital statistics are up to scratch and there's a clever system using key colours for giving what amounts to a visual permutation table for the types of ammo interchangeable among the run-of-the-mill international models, but they haven't yet conceded the obvious point that we need a set of *oblique* head-on pictures at something like ten or twelve degrees from the line of sight and a specially big one from above, because the head's a smaller target and the aim is normally at the stomach or the heart so that you're looking slightly down at the image. The only picture they give us is smack into the line of sight so it looks like an end-on view of a sausage roll with no sausage in it.

But this was an easy one, a Typolt Mk XI short-range sub with sixteen in the drum, and I was looking slightly down at it in the normal way. I couldn't see whether it was at safe or fire but by the look on his face I knew I ought not to move.

He had the intent gaze of a bird, the iris so dark that the eye seemed all pupil; the other one was glass, not too well made. The streaks of white in his ruffled hair, the deep-cut lines in the face, the strong hooked nose, the scratched leather covering of his mechanical hand and his crouched attitude, all gave him the look of an eagle mauled in some foray, the plumage torn but the pride fiercer than ever.

The man behind me shut the inner door of the sound-lock.

"Who are you?" In Polish.

The room was big but cluttered with trestle tables and sagging settees and a vast carved Lublin dresser with a GEC transmitter-receiver stuffed into it. Designer's desk covered with papers, bottle of Wyborowka Vodka and three tumblers, some tins of meat, pair of leather gauntlets with the fleece sticking through a gash, packet of *Sport*. The stacked boxes in the corner farthest from the stove looked like ammo. Thick smell of black leaf.

"It's all right," she told them. She'd come from behind a baize folding screen. I heard a kettle boiling. "He's the Englishman." She came towards me so that he had to shift his aim.

"*Alinka!*"

Impatiently she said over her shoulder—"I've told you he's all right, Viktor." Black sweater and slacks: she wouldn't be wearing the uniform any more. She was thinner than I remembered, or it was that black accentuated the lean lines of her body as she moved towards me with a controlled rhythm and stopped, facing me, her patent-leather kneeboots neatly together. I know that this was how she moved, and stilled herself: I've learned more about people by their bearing than by anything else, even their eyes, because it has a permanency and expresses what they are and not just what they're feeling.

In English she said: "I've told them about you."

"*Alinka.*" His voice was rough with anger. "Did you tell him how to get in here?"

She turned away, this time controlling her impatience, and I sensed that it was something they'd all had to learn: to be patient with Viktor. He'd lowered the gun but his bright eye burned at me.

"No," she said. "He knew."

"How did he know?"

"Does it matter?" She held a tumbler to the light and poured some vodka. "He knew they were going to arrest me but I didn't ask him how he knew. I'm still free, that's what counts." She brought the vodka to me with quick lithe strides. "Can I know your name?"

"Longstreet."

"Drink. I owe you that."

"Who are you?" It was the other man, the one who'd sat with her in the *kawiarnia*, his big confident hands clasped on the table and sometimes thumping it gently for emphasis. But he hadn't eased the fright in her. They were all frightened, here.

I asked him: "What did you say?"

"Doesn't he speak Polish?"

"If he did," she shrugged, "would he have to speak to you in German?"

He watched me steadily, a good face with the eyes well

apart under a wide flat brow, the mouth long and com-
pressed, contemplative. He'd be their mainstay, here, the
one who never panicked; but I thought that at this moment
his confidence had never been under such attack. It wasn't
because of me, I knew that.

She said to me: "This is Leo Polanski."

"My God, do you have to tell him our names?"

"Please, Viktor," she said quietly.

Polanski inclined his head, still watching me. He said:
"You have helped us—"

"*Ich verstehe nicht—*"

"You have helped us," he said, this time in German, "but
we need to know who you are."

I turned and put the vodka, untouched, on the corner of
the littered desk. There were several versions of who I was
but I didn't know which one I ought to give them.

"Is it not all right?" she asked.

"I'm driving."

There was no actual need for me to tell them who I was:
it would simply be for the sake of putting them at their ease.
If I didn't satisfy them they might stop me coming here
again; they could do that easily enough by changing the signal. It might take a little time for them to see that they'd
have to cooperate with me, because a changed signal
wouldn't stop a police squad if I cared to tip them off: they'd
drill right round the door with heavy-calibre rapid fire,
like opening a tin.

Of course it might take them less time to see that I ought
not to be let out of here at all. It made no difference that I'd
been of use to them; in the last few days before a city-wide
revolution there could be a change of fortune and loyalties,

and if it suited my book I could have them dragged out of here and slung into the interrogation cells before they were packed into the special windowless trains for the camps in the Komi Republic.

Viktor realised that much: it was in the burning dark of his one good eye as it stared at me. He was the only professional here, too young for the war but old enough to have manned the barricades in the '56 Poznan riots: maybe that was where he'd trained.

"I'm an observer. You're going to start a war, aren't you? You'll need Western observers."

I'd spoken to Polanski but it was Viktor who answered, limping quickly to the desk and ripping open the packet of *Sport*, holding it against his chest with his mechanical hand. Left leg, left hand, left eye. Grenade or a mine.

"What's your paper?"

"I'm free lance."

"Where has your stuff appeared?"

"Most places."

"What by-line?"

"Pseudonymous."

"You won't leave here unless you can do a lot better than that." The match flared and then his head jerked and he was staring towards the door of the sound-lock and Polanski said:

"Josef."

Three short, one long.

Alinka didn't move. She stood perfectly still, closing her eyes. I could believe she was praying.

Polanski opened the first door, then the second, and Josef came in, stumbling, hitting the acoustic padding with his shoulder and straightening up and looking at no one, a white face bright with sweat and the eyes flickering from shock, his breath coming in gusts as he stood in the middle of the room, a short clownish figure swaying with the uncertain stance of a bear on its hind legs, his thick coat hanging open, blood on the sleeve.

"It wasn't any good."

The neck of a bottle trembled on the rim of a glass.

"Never mind, Jo," Polanski said.

"Are you hurt?"

"No." He took it and drank and she waited and he let out a long shuddering breath. "That's not my blood. We lost Zygmunt and Jacek."

He drank again and she tried to make him sit down but he shook her away and told them all of it, all there was, the main doors breached with five stick bombs according to plan and Jacek and himself in there first with Karol giving them cover and Jerzy standing by with the stolen van, but the alarm had gone off and they'd only had time to open up the first three cells and Jan hadn't been there and they'd had to come away before they were cut off.

She took his empty glass. "Thank you for trying, Jo."

"Next time," Polanski said.

They weren't frightened any more because they knew the worst now and it could have been worse than this: Jan wasn't here but Jo was back.

He nodded quickly, his mood suddenly changing, a wicked smile creasing his clown's face, the ends of his long mouth turning upwards. "Next time, yes. Who's this?"

The *anglik*, she told him.

"So?" He grasped my hand in both his own and I felt the

surprising strength in them. "We need people like you!
Alinka told us how—"

"*Sorry?*"

"Huh? She told us how you drove, Jesus!"

"I drove into the river."

"Well, anyone c'n make a mistake, no? You did a swell
job, no kidd'n."

"Jo. Don't tell him anything."

"Don't what?" He looked across at Viktor. "What like?"

"We don't know who he is yet."

"We can ask him, can't we?" He switched so fast that it
was like two different people talking. "What outfit are you
with, pal?"

The lid of the kettle had started rattling minutes ago and
Alinka went round the screen.

"I'm on my own."

"He's on his own."

"That isn't enough."

"It's enough for me." He shrugged his coat off and dropped
it across a settee and poured some vodka. "Viktor's a wonderful guy, a very wonderful guy, but he took a beating and
it was because some bastard put the skids under him, see,
someone he trusted, so now when his own mother holds out
a cookie he bites her fingers off, you get it. An' now he's
steamed up because it's getting close to the big day, we're
all of us kinda jumpy. You know what I'm talkin' about?"

"Wednesday."

The sounds were distant at first: the traffic seemed a little
heavier, that was all.

"Sure. Wednesday."

He raised his glass, his smile very bright.

"You think they'll send tanks in?"

"They can try. We have the approach routes mined."

"What are the chances?"

"Of what?"

"For you."

Doors slamming.

"Look, this isn't Prague. They weren't prepared. We are. We're taking the initiative, you get it? There's thirty thousand Russian troops in this country and if they're goin' to use them, okay, they're goin' to use them. But if their tanks get in we're not goin' to throw whitewash over them like they did in Prague. We're goin' to shoot back. This won't be a walkover, it'll be a war. They wouldn't have dared to go into Prague if there'd been military resistance. How can the U.S.S.R. let itself be seen fighting a *war* with one of its own loyal satellites? Even if it could win?" The bright smile was frozen now, a rictus. "We've raised an army here. Fifteen units of picked men. Men like Viktor. Okay, men like me. Men who will *not* have the land of their fathers turned into a penitentiary for state-registered juvenile delinquents. Right? We have stockpiles strategically dispersed—subguns, grenades, land mines, you name it. Wednesday morning, 0001 hours, the three main generating stations hit the sky. Will you be here? Don't be here Wednesday, pal."

He tossed back the last of his drink.

Alinka was moving across to us. Halfway she stopped, and stood listening. Viktor and Polanski had been talking together and now they were silent.

"Jo," I said. "Is it the only way into this place? By the elevator?"

"Huh? Yep. I guess we just sweat it out." He'd heard them now.

There was a question I didn't want to ask him.

Voices now, not coming from any particular direction, just through the walls, through the floor. The building had come alive. Doors slamming again but this time inside the building, the doors of the apartments. The thudding of jackboots.

Alinka was very still. So was Polanski. Viktor had gone for the gun and picked it up and now he sat with it across his knees. Joe hadn't moved but his eyes had narrowed and they began flickering as if the light was too bright. He had stopped smiling and his face looked as it had when I'd first seen him come lurching in here: blank with shock. He was a man who lived hot and worked best when he was bombing his way into a precinct bureau and now there was nothing he could do but stand here while his nerves drew thin and the blood receded, leaving a mortuary pallor. Perhaps he knew it now, the question I didn't want to ask him: had he been followed here?

Listening, you would have said there were rats running behind the walls, their sound magnified.

Last night I'd gone half a mile through the shadows of the river-walk before climbing and cutting across the city centre to the hotel, and on the way I'd seen this taking place in a quiet street near Dworce Srodmiescie. They didn't hurry—there were no klaxons or shrilling tyres—yet the operation was incredibly fast: three Warszawa saloons pulling up near the middle of the street with an M.O. riot-squad Jeep at each end to block it off. Ten seconds, and five hundred people made captive as if a net had dropped from the night. Most of them hadn't even known. In the privacy of their apartments, at their ease in the intimate light of the television screens, nothing had told them that for fifteen minutes a paralysis had held them powerless, that there had occurred a visitation of the State.

Some had known. It wasn't a general search but a raid with specific objectives. You are Franciszek Labedz? You will come with us. Five or six of them guided across the pavement to the waiting saloons, the sharp click of the doors, the jab of starters. A child had run after one group and its mother had pulled it back. I remembered the child's voice piping across the snow; more than other things I remembered that.

I found Polanski's eyes on me; we looked at each other without communication; we were looking in our minds at what we heard. This was a general search, noisy and with nothing in the orders about discretion. Most of the sound came to us through a lightproofed ventilator high in the wall above the Lublin dresser: the patter of boots on the stone stairs, the rapping on the doors, music from a radio out of tune with events, voices, surprised.

Co się stało?

Policia!

Far away, under the same sky, the moan of a tram along the Krakowskie Przedmiescie.

There'd been a door here in the wall opposite the stove, and two windows, one each side of the dresser; the edges were still visible but there'd have been a better job done on the other side, the door sealed and plastered over, the windows bricked up.

Teraz—natychmiast!

Iron knuckles in suède gloves: open your door. The State is here and you are State property. I am the State. Open. Boots tramped along the wall where the door had been and Polanski's head turned slowly as he listened, as if he saw their coated figures. His eyes were steady. It was Jo who moved, jackknifing slowly like a puppet with the strings suddenly cut. I was near enough to break his fall and Alinka came and crouched by him, whispering.

"He's been giving too much blood. He goes twice every week to the clinic."

Blood for Wednesday. I'd seen the queues, patient in the snow. Blood for Sroda.

The sudden scream of a woman.

Wladvslaw! Uwazaj!

Viktor's right hand was stroking the submachine gun, his head lifting as he heard the cry.

Jest pozno!

They'd got a man.

The scream fell to a dying cadence, becoming sobs.

I'd never seen such rage in a face as I saw now in the face of Viktor, his eye the eye of an eagle, caged and goaded. "Sroda," he said to the wall, to the boots and the belted coats, "Sroda," he promised the woman who tonight would sleep alone. Polanski heard him.

"Sroda," Polanski said.

Then they left the building, their sound ebbing as when a wave fills a gulley and drains away. Someone had switched off the radio and there was no more music from it. Faint voices called among the corridors, as if people had lost their way. Engines in the street.

We'd got Jo onto one of the settees, legs raised and head

down. Droplets of sweat sprang as fast as Alinka wiped them away.

"If they let me out of here," I said to her, "they might change the signal. The day—"

"I will not let them," she said quickly.

"They might not listen. The day after tomorrow your new *karta* should be here. If they change the signal you'll have to get someone to fetch it; I'll be at the Bar Kino at nine in the evening. Ulica Czackiego. Saturday."

I had to get clear now. Jo had confirmed the overall situation as reported by Merrick and it was all I needed and I didn't want to be still here when the rot set in; at any given minute in any given U.B. bureau someone else was going to break under interrogation and this building would be opened up again and sixteen rounds from a Typolt Mk XI wouldn't do much more than fill the place with smoke— they'd send in riot squads if they had to.

"The Kino," she said. Then Jo began lolling his head from side to side and we sat him up. It was no good telling them to get out of here with me because there wasn't anywhere they could go: wherever they went they'd risk exposure. Jan Ludwiczak hadn't been told where this safe house was located or they'd have smashed the mirror by now, but every time one of them left here, the rest were at risk. It would be the same anywhere else.

Polanski stood looking down at Jo. Viktor hadn't moved; the gun was still across his knees. He seemed lost in some other time and some other place, maybe the barricades of Sroda.

"All right, Jo?" Polanski said.

"I don't know why it happens."

"It happens because you keep going to the clinic. From now onwards you'll keep away."

I began moving to the door. Halfway across the room I heard the slight clink of a sling buckle as Viktor swung the gun but I went on moving because this side of a verbal warning I thought I was probably safe. I didn't know how stable he was but I'd seen they had to handle him with patience.

"*Stoj.*"

I turned round.

In German, Polanski said quietly: "All we want to know is who you are."

Jo was trying to get off the settee but Alinka stopped him: it looked as if you didn't go too near Viktor when he had his finger inside the guard. But she was angry, brittle of speech.

"Vik. You know what he did for me."

Polanski said to me: "We don't want to make any conditions." He wet his lips, compressing them. "You'd be free to go, if . . ." he moved a loose hand, the one nearer Viktor. "We trust you, but we want to feel safe here, and you knew how to find us. Who told you? That's really what worries us. We know the British are on our side to the point of actual diplomatic backing and we know what you've done for us personally, so it must seem we're being mean with our thanks. But if you'll just give us—"

"Vik," Jo said with his eyes squeezed into bright slits, "you've got ten seconds to put that damn' thing down and then I'm coming to get it."

Alinka murmured something to him. Polanski watched me with worried eyes. I didn't know how much logic Viktor was capable of following but it had to be tried.

"One of you led me here."

I looked away from Polanski and down the length of the room at the ravaged untrusting face above the snout of the Typolt.

"That's how I knew. Nobody told me. You exposed your safe house because you're amateurs: you don't know when you're being followed or when the police are moving in to pick you up, and when one of you gets pulled in you don't know where he is till somebody tells you and then you go in with bombs instead of a blueprint, so you never get near enough to spring him. You've no source of counterfeit papers, so the minute you're on the wanted list you've got to get off the streets and where do you go? To a refuge with only one exit and not even a Judas hole, and my name for that is a trap. The day I arrived in this city I didn't know you existed: I'd only been told. But my job was to locate you and within forty-eight hours I'd done that. I'm a professional and for me it was routine but for you it could have been fatal; none of you would be here now if my interests didn't coincide with yours. But it happens that they do, so let's put that thing back in the toy cupboard and go through our twice-times again. You've struck some luck when you need it most: I've been useful to you and I can be useful again. But not on your terms. On mine."

Viktor hadn't moved. I met the fixed black stare of his eye but learned nothing from it; there was courage in this face, and suffering, but no sign that it could recognise an appeal to reason.

I said: "I'm going now. If you shoot, remember you'll be shooting away one of your own barricades."

As I turned my back on him I heard someone move behind me but it was too late to do anything except keep on going and it wasn't until I was through the sound-lock and shutting the outer door that I saw her lean black figure standing across his line of fire.

It took nearly fifteen minutes to check and recheck for surveillance because of the light conditions and wall angles and the lack of effective cover. They'd only raided one side of the building and they could have posted some people in the area to observe later movements. The damned place was a trap.

Then I was filtering through the network of narrow streets where the snow was thick and the lamps few and the night quiet, encoding in my mind a fully urgent signal to Egerton telling him that tonight the whole pattern had shifted and that something was wrong, hellishly wrong.

9

RENDEZVOUS

Steam burst across the red lamp and left its bloodied plumes blowing in the dark, and wheels rolled, iron on iron. No one was there, it had gone, and he crouched in front of the ammo boxes, rubbing his cobbled fingers, and steel rang, dull as a cracked bell.

See him and pull him out, it was getting too close, they wouldn't like that, but he was no better off than I was. He couldn't even take care of himself: they'd only got to bust open one of the Czyn places while he was there doing his homework like a good boy, and they'd clink the poor little sod for aiding and abetting dissident factions clandestinely engaged in activities against the *Polska Rzeczpospolita Ludowa*, so forth. Make His Excellency the British Ambassador look a right lemon.

Soot clouded between the massive spokes and he blew his whistle, his black bright eye watching me above the drum of the Typolt, no go I said, not even a Judas hole. They ran right to the horizon, leaning together till their tips touched in a point, one of them was coming.

It was small at first because of the distance, and you wouldn't notice it if you hadn't spent years ferreting in the back streets of the political hinterlands, then you'd see it sticking out a mile. There'd been a definite pattern and it had shifted suddenly as if his finger had tapped a kaleidoscope: *we know the British are on our side to the point of actual diplomatic backing.*

Oh are they really, well that's very interesting.

It came fast and grew gigantic, a black mountain on the move towards me, and she lay there with her lean body stretched under the lamp, her shadowed ivory breast tipped with blue in the deathly light and a dark curl creeping in the wing of her arm; then the sky was blotted out and it was on me with a shriek and I was down, too many friends, next time they'll make sure his head's under the wheel.

The long sound of it drew out, thinning to silence, and a signal clattered. The ceiling was dark again. Polyphasic sleep had left me surfaced and I leaned across her, a dream fragment persisting, and checked the time: 0015. The 0015 to Krakow via Lódź and Czestochowa, a black brute loosed southwards across the snows.

Fqb fqqi lup ddqb gjuu hhr ixxn gls eedf nlqq jri srrw hqw oouh yoxx wqk huuh.

I'd seen one this morning, with weak sunlight throwing clear reflections on the windows because all the blinds were down. It had drawn away slowly eastwards towards the Russian frontier.

Third series with fifth-digit duplications and recurring blanks, normal contractions: *Can you confirm any degree of UK diplomatic backing of potential revolution here.*

But I wouldn't send it. Somewhere on the crest of a sleep

curve the thought had come: Egerton knew. And he expected me to know, to have found out. All he wanted was for me to do something about it. He was waiting for some raw intelligence to give his analysts, not for a signal saying look my drawers are all wet how did that happen.

There wasn't a lot of time. Merrick might get me some stuff on this but we were both moving into the red sector by now and I'd have to pull him out before long; behind the official preparations for the reception of the Western delegates there was a much bigger operation running. And the trains were rolling east.

The thing was that Czyn was being fed with doped sugar. The U.S.S.R. wasn't alone in hoping for the total success of the talks: the U.S.A., Britain, France and the Benelux states had been grooming their spokesmen since last August and the message was perfectly clear. The cold war had been devalued from the moment it was seen that short of global annihilation a hot war couldn't be won. Détente was back in fashion and when the Bonn delegation arrived in Warsaw there'd be quite a few bricks of the Berlin Wall lying on the ground. If the talks succeeded they wouldn't be the last: they'd open the way. And the U.K. would give diplomatic backing to a full-scale revolution in Poland as promptly as it would put the whole of its sterling reserves on a three-legged hundred-to-one outsider with its arse to the tapes at the off.

They'd know this, if their minds weren't inflamed with their dreams of manning the barricades in the holy name of the motherland.

The smell of the soot came now: it always took a few minutes. The building was old and decade after decade the trains had shaken it, loosening the tiles on the roof and the cement round the doors and windows and making cracks in the brickwork so now it was like a sponge, absorbing the smell of soot and diesel gas and exuding the smell of *bigos* and *karp po polsku* from the kitchen below.

Assumption: the doped sugar was being fed to Czyn by an agency purporting to be British and spuriously offering diplomatic backing in exchange for information. This agency served a state considered alien to resurgent Poland or it wouldn't have to assume British identity. Rule out the West: the CIA and the Deuxième Bureau and the Gehlen Organisation and the little mail-order firm in Geneva that sent all its bills in plain envelopes to NATO.

What information? Information on the activities of Czyn. We were getting that without any offers of backing. Egerton had meant what he said to Merrick: 'Nor must you lead them to feel that the United Kingdom is in any way prepared to assist them in whatever projects they have in mind, morally, physically, officially or unofficially. You must not even let them infer that such is the case, from anything you say; and if you think that despite your caution they have so inferred, then you must negate it. Is that perfectly understood?' He'd been so specific that he'd clearly known, at that time, what I'd learned only last night: that someone was soft-footing it round the Warsaw cellars with a borrowed Union Jack poking out of his breast pocket. And Merrick would follow that explicit order to the letter: his anxiety to make a good showing in his first mission was half-killing him. From behind me, his numbed face reflected against the dark trees of the park, he'd said with fledgling courage: 'I won't let you down.' That was his one fear.

Recheck and rule out the hairline possibility that it was MI6, and not a foreign agency. The Bureau doesn't exist, publicly or officially, simply because it's empowered to do things that could never be admitted, publicly or officially, to have been done; and built into its anatomy is a self-destruction unit triggered to go off in the instant when any one of its operations runs wild enough to risk exposing it. We all know that. Each of the shadow executives in the overseas missions echelon has the suffix-9 after his code name to indicate his proven reliability under torture, and among the facilities available to agents in clearance is the death pill. Because one single operative, nosing his way through the warrens of a sensitive area in Manchuria or Paraguay, can hit a counterintelligence trip wire and blow up London Control. That was why there'd been a death-house chill over the Bureau last week when a wheel had come off in Gaza: they didn't know where it would roll. And that was why Merrick, for all his tail-wagging eagerness to bring us the right bone, would have to work through half a dozen missions of increasing complexity before his director would brief him anywhere but in a taxi.

The situation that ruled out MI6 was that despite its official non-existence the Bureau was responsible to the same Minister and therefore subject to the same policy. Syllogism: the Minister dictated policy to both agencies. The Bureau had orders to negate any inference that the U.K. might assist Polish insurgents. The same orders would have been received by MI6. Ergo, MI6 could be ruled out. QED.

It wasn't the U.S.S.R. For one thing the setup was untypical of Russian thinking and for another thing they'd rather tuck a broken stink bomb into their breast pocket than a flag of the decadent capitalists even for the indirect purpose of hurrying their ruin. If Moscow wanted information on Czyn it didn't have to get it by subterfuge: the trainloads quietly leaving the city for the frontier at Briest would be passed through the interrogation centres before their dispersal to the camps. The snowball effect was already in operation: one member of Czyn, efficiently grilled in the detention cells, would buy an eastbound ticket for at least two of his fellow crusaders.

So there was no one. No one with any reason to use the U.K. as a cover for extracting information from Czyn. Yet it was being done.

The room was too small, shutting me in. The window was opaque, coated with ice, and I couldn't see beyond it. I got off the bed and pulled my coat round my shoulders, standing by the window to scrape at the ice with my nails. A ragged hole grew against the glass and I went on scraping until I could see a lamp below in the station, and then other lamps beyond, and finally the soft blue haze of the city thrown by the sodium lights and deflected upwards from the snow against the faces of the buildings. And the farther my eyes could reach, the farther my mind could range, and I knew with sudden tingling clarity that tonight I'd arrived at the edge of the area that Control wanted me to explore, and that once inside it I must tread with infinite care.

"The Bar Roxana."

He didn't know where it was.

"On Jerozolimskie."

The line wasn't bugged. I'd got the picture on the Embassy before leaving London and part of it was that three weeks ago the clicks and echoes had become so bad that they'd interfered with the actual conversation, so they'd fired a diplomatic rocket at the Polish Foreign Ministry suggesting they took a look at Clause 19(a) Para. II of the Instrument of Convention, reference facilities granted to foreign missions: *and that such telephonic installations shall at all times be free of technical modification.* Everyone does it, of course; there's a jukebox in a cupboard within sight of the Cenotaph where you can enjoy a do-it-yourself Linguaphone course right round the clock, but now and then a rocket goes in and for a few weeks His Excellency can date his Bunnies without it actually getting into Hansard.

When did I want him to be at the rendezvous?

"Say half an hour."

He sounded worried because it was the first specific rdv we'd made and he was wondering why I couldn't just pick him up in the street as I'd done before. He didn't say anything about this; he just said that he'd start out for the Roxana straightaway.

Before he could ring off I said: "Use a taxi. Get it to drop you off somewhere neutral like a post office and then do the last few blocks on foot. They put a tag on you from the Residence to the Chancellery this morning, so make sure you're clean."

I'd used a phone box midway between the hotel and the bar so that I'd be certain to get there first; there was a bus queue opposite and I stood there for nearly thirty minutes in the cutting wind before he came; then I gave it five minutes and it was all right, so I followed him inside and ordered Vodka grogs.

"It took you long enough."

"I'm sorry." He looked like death.

"How many were there?"

"Only one, I think."

"You think?"

"Only one." He couldn't look away from the door.

"Don't worry, I checked."

He looked away now, his eyes red from the wind that had cut behind his glasses, his glasses magnifying them, magnifying the fright in them.

"Did you?" Then he got the thing out and pumped it. "Excuse me."

"I'm having you pulled out of Warsaw."

He looked as if I'd hit him.

"What have I done wrong?"

"Nothing. This isn't your game, that's all."

It was the first time he'd had to flush a tag and if it had left him shot to shreds like this, then how in God's name was he ever going to survive until it became just a natural act like blowing your nose?

"I haven't been at it very long."

"The best time to pull out."

But the thing was that I couldn't do it to him and I knew that. Check his reports, keep him out of trouble, those were my orders, and I could signal London till the Telex seized up and it wouldn't do any good because they wanted him out here and they didn't care if it killed him and they didn't care if I had to stick here and watch them do it.

"I'll get better," he said, "as I go along." He couldn't get his breathing right and I knew by the way he hung on to his mug of grog that he was fighting the urge to fetch out the atomiser again and shame himself with it. "Don't send me back."

I looked away. "It's not in my hands. I just wish to Christ it was. Have you got anything for me?"

It wasn't much, a couple of sheets. Certain changes of plan in spearhead deployment, reduction of present radio contact to minimise risk, increasing importance of person-to-person liaison (he meant cut-outs), so forth. Nothing about what I was looking for.

"Which unit was this? The one they wiped out yesterday?"

"The one in Tamka."

"Where the power station is."

"Yes."

"Where they'd fixed up radio-controlled detonators?"

"Yes."

His tone was numb and he sat hunched in desolation and I was fed-up with it.

"Well, they won't go off now, will they? Let there be light next Wednesday, and there will indeed be light. It's a bloody shame, isn't it, Merrick? It'd be nice to think we were looking at a report on something that's going to make history, a glorious revolution wresting the independence of an oppressed people from its despotic overlords and pre-cipitating the collapse of Russian dominance in the whole of Eastern Europe. But what we're looking at is the autopsy on a dead duck."

I think he hated me then. His head jerked and his eyes opened very wide and he stared into my face, wishing me dead.

"That's what you—" and a spasm took him and he sat with

it and I waited and finally he managed to get his breath without using the spray and I liked him for that, he'd got pride. "That's what you want. Isn't it?"

"No."

"Then why—"

"Because I'd like to see them do it and I know they can't."

The tension went out of him and he looked down.

"But they ought to try."

He said it very quietly and not really to me. And I knew he was saying it about himself, no one else.

"They'll try all right. Christ, so would I. It's just that we're not going to get much of a kick out of watching them fail."

Two men came in and I checked them in the mirror. It was routine but I did it a fraction quicker than usual because until tomorrow it was important that nobody asked to see my papers.

"Did that stuff go off?"

"I'm sorry?"

"To London."

"Oh yes."

"What time does the Queen's Messenger get in?"

"He'll be on the three-fifty plane."

"Cleared by four-thirty, Customs and entries, all that?"

"A little sooner, unless there's more snow and the roads get—"

"Look, just keep it on you and leave at the normal time, about six. Make for the Residence and if there's a tag you'll have to flush him."

He nodded, swallowing.

"It gets easier every time. You only had a standard gumshoe this morning and you'd have peeled him off all right if you'd wanted to. Thing is to know they're there." I folded his report and gave it to him.

"Don't you want it?"

"Hang on to it for the moment." He put it away clumsily, catching a corner and having to smooth it out and do it again. "It's on the ball," I said, "don't worry. But there's no mention of the U.K. diplomatic support they think they're going to get. Why not?"

His face went blank. "Support for the revolution?"

And the pattern shifted again and I wasn't ready for it any more than I'd been ready the last time and it took me a couple of seconds to steady up.

"That's right."

"They must be out of their mind. Why should the U.K. want to disturb the balance of East-West relations just when there's the hope of—"

"How many people in Czyn have you been in contact with, a rough count?"

"Fifteen or twenty. The Ochota unit near—"

"And none of them have talked about it?"

"Not to me, or I'd have put them right. You remember what Mr. Egerton told me about scotching any ideas like—"

"Let it go."

He shut up and I tried to think of a snap answer because sometimes it'll work if you just let your mind take a jump in the dark before you have to inhibit it with data and do it the hard way, the logical way. Sometimes it works but not always. Not now. The thing was that it would be very important to Czyn if there were even the slightest hope of Great Britain lending support to what they were trying to bring off, and if one unit knew about it they'd pass it on to the whole network, priority flash. And they hadn't.

I finished the hot vodka. It had sped up the circulation and I could feel my fingers again; it had even given a bit of colour to Merrick's face though the effect was macabre, like rouge on a cadaver's cheeks. It'd be interesting to know why he related his bid for freedom from paternal dominance with the Polish people's attempt to get out from under the Muscovite boot to the point where the bare idea of their failing was breaking him up.

"*Ile się należy?*"

"*Dziesięć zloty.*"

Merrick got off the stool. "Thank you."

"Wait five minutes. Be in touch."

He stopped me halfway to the door. "Are you going to ask London?"

"Ask them what?"

"To take me out of Warsaw." His eyes were vulnerable, ready to flinch.

"We'll both be getting out before long. You're here to get info on Czyn, so you'll stay till the last train leaves for the camps but I don't give it beyond Tuesday. Till then we'll be treading on eggshells. If you get caught in a raid don't count on your diplomatic immunity because it doesn't cover your involvement with elements hostile to the state. And don't count on me, because you know what I told you in London: I'll throw you to the dogs."

The street was clear when I went out. The only danger was from the uniformed M.O.'s because the secret divisions didn't have anything on me. I turned left, going westwards through the failing light and picking my way over the sooty crusts that still covered most of the pavements. There hadn't been a thaw to make any slush and they couldn't do much with shovels.

Proposition: an agency was using the U.K. as an infiltration image and promising diplomatic support. Remarks: impossible because no one had any reason to do that. Proposition: the said agency had convinced Polanski and therefore the whole of his unit that the U.K. was in fact allied to their cause and the unit had kept this highly encouraging news to themselves. Remarks: impossible because they would have passed it on. Problem: relate two impossibilities to reality.

Most of the shop windows were lit. There was no real daylight here: night came at any hour after noon and covered the buildings until late morning. They said that if the wind blew from the southwest there was sunshine here, even in winter, and the forests ringed the city with jewelled ermine. Today the wind sliced through the streets from the north, numbing the bones.

One other question circled my thoughts: it looked as if Czyn was going to have its lifeblood drained away before it could spill it at the barricades. If so, why did the Bureau want information on its activities? Why take the pulse of the dying?

Towards the Plac Zawiszy I turned right for safety's sake and crossed the railway bridge and went left again along Ulica Vrodz and that was where they got me.

10
FOSTER

It was just bad luck. They came round the corner and we were face to face before I could do anything.

"*Dokumenty.*"

They were young and their faces weren't quite composed: I think they'd been laughing about something, perhaps girls, and now they'd got their duty to do but the amusement was still in their eyes as they looked at me, waiting. They would check my papers and walk on again, their secretive laughter coming back as they talked.

"I have lost them."

One of them smiled at my joke. It was almost as good as the one about the girls.

"Dokumenty," he said, and showed me his police card, tapping it. My Polish had been halting enough to assure them that I couldn't have understood. You do not lose your dokumenty. It is all you are.

"I am trying to find my way to my Embassy, so as to report the matter. The British Embassy. My best way is along Ulica Jerozolimskie, isn't it?"

He put his police card away and tapped the lapel of my coat, his eyes very intent now. The other one, taller, leaned forward to listen. I could smell the damp cloth of their uniforms, the leather of their belts.

"You have no papers?"

"I have lost them. I am on my way to the British Embassy to report it. This is a very serious matter for me."

Crossroads and two vehicles opposite directions a few people in a queue conditions awkward a clear run fifty yards but their guns: quite often the classic maxims of training duplicate natural instincts but there has to be brain-think as well as stomach-think and the chances here looked remote and it could be lethal. In the early days it strikes you as clumsy, the idea of making a run for it, inelegant; then you come to know what it's like, their tonelessly barked questions, the clang of a door, the half-lit passages, the grille where they come to watch you, and the moment when you think: my God, I could have run, now it's too late. But you can swing too far the other way and there's a new one to learn: that you mustn't let the thought of interrogation worry you so much that you'll make your run blindly.

"You have no papers."

"No."

They leaned close to me, attentively, needing to get it quite right, to believe the incredible, because in a police state if you have no papers you have no face, no name. You are guilty of not existing.

"Come with us."

Recheck. No go. The discretion factor was the only advantage, firearms will not be used unless, so forth. The rest was all on the debit side and even if they didn't shoot I could come unstuck and go sliding under one of the vehicles.

"Will you please show me the way to my Embassy?"

The basic rule is to try anything but there's no guarantee it'll work.

They used the telephone point on the far side of the crossroads and we stamped our feet till the car came, a black Warszawa with M.O. on the side.

It was down in the Ochota precinct, a nineteenth-century building, once a private house but with a portico added on later and the doors doubled. The guard followed us in. Big portrait of the Chairman of the Presidium of the *Soyuz Sovetskikh Sotsialisticheskikh Respublik* and a smaller steel engraving of the Chairman of the Council of State of the *Polska Rzeczpospolita Ludowa*, several others, one of them behind the desk, Janusz Moczar, the Minister of the Interior; he was the man I'd want.

There was a stove in the corner and the dry air was opening up the guard's sinuses: his post was outside in the raw sooty wind. Long bubbly sniff and mouth exhalation, long bubbly sniff, five-second frequency.

"What is your name?"

"Bodkin."

"Other names?"

"Alice."

In the old days it was easy. You'd say your name was Need Help and when they rang the Embassy for information on a British national who'd lost his passport, the clerk would twig it and send a secretary along and you'd all go home and have tea. These days the intelligence services had so much on that they kept most of the embassies in a state of quiet hysteria and if an agent got copped they just sent out for champagne.

"You have lost your papers?"

"Yes."

He was a police lieutenant in uniform but not an M.O. and I couldn't quite place him. In the Eastern bloc states the uniformed branches are the Civil Police, Civil Police Volunteer Reserve and People's Militia, but the secret divisions can add up to a dozen or more, each with its specific interests: surveillance of political factions, infiltration of foreign missions, active suppression of Church influence, monitoring of the state apparatus, maintenance of files on the population, with a few top-level divisions directly responsible to Moscow. In some cases there's considerable overlap and you can be trundled from one detention centre to the next while they try to work out who's job it is to give you the chopper.

The other man didn't say anything. He sat near the stove with his pale hands dangling over the ends of the chair arms, a secret-division executive in a black suit and pointed shirt collar and his tie in a very small knot: a dough-faced middle-aged Party official with eyes like a fish that watched me all the time but never looked at me. He would be a Moczar man but that didn't tell me anything because the Minister of the Interior was the head of the police power and he could be in any one of its divisions, but he worried me because they're always on the lookout for exchange material and this was a suitable time: an international conference tends to cosy-up the atmosphere and that's when people, like fringe-syndicate journalists, step out of line and get hooked, in addition to which we had Blok and Shelepov in the Scrubs and they were both valuable enough for Moscow to try setting up arrangements.

"What is your business in Warsaw?"

"I cannot tell you that. I require some paper and an envelope, please. I wish to send a message to Comrade Janusz Moczar immediately."

The first thing was to get into the open. There'd be an armed escort but a chance could come up. In here there was no chance at all.

He looked at the dark-suited man and one of the pale hands lifted and fell by a fraction. He didn't speak.

"You wish to approach the Minister?"

"Yes. To demand my immediate release."

"On what grounds?"

He was writing a kind of shorthand. The atmosphere had changed: it was bound to. In a closed society with strictly ordered disciplines there's always fear present: particularly fear of those in power because they don't need evidence or warrants or public acquiescence to proceedings before they can act. They'll slam a man in and throw the key away, even if he's a major general with a brother the chairman of the National Assembly: *onset of acute paranoid manifestations,* a signed certificate, all quite circumspect. Fat chance for a police lieutenant if he didn't notice the soap.

"My reasons are private. They concern the Minister of the Interior and no one else."

Meaning that he was already on dangerous ground.

A pale hand lifted and fell but I only saw it at the edge of the vision field and I couldn't tell if the signal differed from the earlier ones. The man I was really talking to was that one, in the black suit; the other was only a voice.

"You are personally acquainted with the Minister?"

"Of course."

If it wasn't going to work it was at least keeping his mind from the standard questions and that was a help because I couldn't answer them. P. K. Longstreet was floating under the ice of the Vistula and he'd have to stay there. I'd given them a name but it didn't make any difference: when did you arrive in Warsaw? By what flight? Where are you staying? He'd check and draw blank and they'd know I couldn't tell them my business, so the best thing was to point that out before they'd got round to it.

His belt squeaked as he reached for the cheap wooden letter rack and tugged out a sheet of sepia-coloured paper with the police crest in the top left corner and a smudge near the edge.

"You may write."

"That piece is not clean enough. This is for the Minister, I have told you."

He got another piece and turned it to the light and laid it flat on the desk and I nodded and got my pen. They were going to steam open the envelope somewhere along the line but they wouldn't expect me to know that so I said:

"Please place yourself where you cannot read what I shall write. I must remind you again: this is for the eyes only of the Minister."

He turned his head and the hand instructed him. As I reversed the pentop and stuck it on, he got up and paced towards the doors, his jackboots creaking.

Go outside and blow your nose and come back.

As I began writing I heard one of the doors open and the guard go out; and even after these few minutes I sensed the street and the sky with the hunger of the trapped animal, because it might be months or even years before such a door would open for me.

At midnight I used three *asanas* to combat the cold: *uddhiyana, jalandhara* and *vajroli mudra*. They'd taken my watch but the chiming of a town clock came hourly through the high ventilation grille, and the acoustic effect had a freak quality because the space was small: it sounded as if the clock were in here with me, its volume diminished, or that I was listening to it in the open.

It was only the watch they'd taken. The rest had been checked and handed back: wallet, pen, money, where are your keys? I do not have any. Why not? My room key is at the hotel and I have no car here and I do not require the keys that I use in my home country. Handkerchief, *Angielski-Polsko* pocket dictionary, penknife, nothing else; the poor little devil had thought he'd got his sums wrong when I'd given him back his report but it was just that between blowing your cover and getting a new one you've got to watch what you carry.

The search had surprised me. They ought not to search a personal acquaintance of Comrade Moczar and they ought not to take his hat off and shoot a full-face and profile against the white board but they'd done that too. It was all right because those pictures are useful only when they've got you inside, and if you can get out again they're no good as an image to work with when they're looking for you in the street, especially in Warsaw in winter when everyone's identical in a fur képi but all the same they ought not to have done it.

The lieutenant had given me an envelope and I'd sealed it myself. I must tell you that if this message is not delivered immediately by hand you will invite serious trouble for yourself. If it is intercepted or opened before it reaches the Minister, he will learn shortly from my associates that I have been apprehended and will know that my first action would have been to contact him and demand my release.

He'd gone off with it himself, cap, greatcoat and gloves and a salute for the wax-faced man in the black suit. Then I was taken to a smaller room with barred windows for the search and the photographs. That was nine hours ago.

From here to the *Najwyzsza Izba Kontroli* it was twenty minutes by car, but of course he could be absent or busy supervising the clearance of the underground forces from the city. But it didn't look good.

Some hot stew and black bread at half-past eight, then I'd spent a few minutes facing the possibilities: a full-scale interrogation and the subsequent workout when I wouldn't talk. Solitary detention, sleep and sensory deprivation, stress-imposition and the ordering of painful postures, sudden switches of attitude from the accusatory to the benign, physical strictures: and they wouldn't be the worst. Within a few hours you can turn any man into a mad animal, but there's a break-off point because the object is to get information and they can't get it if they've gone too far and wrecked the personality. It's up to that point where the suffix-9 has a value: beyond it you're lost and so are they and they know that, the good ones. And that's your only hope.

But nobody likes the dentist.

Keys again. He was a big man but thin about the face,

and his eyes were never still, showing their whites like a kicked dog, watchful for a boot.

"*Dobrze?*"

"*Dobrze.*"

He took the tin bowl and the spoon away, snatching them suddenly and hurrying out, frightened that someone might have heard him offer a word to me out of his inborn peasant courtesy. His hands should be on a plough as his father's had been: what was he doing here among bricks and bars?

The cold was depressing. Cold is for the dead.

In presenting my compliments I request my immediate release from detention in the Ochota Precinct and your personal guarantee that I shall not in future be molested in any way by members of your police services. Their action in questioning the loss of my regular documentation was fully justified, but I wish to avoid similar incidents during my stay in Warsaw, and therefore require the use of a provisional laissez-passer bearing your own signature and seal, which I shall be prepared to surrender on leaving Poland. I have no wish to jeopardise your high position in the Cabinet at a time when critical pressures menace the stability of government, but since I am in possession of certain facts at present unknown to your political opponents I find myself obliged, in my own interests, to ask your immediate attention to those matters stated above.

A light burned in the corner near the latrine channel, a low-power unshaded bulb that hung within an inch of the wall. Its warmth had been melting the frost on the brickwork since the beginning of winter and now an icicle clung there, reaching to the concrete floor. In it the bulb glittered, many times reflected, gilding it and giving it the semblance of an ikon, here for the prayers of the wretched.

Working principle: to the cupboard of every man, a skeleton; and the greater the man, the more need to keep its door locked. In the hierarchy of government the truth has no exclusivity, but in the state apparatus of the communist world it has particularity because the discipline of the Party credo leaves scant room for human error, and as the comrades labour their precarious way up the pyramid of power, a thumb in the eye and a boot on the neck of their nearest competitor, they know that a slip will send them pitching down again.

Tell any man *I know what you've done* and he'll think at once of his worst indiscretion: fear and guilt will persuade him automatically that if anything is known then it is the worst that is known. I thus expected that if Comrade Janusz Moczar ever received my message he would send for me. I might be bluffing but how could he risk that assumption? Once in the privacy of his office all I could do would be to use his face as a guide, making oblique references to black-market manipulation if greed showed there, hinting of mistresses if he looked a lecher.

Comrade Minister, the regulations controlling foreign currency exchange have always been subject to certain evasions, as I'm sure you know, but few people realise that a large part of the profits made by the touts in the big hotels finds its way to the coffers of those empowered to stop these widespread transactions, if they chose.

Comrade Minister, the private affairs of the members of the Polish Cabinet are of course not my concern, but the world is sometimes inconveniently small, and a certain lady of my acquaintance—here in Warsaw—recently proved herself regrettably unentitled to the confidences extended to her by others. You know how it is, when an exclusive little party lingers on . . .

Delete where inapplicable.

And use his successive reactions as data feedback to correct my course to the target. It could be done. It has been done. Braithwaite is particularly good at it and whenever he shows up at diplomatic receptions a lot of the guests take out instant insurance by cabling their wives through Interflora. He works, as I would work, by the elementary rule that the surest way of extracting information is to imply that you know it already. Moczar would come out strongly for proof and he wouldn't get it because I hadn't got it, but the aim would be to convince him that he couldn't take the risk of throwing me back into detention; he'd be smart enough to know that even a fragment of evidence against the head of the police power could be worth a lot to the officer responsible for my safekeeping if I took a crack at trading it in for an arranged escape.

The gilded ikon glowed. Perhaps I was dazzled by its light or by the wishful thoughts that some call prayers. But the throw I'd made could get me out of here and into the open where the clock chimed under the sky: it could at least do that, and give me the chance of a break.

Keys.

A different man, older and less scruffy, a professional imprisoner, impersonal, his remote eyes playing directly on my face. I have never been taken out of a cell for abortive execution but I thought I recognised the look he gave me.

Hearing already the predestined crackle of shot among the walls outside, he seemed puzzled that I still had movement. Perhaps he looked at us all in that way, his time sense dislocated by monotony.

Two guards. Come with us, they said.

In the room where they'd taken my watch away they now handed it back and I fastened the strap: it was an hour before dawn and the window was still dark. There were four of them now, a captain of the M.O. and three sergeants, all in spruce uniform and waiting punctiliously while I fixed the buckle and pulled down the sleeve of my coat.

"*Eskorta!*"

Two ahead and two behind as we clumped down the passage and through the office and out by the double doors, salute from a rifle butt and the bang of heels. The air smelt of steel and I saw a star caught in a web of cloud high over the skyline. The tang of low-octane exhaust.

They swung the step down at the back and we climbed in: there was no hustling. One of them put a hand on my arm but only to help me up the narrow steel step, as if I were infirm, or to be valued. We sat in formal rows along the side benches and no one spoke; it was all very official and through the heavy mesh on the windows I sometimes caught the reflection of the amber swivelling lamp on the roof of the van. Beneath us the chains flailed softly at the crusted snow.

Raszynska and a right turn into Ulica Koszykowa, the Czechoslovakian Embassy with its windows dark and the flag still frozen into the folds left by the last wind before winter.

North along Chalubinskiego and in silence something

smashed and I knew it was hope because this wasn't the way to the *Najwyzsza Izba Kontroli* where the Minister of the Interior was going to give me the freedom of the city in recognition of the fact that I had him across a barrel. He had me in a mobile cage and I was no better off here than where the light of the yellow bulb was turned to false gold and the mind was moved to false hopes.

"Wolniej!"

"Tak, Kapitan!"

We swayed sideways as the driver obeyed. The surface was treacherous and it wouldn't do to have an accident when carrying a prisoner. The street's jigsaw slowed across my eyes, cut into a matrix of images by the mesh at the windows. It was no good thinking *when they take me out* because when they took me out they'd be ready for an attempt, and if I broke clear they'd shoot and there'd be no point in facing the sky with a hand flung out, no answer to anything.

Then they were moving their positions slightly, straightening up, and the snow at the edge of the roadway crackled under the tyres. I couldn't see where we were because the name of the street had swung past in parallax behind the stem of a lamp, but I knew we'd crossed into the Wola district, north of the railway.

The captain and a sergeant climbed down and turned and I knocked the hand aside as it tried to help me and they closed in quickly as we stood in the rising gas, my arms pinioned now because the sudden movement had worried them. A good escort works like a blind-dog, regarding his charge as an extension of his own body, and there was no chance for me here.

When the prison van backed away I saw the big Moskwicz saloon by the kerb. It was in the Russian style, amorphous and lumpish and with curving quarter lights at the rear and domed hub plates; it stood on the snow like an immense polished beetle and above its roof I saw two men in black astrakhan coats coming down the steps from the pillared entrance to the building, the guards at the top still holding their rifles at the salute. The whole thing went smoothly, as if rehearsed: I was led quickly to the saloon and put inside, my escort shutting the door and standing back to keep orderly station along the flank of the car as the two civilians entered it from the other side, ducking their fur képis and taking their places, one on the occasional seat and the other beside me. The doors clicked shut and the engine was started and we got under way.

"Jolly cold, isn't it?"

He fished out a whisky flask with the ease of habit. He was the one facing me and I thought I'd met him before, as one does when one has seen so many pictures of a face in the newspapers. This one was crumpled rather than lined, as if the tissue-paper skin had been crushed into a ball and then smoothed out again; the large eyes were pink-rimmed, their whites laced with red rivulets, and the mouth was long, thin-lipped and set in an expression of irony as distinct from cynicism: it was the mien of a man who had long ago discovered, with secret delight, that the follies of others matched his own. His name was Foster.

He held out the flask. "Warm the cockles, old boy?"

I shook my head and he made a token gesture towards the man beside me before he unscrewed the top and with studied formality poured a tot and drank it at a gulp. I looked at the man beside me and saw that he was Russian, with the flat heavy features of its eastern peoples, a son of Irkutsk or Krasnoyarsk, more northerly. He sat with a rocklike equilibrium, watching the Englishman.

We drove through deserted streets towards the Vistula, the glass division isolating us from the chauffeur and his uniformed companion.

"How's the old country these days?"

"Keeps going."

He nodded, putting the flask away, not yet quite ready to meet my eyes. I supposed it was courtesy, to ask about England, not wistfulness, because to do what he'd done must have needed hate of some stamina. Love of country is only love of oneself, a grand form of identification, and that wouldn't have worried him; but to turn his back on the love of friends might have been more difficult.

"Are you here for long?"

"A few days."

"Picked the wrong time." His nerves showed behind the faint rueful smile and he looked away again. "I mean the winter."

"Which one?"

"Ah," he said, "yes." He stared through the glass at the slow parade of the buildings. "These people would be all right, you know, if they'd only get down to their work and show a bit of faith in those who are trying to create the new world. But they're too proud of their past, warrior nation and all that, it's old hat these days. Things have changed, and they're going to change a lot more. The past's all right, but you won't get far if you spend your life in a museum." He turned his face to me. "There's such a lot of good in them, though, just as there is in everyone, and it's a shame to see it go to waste."

I sensed the unconscious appeal, not for the Poles but for himself: he believed he didn't give a damn whether I thought there was some good in him or not, but he hadn't been long enough away to get a perspective on his convictions, and the shock alone was going to take time to dull off; twenty years in Whitehall with a solid reputation and a circle of friends who'd admired his two conflicting qualities of modesty and brilliance, then he'd been sent out to Port Said on a piddling little extradition job and by sheer chance had got blown, less than six months ago, with just enough time to get aboard the *Kovalenko* before she sailed for Odessa. And in London the headlines breaking the news he'd hoped never to make.

"They give you any grub, old boy?"

"Yes."

He nodded, satisfied. "Sorry they kept you hanging about like that. I only got called in a couple of hours ago." He leaned forward suddenly, his head on one side. "Thing is, it's quite a chance for us to talk to someone like you." We watched each other steadily for two or three seconds before an innocent smile touched his eyes—"I mean someone of intelligence, from the U.K. I dare say you've got a better idea of what's going on than any of these smart-aleck businessmen who think they know all there is. These talks, now —they're just as important to you as they are to us. We all know what they could mean, don't we, if they're given half a chance—virtual end of the Cold War, put it that way, aren't I right?"

The tone was easy, the eyes lit with the warmth of fellow feeling. This was the charm the popular Sundays had plugged six months ago, when the *Kovalenko* had been steaming through the Bosporus, the 'dangerous charm of the archdeceiver.' He was laying it on a bit thick but to a certain degree it was genuine and the real danger was there. At dawn in the capital of a police state east of longitude 20, I was being vetted by two KGB men of the Soviet State Security Service and if one of them happened to look like an amiable barfly in a London pub it was the more necessary to remember that in fact he was a man who'd sold his country and his friends for a coin he'd valued higher, a man who was going to send me back into the cells when this little ride was over. The van with the meshed windows wasn't keeping escort station fifty yards behind us just because it hadn't got anywhere else to go.

"Of course you know we're having a spot of bother here, these hot-blooded young rowdies. All they want is a bit of excitement now there's a chance, boys ourselves once weren't we?" He gave a short good-humoured laugh and this too was partly genuine; I remembered reading that thirty years ago he'd been sent down from Oxford for the traditional prank of sticking a jerry on top of a weather cock. Boys will indeed be boys but I also remembered the silver-haired man they'd half-carried out of the airport like a waxwork doll; he hadn't been a 'young rowdy.' "It doesn't add up to more than that," he said comfortably, "as I'm sure you realise. That's why we're a spot puzzled by these rumours going around, you know what I mean?"

We were still heading east, nearing the Vistula. There'd been a new prison established some eighteen months ago on the other side, in Grochów I.

"No."

He looked at me steadily for a moment and then sat back with a shrug. "There are so many rumours, aren't there, at a time like this, journalists in from all over the place, keen to jump the facts." Without any change in his tone, his eyes still sleepy—"I mean the one about the U.K. looking kindly on whatever shindy these young asses can kick up, if we let them."

So I could have wasted my time busting a hole in the ice with the Fiat because the proposition was that Polanski's unit was the only one that had been fed the dope about the U.K. diplomatic-backing thing, and now the KGB had picked it up and the KGB picked up most of its stuff by augmented interrogation, so who had they grabbed—Polanski? Viktor? Jo? Where was Alinka now? The trains were rolling east. I could have wasted my time.

I said: "Can you spell it out for me?"

Her lean body, a dark curl creeping in the wing of her arm, all she would ever be, a dream fragment persisting.

"We don't want to tell you things." His smile was faintly coy. "We want you to tell us things."

"If shindy means a full-scale revolution and young asses means half the population of the Polish Republic and looking kindly means the explicit patronage of Great Britain at Foreign Office level, I'd say it's worth about as much as any other rumour wouldn't you? I come from a country where—we both do, I was quite forgetting—where people would get a certain kick out of seeing the Poles chuck the Kremlin off their backs because we've always had a soft spot for the underdog whoever it is, but that's not enough to make us queer the pitch at a time when there's a hope of an East-

West *détente* in the offing. But you ought to know that, so why ask me?"

A spark had come under the heavy lids but now the eyes were sleepy again, full marks for that. The Russian hadn't moved but I sensed a reaction in his total stillness beside me: his grasp of the idiom must be pretty fair.

"I see, yes. That's what we thought."

"Then I haven't been much help."

"You mustn't think that, old boy. You're being most co-operative. Just what we were hoping for, bit of cooperation."

Lamps swung above us, their glow lingering wanly against the first milky light of the day. The span of the bridge curved upwards across the wastes of ice as we were lifted, losing the skyline, finding it again. In the glass division the side lamps of the prison van floated higher, two bright bubbles, and floated down.

"That's where someone went in." He was looking through the side window. "Couple of days ago."

"Went in?"

"Down there. In a car."

"Bust the ice?"

"Yes. I think he was trying to get away from the police. They say there was quite a chase. Poor chap, what a way to go. But he shouldn't have been so silly; the police here are very good. We've got to keep order, that's awfully important."

We slowed down the long descent towards Wilenska Station, having to use more of the shoulder because the first trams had started running.

Of course it could be the other way round: the KGB might not have picked it up—it could be their own man, the one

with the borrowed Union Jack poking out of his breast
pocket, feeding the stuff in. Why?

"It's like Wales," he said, turning to look at me, "and Scotland. You must try seeing it that way. They've kept their
spiritual independence but they've willingly helped England
fight her wars. Bit of flag-waving goes on at the Cup Finals
but there's no harm meant, is there? Charles went over
pretty big at Carnaervon, proof enough."

By rough reckoning I had ten minutes. I didn't know why
they'd switched me from the van to the saloon: it wasn't
so that they could vet me because they could have waited
until we were inside Grochów, where the grilling was going
to start. Perhaps it was caprice on his part and his masters
had indulged him: he was a first-ranker of high value to
them, twenty years' loyal service on the books.

What then had moved him, in the shadowed psyche below the brilliant mind, to offer me a ride in his comfortable
motorcar since we were going to the same place? Not his
sense of irony: that was too cerebral. Something deeper:
they'd said of him, those who'd been his friends, that if
he'd ever gone right over the edge he would have been a
schizoid, that the strain of his critically balanced double
life would have led him sliding into a world of phantasy.
But there was no real edge, no borderline: he was the type
who would order a cleanly laundered shirt for the con-
demned on his way to the gallows, to give his death a
token dignity; or choose that on my way into Grochów and
beyond I should hear the accents of familiar speech, here
in a foreign land, and know the comfort of being called
'old boy.' Or it was something more basic: self-justification

on the infantile level—here are you, a captive, and here am I, a free man, so who's the better?

Ten minutes—but it was a question of chance, not time—hit the door open and pitch out and hope not to break a leg and try to run before the snow was pock-marked around my feet and they corrected the aim and I knew it hadn't been worth it. Smash the glass division with a rising kick and connect with the driver's neck and send the lot of us sliding wild and hope to get clear of the wreckage and use the confusion as flying cover.

Not really. There was too much against it and I was only making sure I could answer the question that later, days later, would needle me when they got round to the advanced stuff and I'd give my soul to be free: hadn't there been *anything at all* I could have done? There had been nothing at all.

"Poland," he said reasonably, "and Czechoslovakia and the others, all keeping their spiritual independence and living in harmony with their mother country, just like Scotland and Wales. Does it sound so odd? It always takes time, of course—the future never likes being hurried. Think what a fuss there was when the Romans came, but they did a world of good, didn't they, gave us good laws and proper plumbing, don't know what England would have done without them. It's the same here, and you really ought to try taking the long view." Looking out at the dark figures huddled at a tram stop he said in a quicker tone—"You know your way, do you, around Warsaw?"

"A few of the main streets."

"You know roughly where you are now?"

"East of the river."

He nodded, tapping at the glass division. "That's right. Not far from anywhere, really."

As the big saloon began slowing, I saw the shape of the police van reflected beside him, closing in and then dropping back a little, keeping the distance.

He leaned towards me, his tone intimate now, the whisky on his breath. "The thing is, old boy, we don't want you to rock the boat. Moczar's got his hands full at present, cleaning things up for the talks, and we'd rather like him to be left alone."

He swayed back an inch as the saloon came to a halt by the kerb. The reflection of the van had also stopped, but none of its doors were opening: they were just sitting there, holding off. It could be a trap but if they wanted to rub me out they could do it quietly inside Grochów; the only point in this setup would be to establish public testimony to the fact that I'd been shot while trying to escape and it didn't seem logical. It looked like a chance and this time a real one and it'd have to be done explosively within the next few seconds, the right elbow driven hard and upwards to paralyse the windpipe of the man beside me and the left foot kicking for the face in front of me as the weight came back, difficult because of the balance factor but only difficult, not impossible; Kimura could have done it without any trouble, this or nothing, this or Grochów.

"So we're hoping you'll be a sport." He leaned forward, head tilted, the tone engaging. "We've got your name, and we'll see it's passed round to all the M.O. stations, so if you get picked up again just tell them who you are." A smile narrowed his eyes. "Bodkin. So English—and so Russian. Alexandrovich Bodkin, yes. What I mean is, you won't

need a pass or anything; we'll tell them to leave you alone."
He pulled at the chrome handle and the door swung open.
"Mind how you go: the streets are so treacherous, aren't
they? Because of the snow."

11

NIGHT

The cups had been specially designed, *Bar Kino* in white letters on the black ground of some 16-mm. negative that went right round the rim.

"*Proszę o rachunek.*"

Half an hour was fair enough.

She made out the pay check with the indifference of fatigue, her thigh against the edge of the table as she took the weight off one foot. A lot of them took two jobs, Merrick had said, to earn enough to buy clothes.

Western jazz of the thirties pumped from the walls. It had been a waste of time, the Fiat thing. Someone should have been here at nine and it was half-past now and I was going because I didn't want to sit here thinking about what they were doing to her.

"*Dziękuje.*"

Or what they were doing to me. They had me in a bottle. *I'll see you in my dreams.* One of the big bands, New Orleans, another world and another time. But you won't get far if you spend your life in a museum.

The thing was to avoid the attractions of the *idée fixe:* it can throw you. So we're hoping you'll be a sport. He needn't have said that. It had been quite enough to name the deal: they'd leave me alone if I'd leave Moczar alone. That was all I'd asked for and I'd got it and Alexandrovich Bodkin was now *persona grata.* And I'd been so glad to get off the hook that I'd fallen for an idée fixe: that my threat to the Minister of the Interior had worked, and worked even better than I'd expected. They'd not only given me the freedom of the city but had shown concern that I'd be unsporting enough to tread on his face just for a giggle.

Another thing to avoid is low blood sugar; a bowl of stew won't last you twelve hours and you can get lightheaded and it wasn't until I'd had some food that I'd seen the bottle they had me in.

He'd never received my note. They'd opened it and turned it over to the KGB when they saw what it said. A foreign national gets picked up and says he's lost his papers, and instead of answering questions he threatens to kick the head of the police department off his perch if they won't play it his way. An interesting case for investigation and they'd started to investigate it and they hadn't finished yet. It had been for the Englishman to make the decision: they could transfer me to a top-security prison and take me slowly to pieces and see what was left or they could let me go and let me run and see where I went. Classical Russian thinking and often highly effective and that was why I didn't like it.

It had been unnerving, getting out of the car and walking away, remembering it could be a trap and even believing it was a trap, the nape of the neck going cold, Western secret agent shot down in street, the crusts of snow skittering in front of my shoes like sooty sugar, the tram queue and the throb of the big saloon moving away, the higher-noted gear-whine of the van. Standing under the open sky where I'd prayed to the ikon to let me be, free and alone, the long night gone and the day beginning.

Later I'd done some brain-think. The city was mine and I could go where I liked, but if I tried to get on a plane or a train or an Orbis coach or took a car too far I'd find out how free I was. As free as a fly in a bottle.

We've got your name.

Also my photograph but he hadn't mentioned that. Pictures like those are normally useful only when they've pulled you in and start hunting you in the files instead of the streets, but this was a special case and by now they'd have been processed, life-sized blowups with a superimposed képi, pride of place on the notice boards in every M.O. station, subject: image assimilation by all patrols going on duty, remarks: report on movements and whereabouts, do not question or ask to see papers.

The only point they hadn't covered was too clear to miss and this afternoon I'd started research on it. Because they couldn't have just left the cork out.

I put down three zlotys and edged between the small round tables to the swing doors, then came back.

"Christ, I told you to send someone, didn't I?"

It was over a mile from there and if they'd picked her up they'd have booked her for the trains.

My cup was still there but it wasn't the same place.

"There wasn't anyone else."

"You could have sent—" then I shut up. She sat very still,

her dark eyes not really seeing me, a nerve alive at the corner of her mouth. I went over and said I wanted a cognac, meaning I wanted it now. She hadn't moved.

"When did it happen, Alinka?"

"An hour ago. Viktor is dead. I don't know where the others are—"

"How did they blow you? How did they find out?"

"He said he would never let them take him—"

"How did they find out?"

She began shaking and I shut up again, pushing the glass against her hand where it lay like a dropped white glove. It was a pointless bloody question anyway; they'd been wiped out and that was that, boots on the steps and the mirror smashed and the Typolt giving shot for shot, the dead eye of an eagle with the rage still in it, trust an amateur to make a mess of things: he'd looked like a professional but he'd been a professional suicide, that was all, the city was full of them.

"I was afraid you would have gone," she said.

"You weren't actually there, were you?"

"No. I had gone for a walk, and Leo was with me; he wouldn't let me go alone, even in the little streets. There were cars there when we went back, and Josef was running. We all ran, then, and Leo said we must separate."

She drank some of the cognac, both her hands round the glass, her eyes closing as she put it to her mouth.

"He wouldn't have lived longer than Wednesday. He was going to do it then. He was a born martyr."

"I know," she said.

I gave her the folded green card. "Don't look at it now. Look at it later."

She put it into the side pocket of her coat.

They'd been a bit pressed but it looked all right, thin cheap pasteboard and faint print, the photograph peeled and backed and stuck on slightly off-centre, not difficult but give them credit; it's the ageing process that takes most of the time because if you hurry the machine it'll just shred the thing up instead of reproducing the right degree of wear and tear. They'd even got cocky and put a lipstick smudge.

I'd told Merrick to send out one of the female clerks with the package from London in case he was tagged again. That was the reason I'd given him and it was partly true, but more important than that was the danger of my exposing him to the KGB. I was contagious now. I'd used the girl as a cut-out for protected contact: if an M.O. patrol or a U.B. agent had seen us meet, it wouldn't get them anywhere useful; they'd know I'd made contact with the Embassy and that was all: it wouldn't expose Merrick. And they'd expect me to trade with the Embassy because that was where they'd left the cork out.

The line had been safe, so I'd told him to start the research for me: "I want you to vet the cypher-room staff. Get the Ambassador to give you plausible facilities and tell London what you're doing so they can lend a hand. If you turn anything up you can hold it ready for me."

He said he wasn't quite sure what I wanted him to do.

"You assume that the cypher-room staff has been infiltrated and that incoming and outgoing signals are being copied and passed to the opposition either as a routine measure or as a special-surveillance operation. If you tell London to cover dossiers, they'll turn up the last screening programmes and they'll automatically monitor all signals for evidence of tampering. At this end you can give them the idea that you're in trouble because one of your signals was inaccurate or that you broke a security regulation and you want to check what you sent. Make it a recent one and give the impression that you know you've dropped a brick and that it's not their fault, in other words that they didn't make a duff transmission. What's your code?"

He said it was fourth series with first-digit dupes.

"All right, send off a couple of signals using the ignore key and tell them they're fully urgent and that they've got to send them while you're there. If they kick up rough because the tea's getting cold tell them it's on H.E.'s orders. Ask them to give you back your own originals and tell them you want their recoded originals and copies as well. If they let you have them, send another signal informing London they've done that and for Christ's sake leave out the ignore key this time. Watch their reactions at every stage and see if they fit your idea of people who've got nothing to hide."

He said he understood. He also asked what he should put in the ignore signals; I suppose the poor little tick had never had to send one before.

"Tell them you've caught it in the zip again."

The frightening thing was that it could be important: I wanted to know why they'd bottled me up in Warsaw but hadn't cut my line of communication through the Embassy. I didn't need to go there if I wanted to send anything out: within fifteen minutes of picking up the telephone in the Bar Kino the clerk in London could be decyphering. And they wouldn't want me to do that. Correction: they'd want me to do it but only if they could know what I was sending.

So I'd moved an untrained recruit into a highly sensitive area and it had felt like putting a match to a fuse, because if Merrick exposed an opposition agent actually installed in the cypher room of the British Embassy it was going to make a nasty bang at a time when the East-West delegates were sending each other roses. Merrick would be all right but I'd get the chopper; I was out here to local-control his mission and his mission was circumscribed and didn't provide for my pitching him into an area with this much potential for blast.

There'd been no choice. The Bureau doesn't like commandeering facilities in Her Majesty's embassies unless there's something big in progress and even if London sent me a ticket for the Warsaw cypher room I couldn't go in as young Merrick could, the image already established and the cover story dependent on it: I'd have to go in as a stranger with inspectorate powers and if in fact the opposition had placed someone among the staff he'd scare so fast that the next morning his desk would be empty and so would the filing cabinets.

I had to know their minds, to know if they'd said: *let him run and we'll watch where he goes, let him signal and we'll read what he sends.* The fifth series comes fairly high among the international unbreakables but a code only stays locked till someone finds the key.

Her glass was empty and she was watching me, the shock still dull in her stone-blue eyes, their quickness blunted.

"Are we useful to you?"

She wanted to know why I'd gone to the trouble of getting a new karta.

"Not really."

"If we can be useful, tell us."

"All right."

She gave a little nod and was still again. I could have learned something from this woman, from her ability to sit like this, her calm containing her anguish, a brother for the camps and a friend for the grave and the known world falling away like a city going down.

I got the girl over and paid.

"You've got somewhere safe you can go?"

"Oh yes." But she looked at me blankly because she hadn't thought of it yet: that there had to be somewhere safe she could go.

Perhaps there was nowhere now. The people who had rebuilt this capital from the ruins of the war were being smoked out of it like rats.

"Don't take any risks. Keep low for a few days."

"Yes," she said.

"Go to your parents. They in Warsaw?"

She answered in Polish because it was all she still remembered of them, the language they'd spoken together.

"There are friends you can go to." She nodded and I said: "I don't mean People in Czyn. Forget Wednesday, it's been called off. Forget the barricades, there won't be any. Just save yourself, Alinka."

I got up and she lifted her head, watching me, as I sensed she'd go on watching me when I left here, until the door blotted me out and another bit of her known world broke away.

"You'll be all right now. You've got your papers."

She nodded again. Standing over her I noticed her hand

sliding towards the empty glass, the palm flat on the table and the fingers parting and covering the round glass base as if to hold it down so that no one could knock it away and send its fragments dropping among all the other fragments of once-familiar things.

Papers weren't any use to her now. Even her name had been taken away for pulping in a destruction machine. Wanda Rek was no one, meant nothing.

I got a pencil. "If you need me you can phone this number. Just leave the message; they'll know who it's for." Then I left her and went through the swing door and crossed the street. The wind blew from the north and the tall lamps swayed at the top of their stems, sending shadows on the move. I thought it would have been possible to keep on walking, then I had to find a doorway and shelter there, not from the wind, from the idea of going on. There weren't any people about: they didn't fancy being out in this killing cold. The windows of the state supermarkets were bright with cheap goods to impress the visitors with the wealth of Polish production; the lamps kept the dark sky hidden and made it look as if the city were still alive or at least had once contained life, but from here it seemed more like a fairground hit by plague, a lone tram running blindly on its tracks into the distance as if there hadn't been time to switch it off, the perspective of neon signs winking for no one, for nothing. What a bloody silly time, I'd told Merrick, to open talks here, but he'd said they were expected to last for a good six months, well into the summer.

Then the movement, quite a long way off, of the only living thing that seemed to be left. Coming out of the bar she put her gloved hands to her face as she felt the cut of the wind, at first moving away from me and then coming back, not sure where to go in a world she no longer knew.

From where I lay, the window made a blank parallelogram, a screen where light came as a train went by, fading in the intervals to the background glow of the city. The glass had frosted over again, covering the clear patch I'd scraped with my nails, but it wasn't symbolic: I could see even farther now than I'd seen then. And I didn't like it.

There wasn't any light from the freight trucks, only their noise and the shake of the building; the light came from the passenger trains, though not from all of them because some had their blinds down, those for the east.

I didn't like it because most of what I could see was based on mission-feel and I couldn't discount it. Assumptions were unreliable: I assumed that there was an adverse party working the same field as Merrick and I and feeding the Polanski unit with doped info until its turn came to be wiped out, and I assumed that the KGB had chosen to vet me and let me run and both these assumptions could be wrong. Mission-feel is never wrong: it's the specialised instinct you develop as you go forward into the dark like an old dog fox sniffing the wind and catching the scent of things it has smelled before and learned to distrust; and in the concealing darkness the forefoot is sensitive, poised and held still above the patch of unknown ground where in the next movement the trap can spring shut.

The feeling I had was close to that; but a man, being a more sophisticated beast, is caught with traps of greater complexity, and what I sensed was that behind all the logic I was trying to bring to the few facts available and all the attempts to make a pattern from random pieces, the opposition had a programme running, its engineering as smooth and massive as the iron wheels that rolled past here on their predestined rails; and that I was in its path.

Egerton didn't know what it was but he knew it was there and he'd sent me to find it and blow it up.

"Is it morning?"

"No."

"I don't want morning to come."

She'd told me before in a different way, saying she didn't want the night to end, crying for a long time naked against me, the saltiness on my face, asking me to hurt her, as if the mind's hurt wasn't enough: guilt for the dead, the abandoned, her leanness quivering and her mouth avid but far from love. Later she forgot and the body was enough, her skin burning under my hands and her thighs alive: she made love as if time was running out. Later still she told me about herself, speaking in Polish and half to someone else: to the person who must one day find again and recognise these pieces of identity and try to make them whole.

"They wanted Jan and me to go with them, but Israel was only a place on the map and we had all Poland, where we were born. They sent long letters at first, saying what a solid future there was for us if we'd go out there, and how kind the people were, and finally we got sick of reading their letters and just tore them up, still in the envelopes. To me it was a kind of—not disloyalty exactly—a rejection of all we'd been as a family; they'd turned their backs on everything we'd known and loved and grown up with, the music and the forests and the fires in winter, and our friends. But I missed them, so did Jan, and when I got married it was partly to make a new home for him, though I think I was in love for a time. But Michal"—she paused on the name, finding an odd-shaped piece that she knew would never fit— "Michal started getting letters from my father, the same kind my brother and I used to get, and he said we were obviously missing a big chance, and tried to convince me, and couldn't. So he went out there to join them."

Thus it is in events that thy tribe shall forever wander, finding in the shade of each tree a seeming haven till it be shewn that as the sun moves, the shadow moves, leaving thee unsheltered.

"He said that since the Russians had taken over our country a Pole couldn't be a Pole so he was going where at least a Jew could be a Jew. I think he was sure I'd follow him, but I threw his ring from the Slasko-Dabrowski bridge."

Then for a time she slept and so did I, and when I woke towards dawn she'd moved away a little and leaned watching me in the grey light from the city, her face still stained from the tears that had dried, her eyes dark in thought as she asked me again who I was, who are you please.

"No one you'll remember."

I left her warmth, breaking the thin film of ice in the big copper pan. Putting my things into the airline bag I remembered thinking, somewhere in the night, that she'd have to stay here if she were to survive the next few days because the only friends she could go to were at risk themselves.

"I need a contact in Czyn. Someone I can phone any time between now and Sroda. This is a safe place. You told me to let you know if I wanted any help."

"You would like me to stay here?"

"Yes."

"I will stay."

"Have you got any money?"

"Some."

"You'll have to buy a few things. Ask the man to get them for you. Take a walk when you need some air but don't go far." I zipped the bag shut. "I'll phone always at an even hour, eight, ten, twelve, so be here then. If I don't phone, don't worry. I'm not sure how things will go."

I went to the bed and she raised herself, kneeling and twisting against me, biting gently at the pad of my hand, her black hair hiding her face from me till I left her and looked back once at her stillness, her arms crossed against her breasts and her hands clasping her shoulders, head on one side as she said:

"I shall see you again."

"Yes." The first lie of Sunday.

12

TRAP

The few people in the street wore black, and bells tolled, hurrying them across the rutted snow to where a spire poked at the low grey sky. The wind had died in the night, leaving calm. I walked southeast towards the river.

I'd given him some money.

"Let her have my room. Her papers are in order and you can put her name in the register. Give her what's left of this when she leaves." She wouldn't find work again until there was an amnesty.

Three patrols in two miles but they didn't stop me.

Karl Dollinger, journalist, born Stuttgart 1929. The immigration franking tallied with my actual arrival on LOT 504 and they'd put in a slip showing booking confirmation West Berlin, January 6. Reason for visit, to cover talks for *Der Urheber*, left-wing weekly. Various letters and memos, editorial recaps, Telex facilities, press-club card, so forth, nothing to fault.

Security was important now but that wasn't why I was switching base: if I'd needed to stay on at the Alzacka I wouldn't have taken her there. A new cover required a new address and the hotel I wanted now was the big state-owned Kuznia, nearly opposite the Commissariat in the Praga district. That was where they'd been going yesterday morning; from the distance I'd seen the security van keep up speed towards the next traffic lights but the big black Moskwicz had pulled in again soon after dropping me off. They'd gone into the building on the south side, Foster and the man from Irkutsk. I hadn't gone back because they could have slapped a tag on me, but the map in the City Library showed what the building was. It might not be their base, but if it wasn't I'd have to start my search from there.

I'd known yesterday what I'd got to do, but I suppose I'd baulked it because it wasn't a thing you could do in a hurry and I'd have to hurry: we stood three days from Sroda and Sroda was the deadline for Czyn, for the opposition and for me. I knew now what Egerton wanted and his tacit signal was clear: *define, infiltrate and destroy*. And I couldn't do it by standing in the way of the programme they were running: I'd have to get inside and blow it up from there.

A hundred and fifty rooms, fifty with private bath and outside telephone connection via the desk. This one had two windows facing the Commissariat at something like thirty-five degrees oblique, good enough and close enough to observe without binoculars. There was a spillover from the other big hotels nearer the hall where the talks were going to be held, but I managed to get a second-floor single and the timing estimate from the room to the street was fifteen seconds at a pace that wouldn't look hurried.

For three hours I drew blank. Some of the Commissariat

staff showed up before noon and lights were switched on,
so I began filling in the front-elevation sketch I'd made:
records, general admin., public interview, M.O. liaison, so
forth. Not many of the public went in, perhaps half a dozen,
most of them lost-looking, one of them frightened; they
were given an upright chair, fourth window left of central
staircase, third floor, and a big fur-coated woman spoke to
them without a pause and they didn't interrupt; her mouth
was rectangular like a ventriloquist's, opening and shutting
at irregular intervals while they sat watching, sometimes
giving a nod. There were two clerks in Records, both girls,
one of them slightly lame; they plied between the desks
and the filing cabinets, stopping sometimes to laugh together, their work routine and their thoughts on personal
things. Six uniformed M.O.'s reported to the second room
right of staircase first floor, handing some papers to a civilian
who sent them out with a messenger to a room at the back
of the building. The work of these people, routine or not,
was important enough to bring them here on a Sunday, and
it looked reasonably clear that the pressures driving towards
Sroda had opened the doors of every Commissariat in the
city.

I had the impression that if I could have persuaded the
two girls to leave the room with the crowded shelves, while
I lobbed an incendiary bomb through the doorway, a few
hundred thousand citizens of Warsaw would be better off.
It might even be worth doing once I was in there.

1305 seventh M.O. reporting. 1312 ninth interview. 1324
lights out fourth right third floor and the corollary: two
clerks down the steps. 1330 guard on the entrance relieved.
1341 Moskwicz.

The big black Russian-built saloon came in from the west, from across the Vistula. Foster and another man, not the man from Irkutsk but the political agent who'd conducted the interrogation in the Ochota precinct, his pale hands lifting and dropping on the arms of the chair. They got out and climbed the steps and this was very interesting because he must be high in the echelon to travel with a top kick like Foster in his turd-shaped de luxe saloon. I couldn't think about it now because I had to see where they went, and they went to the double-windowed room at the left end of the third floor and when I'd seen the lights go on I began thinking about it.

Findings: a routine M.O. patrol had picked up an unremarkable foreign visitor in the street and pulled him in for not having any papers, but by the time he was inside the precinct bureau there was a high-echelon agent sitting-in to conduct the interrogation and by dawn the next day he was under discreet vetting by the KGB.

They took off their coats and fur hats and Foster sat down and the agent took a folder from a cupboard, dark green folder, cupboard not locked.

Working backwards: I'd realised I was being vetted in the Moskwicz and they hadn't tried to cover it. The new material now coming in and making me sweat concerned the events that had led up to that: at some time between being picked up as a routine measure by the M.O. patrol and my arrival at the Ochota precinct fifteen minutes later, there'd been an alert situation. Someone had known, without seeing me, that I wasn't just one of the hundreds of foreign visitors in Warsaw on private business or with an interest in the forthcoming talks.

They'd known who I was.

The Moskwicz was still at the kerb and the driver and escort were still on board, black leather coats and civilian képis. Note this. Note everything and think fast in the intervals.

They couldn't have known who I was.

And make corrections. The wire had burned out and I'd have to twist the ends together till it glowed again and the analogy came to mind because the mission was suddenly electrified and Egerton was close to me, Egerton and his bloody lies, everyone else has refused, I'm really most grateful to you for helping me out.

Foster. Christ, had he sent me to bring in Foster?

Turn the coin. Foster had been sent to bring me in.

Because he'd been flown from Moscow, part of the alert situation. That was why they'd kept me caged, to give him time to get here. He lived in Moscow, the Sundays said, 'a modest existence in a flat not far from the domes of the Kremlin, once an Old Etonian and now a hero of the Soviet Republic with an alloy medal somewhere in the top drawer with his handkerchiefs and cuff links'; a rumour about a Hungarian woman, 'a simple daughter of the proletariat content to share his uneventful life.'

Until less than forty-eight hours ago he'd been given the signal: *Contact established Warsaw please proceed.*

The fly had hit the web and the web trembled.

They hadn't needed full-face and profile blowups for the patrols. They'd known where to find me *at any time*. That was why they could afford to let me go.

Brain-think. Stay on brain-think because there's a lot coming up and it's got to be looked at and there's not much time left now.

Let him run and we'll see where he goes. It still stood up: it was based on mission-feel and mission-feel is never wrong. But I could extend the certainty now: they already knew where I was going to run because I was in Warsaw to find things out and the only way to do it was to close in, get near them, as near as I was now, just across the street, observing and surveying and trying to work out how to close the gap and get right inside, into the double-windowed room over there where they were quietly running their programme. *Let him run and he'll run to us.*

Into the trap.

I came away from the window. The light in the room was winter-dim but there was nothing here I wanted to see: the moves had to be made in the mind, the next in my own because they'd already made theirs and they were waiting.

It didn't matter that at this moment, at 1405, my security was total. No one in Warsaw knew that a British agent from a non-existent bureau in London was at this tick of the clock holed up in Room 54 at the Hotel Kuznia under the cover of Karl Dollinger, journalist, born Stuttgart 1929. No one. Not even the two men over there with the dark green folder on the desk between them. But it didn't matter because they weren't trying to find me; they were prepared to wait for me. They could have left me to rot in the Ochota precinct or thrown me into Grochów and left me to rot there instead or they could have put me under the lights and broken me open to see what was inside, but the time hadn't been right.

They hadn't known enough. They wanted to know more.

In any capital where international talks are being convened there's always a fierce light focussed on the central
assembly of delegates and plenipotentiaries and secretaries
and interpreters, and in the peripheral glow there are shadows and in the shadows there are always the nameless, the
faceless, the eyes and ears of the intelligence networks
whose job is to peel away the laminations of diplomacy and
protocol and deceit and counterdeceit until they can form
a picture of the realities beneath the maquillage and pass
it back to Control for data processing **and onward** transmission to the overt departments of government where policy is formed. There is nothing adventurous about this: it's
an art becoming so fine that a great deal of what is said
at the conference table is indirectly dictated by those un-
seen in the shadows; and in some countries the liaison between statesmanship and political intelligence is so closely
linked that the first would fail to operate without resource
to the second. This was exemplified in a coded cable from
the Élysée to Whitehall during the Fourth Summit of 1970
and the decoded version is framed on the washroom wall at
the Bureau. *Spent an hour in private discussion last night
with the Persian Minister for Foreign Affairs. Please let me
know what he said.*

Here in Warsaw the talks were to be staged between the
two halves of a divided world and the spotlights were thus
blinding and the shadows, by contrast, darker. The area, by
this situation rendered highly sensitive, was charged with
the explosive element of Polish dissension. In these circumstances Moscow had been driven to devise two programmes
aimed at the protection of its own interests and of the talks
themselves. One of these programmes was already running:

the streets were being cleared and the trains were moving east. The other was also under way.

This was the one that Egerton wanted me to destroy and I hoped to God he knew what he was doing because the talks were as vital to the West as to the East.

Not my concern. Discount the shivering fit of the nerves, the goose-flesh fear that somewhere I'd wandered into a mine field that *even the Bureau didn't know was there*. Discount every consideration that had nothing to do with the mission itself, to do with the implicit instructions: *define, infiltrate and destroy*. Do what you're bloody well told.

Or at least try.

They didn't know enough about me, but they'd know enough to damn me, to kill me, once I'd found my way inside. All they'd need to know was that I was trying to blow up their programme, the second one, the silent one. Then they'd knock me off. They'd set the trap and that was all they'd had to do: they knew, as I knew now, that I'd have to spring it myself, and hope to survive.

The main-line station was three blocks from the hotel and I walked there. I'd had to get free of the claustrophobic confines of Room 54 and I'd had to take a first step towards their base and this was it.

He was a thin quick-eyed boy with a lot on his nerves and I'd have preferred an older man, but there was only one rank and his beaten-up two-door Wolga stood at the head of it and I didn't want to waste any time.

"Hotel Kuznia."

The smell of burnt clutch linings filtered through the ripped carpet. After two blocks I told him to pull in.

"This isn't the Kuznia. It's farther on."

He watched me in the cracked mirror.

"You can leave your engine running." We spoke in Polish and I let my accent show. "How much would it cost to hire you for the rest of the day?" It didn't matter how much it would cost because that bloody woman was going to pay the bill anyway, but I didn't want him to think I was a madman. Only a madman would commit himself to this kind of expense without asking how many noughts there were: that would be his point of view because he was half-starved and I wanted to keep him with me.

"I'm on the station run. You'll have to get one from Orbis."

"They're shut today."

It was still there, so we were all right.

"I can't help that."

"Five hundred zlotys. That's fair."

"I haven't got a licence, only for station runs."

"You can check in at intervals. Your friends'll cover you."

He twisted in the seat and looked at me. "There's rules and I'm not breaking them."

"You'll be breaking a few on Wednesday."

His young mouth tightened. We listened to the ragged beat of the engine. He didn't look away. I said: "Put it like this: if you'll keep your car at my disposal you'll be helping things along, firing the first shot. You shouldn't miss a chance like that."

"I don't know what you're talking about."

"You see that big Moskwicz over there? I want you to keep it in sight when it leaves the Commissariat. I want to know where it goes, that's all. You're lucky, you know, got a chance of being a hero of the revolution. But you'll have to do what I tell you. Go on past the Kuznia and make a turn before the bridge and come back and stop when I say the word."

He licked his thin lips, looking away, looking back at me. "Show me your papers."

They didn't mean anything except that I wasn't a Russian but that was enough. He took his time, just for the look of the thing, and I knew he was hooked. They were dreaming of Sroda, those who were left, and I was bringing it closer for him.

I put my passport away. "When you can do it without anyone seeing, break another hole in the front of your driving seat and put the gun in there. If you leave it where it is now they'll find it without even trying, and you haven't got a licence for that either."

He stuffed the yellow duster on top of the bulge in the side pocket and his quick eyes flicked to the mirror.

"You don't miss much."

"You're up against people a lot smarter than I am, so you'd better watch it, that's all."

The smell of the clutch rose again. There weren't any chains on but we wouldn't need any. The filthy snow was permanently rutted now along the major streets and the trick was to settle into them and find traction on the bare tarmac in the troughs. He turned at the bridge and came back.

"Pull in here."

We waited nearly an hour. They came down the steps together, Foster empty-handed, the agent with a full briefcase. I couldn't see the guard at the entrance from here, but I knew all I needed to know about him: he was civil police, not military, revolver, not rifle, and his post was inside the main doors on the left-hand side going up. There wouldn't be any trouble with him because when I went in there I wouldn't be alone.

At this time, 1540, I didn't have an alternative operation worked out but there'd have to be one because the thing was so sticky with risks.

"Not yet. Give them a minute."

It really was the most disgusting design, the rear windows like nostrils and the domed hubcaps protruding like warts.

"Now."

East and north at the first lights and then left again, back towards the Slasko-Dabrowski Bridge. There was more traffic than usual towards the city centre: a lot of the people here for the talks were using their first Sunday for sightseeing in taxis and Orbis cars.

"Don't get too close."

"I don't want to lose it."

"You won't lose it. It's like a bloody elephant."

Orbis was no use to me. You'd got to present your papers and let them record the details and that was how I'd blown the Longstreet cover. Blow the Dollinger and there wouldn't be time to get another one before Sroda and Sroda was the deadline, three days from now. Fast driving didn't figure in the operation I was now setting up, but if something came unstuck and I had to do some it would have to be in a private banger, whatever I could pinch.

The Bureau wouldn't like that. *You were aware of the strict standing orders that in all circumstances the property of private citizens must be considered inviolable.*

Memo to Control: *Since the private citizens of Warsaw were filling the detention cells at the rate of a hundred per day a fair percentage of motor vehicles parked in the streets were going to stay there until their blocks froze so I respectfully suggest you go and commit a nuisance.*

"Hotel Cracow."

"Yes," I said. "Go on past."

It was an old building in the grand style not far from the river and the Moskwicz had turned through massive gates into a courtyard. As we came abreast I took a look and told him to pull in.

After the fumes inside the Wolga the air was fresh. The gates hadn't been shut for a long time: the traffic going through had gradually spread the tarmac to the sides and against their rusted bolts. Half a dozen cars in the courtyard, one of them abandoned, the marks of birds' feet across the thick snow on its roof and bonnet, the block presumably frozen. No one about, no one on foot. The hotel took up one entire wing of the building, mullioned lattices and a hewn portico, griffons rampant, part of the 15 per cent of the city that didn't have to be rebuilt after the bomb doors had closed again.

Foster and the agent were going up the steps and the driver and escort were sitting behind the windscreen with nothing to do but watch people and in a routine situation I would have spent an hour doing this, hanging about for cover and using the rules, but there wasn't enough time and I had to rely on risky premises: that the driver and escort were a relief shift or if they were the two who had driven me across the Slasko-Dabrowski yesterday morning that they hadn't got a good look at me. They were taking a good look at me now, but they could have seen me actually coming through the gates and that had been the point beyond which I couldn't have turned and gone back, so I kept on and made for the entrance with the image rearranged, shoulders a little hunched and the pace shortened, head down in thought, one of the habitual clientele with no more interest in the aspect of the place.

They were going into one of the lifts and I turned to stamp the snow off my shoes and then went to the desk.

"Would you have a private suite for one week beginning next Wednesday? For two people."

A quick glance down. It didn't matter how well-trained they were: mention that day and there was a reaction. He was wondering how I'd manage to reach here through the barricades.

Reading upside down is a fraction easier than mirror-reading because you don't have to dissociate from the familiar and the brain recognises that if you turn through a hundred and eighty degrees you'll be out of the wood, whereas mirror-writing remains gibberish until you've done a mental switch. All I could see was that his name wasn't among the thirty or so on the one and a half filled pages of the register unless of course he was now A. *Voshyov* or K. *Voskarev*, the two possibles among the several Russian entries. He was on one of these open pages if he'd booked in officially because they went back to January 14 and he'd been flown in to vet me on a night flight of the fifteenth.

"On the third floor, sir, overlooking the court." He added without any expression: "It will be quieter there."

It wasn't important: I hadn't come to look at the register; it's just that the eye of a seasoned ferret notes the lie of every grassroot on its way through the warren. *Voshyov* or *Voskarev* could be the agent and Foster's base somewhere else. The important thing was to expose as much data as possible in the short time left and my real concern was the obscene-looking Moskwicz outside: the courtyard was the area we could possibly work in and the facts needed collecting.

He hit the bell but I told him I didn't want to see the rooms now: I would return and confirm.

The pivotal fact was that when the Moskwicz dropped its passengers at the Commissariat and at this hotel, the driver and escort remained on board. They were there when I walked down the steps, backed up to the wall between the end window and one of the griffons, the engine shut off and the louvres closed and their faces watching me from behind the reflected light on the windscreen.

On the way to the Hotel Kuznia I stopped the taxi at a telephone kiosk and spoke to Merrick.

By nightfall I'd gone over the whole thing again and it looked all right: risky but all right. Most of it stood up so well that the one critically weak point seemed less of a hazard. It was to do with the guard. There was a single police guard on the Commissariat, but today was *Niedziela*, Sunday, and it could be that on weekdays when every department was functioning and there were more visitors it carried the normal double guard I'd seen on other official buildings. If tomorrow they doubled the guard it'd be no go.

13

SIGNAL

Poniedziałek. Monday.

They doubled the guard.

It was getting too close to the limit now to do anything except hack out a last-ditch alternative operation and it took till midday to do it and when I'd done it I knew it would only work if the opposition movement-patterns remained constant. And if it worked at all the main objective would be gained, but nothing more. I would blow up their programme by springing the trap but there'd be no hope of survival.

I don't like suicide missions. They're for the angels.

Rethink.

Findings: the only other thing to do was to let the time run out to Sroda and get a plane when the heat came off and take Merrick back to London where he'd be safe and let them put it in the mission report at the Bureau: *objective unaccomplished.*

So out of sheer stinking pride I set the thing running.

One hour's wait. A lot of the major planning overlapped: instead of throwing out the whole of the original operation I'd lopped the dead limbs and done some grafting.

When the hour was up, I telephoned Merrick and made an immediate rendezvous and then went down to the street where the taxi was parked. I'd paid him a day in advance and he was filling the Wolga with cheap Russian tobacco smoke.

"When they come back keep an eye open and follow them when they leave again, find out where they go. Does that gauge work?"

"Sometimes." He tapped it.

"Fill up the first chance you get. You can lose people that way."

I walked on towards Wilenska against a low wind; the sky was blue-black in the north and they said there was heavy snow falling across the forestland and that the city would get it before morning.

He was late of course.

Trucks banged and the echoes rang under the great sooty roof. A mail van was parked on the slip road that ran parallel with this platform and they were slinging the bags in; on the far side a short-haul tender was butting at a line of freight. A dozen people waiting, their backs turned to the M.O. patrol. No one else.

After twenty minutes he came in from the street and began looking for me among the group of people because the poor little bastard had only had two weeks' training and he didn't know that when you make a protected rdv you don't use cover: it wastes time. When he finally saw me he started a half-run towards me and the M.O. patrol turned their heads, so I called out to him in Polish: "It's all right, it hasn't come in yet. They say there's snow on the line."

I waited till he got his breath.

"I'm sorry," he said. He was always having to say that.

I took him into the buffet. Three men, four women, a kid with a red plastic guitar, his fur hat over his eyes. Steaming urns, a door to the street, telephone. I asked for *czosnek* soup.

"What happened?"

He sat opposite me at the table, pulling his gloves off and blowing into his hands. "Someone tried to get asylum, just when I was leaving the Embassy." His eyes were in a stare behind the glasses, still bright with shock. "They followed him up the steps and tried to drag him away but he got free and came inside. There wasn't anything I could do; none of us could help him. But he didn't seem to believe it. We just had to—to kick him out." He fished the thing from his pocket and covered it as best he could with his cold long-fingered hands. "Excuse me."

I gave him a minute because he wouldn't even know what I was saying.

"Listen, Merrick. They didn't turn up."

When I'd phoned him last evening on the way back from the Hotel Cracow, it was to ask for three men, part of the original plan and still part of the new one. I still had to have them.

"They didn't?" His mouth went loose.

"I waited for another hour."

"They were properly briefed. I told them—"

"They've been picked up. That was the risk we took."

"I'll recruit another three. The Ochota unit's still—"

"No. There isn't the time."

Looking down at his hands he said numbly: "I did my best."

"It wasn't your fault." Because he was doing it again, with his numbed words and his raw schoolboy hands and his pathetic eagerness to please and his utter inability ever to manage it, uncovering something again that I thought had been long ago buried in me: a sense of compassion.

He looked up with a slow blink and stared at me as if I'd surprised him and maybe I had; I suppose it was the first civil thing I'd ever said to him.

"What about the cypher-room staff, you got any leads?"

"Not yet, but—"

"Anything positive, anything negative? Come on."

He drew back on his chair, tender as a sea anemone. "I haven't been given much time, and they're making it very difficult. I think they've taken offence."

Christ, the world was full of them.

Then he was pulling something else out of his coat and I knew instinctively that he'd forgotten it until now and was hoping I wouldn't realise.

"This is from London."

I didn't open it straightaway. "You told London to give you a hand?"

"Well, yes, you said I must."

"They given you any leads?"

"Not yet."

"Because I've got to send signals and if you think the cypher room's monitoring your stuff then I'll have to risk a direct line."

Carefully he said: "There's nothing positive. That's all I can tell you."

I ripped the envelope.

It was fourth series with first-digit dupes. PKL was instructed to furnish full interim report and itemise all info on opposition activities.

I read it twice.

It's always useful and sometimes essential to control nervous reaction when the mind, within a hundredth of a second, is galvanised; but it's difficult not to let something show, just a fraction of the shock that has suddenly taken over while the eyes must remain contemplative and the hands perfectly steady and the voice expressionless. It's hard not to blink when lightning strikes close.

I didn't want to scare Merrick. He had enough to deal with.

"London wants a report." I put the signal away.

"Yes?" His hands cupped the bowl of garlic soup and he finished it; he looked less chilled now, less frightened by what he'd seen at the Embassy.

"They'll be lucky to get it. Don't they know we've enough to do?" I thought I'd better put something on record. "Don't worry about the Czyn people I asked for."

"I can try—"

"Won't you ever bloody well listen?" He flinched, his hands pulling away from the empty bowl, but I didn't care, I was fed-up with them, Egerton and the others who'd been scraping away at this poor little bastard's nerves till I couldn't even tick him off without shocking him. "I said don't worry about it. They were to give me support while I tried to break out of Warsaw but there's no need now."

He nodded contritely. "I see."

Looking at him across the table, at his pale boy's face, at the misery that dulled the eyes and turned the ends of the mouth, at the pain that held him still in case movement would aggravate it, I decided to use his innocence for my own ends, just as a pawnbroker uses the poor. "I might as well tell you, so that you can stop worrying, that I'm now in direct touch with London. You know why."

He stared at me for a long time, wanting to find the right answer because if he got it wrong I might hit him again.

"You think the cypher room isn't safe."

"That's right."

He blinked slowly, thankful. "I suppose you—you've got a kind of instinct about these things."

"I'm a ferret. I've learned to see in the dark."

He smiled faintly at my little joke.

I said: "Listen to me, Merrick. I'm telling London to pull you out. Till you get their signal, keep away from Czyn. They're done for and there's nothing more we need to know. I've had new orders and as soon as I've cleared the pitch I'll be pulling out too. At the moment you're all right, you can sign off at the Embassy and get on a plane, just another second secretary being recalled for reasons of diplomatic expedience, but if you go near Czyn again and get caught in a raid by the Polish secret police they'll make a fuss and you'll be kicked out publicly for inadmissible conduct and it'll look messy."

"I see, yes." He was sitting very still.

I got a pencil and made out a slip. *Fleou lmotrwk skkmao plqcv mzoplexk.* "Put this last signal through for me."

He took it and folded it. "Through the cypher room?"

"I've switched the code."

"I see."

First series, prefix and transposed dupes. *Now going into red sector.* It was one of their bloody rules: when you found a hole you'd got to go into without any chance of getting out again, they wanted to know. Among the riffraff rank and file of the shadow executives, it's known as the clammy handshake and we call it that to make fun of it because it scares us to death.

"Make sure it goes out."

With that fledgling courage of his he said: "You can rely on me."

I got up and paid for the soup and he followed me to the door. "We shan't be in contact again," I told him. "See you in London some time."

When we came onto the platform I saw four of them, KGB types in civilian clothes, standing in pairs, two on the left and two on the right, their hands in the pockets of their black coats, facing towards me. Along the platform, parked behind the mail van, was a dark-windowed saloon.

I looked back through the glass doors of the buffet and saw that two other men had come in through the other door, from the street. Then I looked at Merrick.

He stood rather stiffly, his face white and his head down a little and his eyes squeezed half-shut as if he were expecting me to do something to him though he knew I could do nothing. It wasn't much more than a whisper and I only just heard.

"I'm sorry."

14

DEADLINE

"This is Bodkin."

"Oh, hello, old boy. How are things going?"

The line wasn't very good.

"Musn't grumble."

"That's the stuff."

I heard someone being sick, outside. It was probably Merrick.

They watched me the whole time, rather like cows when you cross a field. They weren't dangerous now. They would have been dangerous if I'd tried to run or throw some of Kimura's pet numbers at them, but there wouldn't have been any point: it would have been a waste of time and I had a lot to do.

I suppose they didn't expect me to pick up a telephone: it had floored them a fraction and one of them had got excited, showing me his gun. Guns are no bloody good, they only make everyone jump.

"This line's lousy," I said. "Can you hear me all right?"

"On and off."

Give them credit: they hadn't actually let me make the connection myself in case I was calling the Navy in. I gave the receiver to the thin one who looked as if he was in charge and said if he didn't get me Comrade Foster in double-quick time, he'd lose his rank when they found out from me he'd refused. It was nice to realise that Foster hadn't bothered to change his name, though the nearest the thin man got to it was Vorstor. In London it had meant another cosy party with lots of booze but in Moscow it made a much bigger noise. That was where I was now, right in the middle of them; I might as well be standing in Red Square.

He wasn't at the Commissariat. He was at the Hotel Cracow.

A stray thought came: they'd probably done it with photographs.

"Look," I said, "you're rocking the boat."

"Sorry about that, old boy."

"You should be. It's your own boat."

"Ah."

He sounded quite interested. The helpful thing was that I was talking into a brilliant brain that could add up things for itself once it was given the data. If I'd had to talk to some cow-eyed clod they wouldn't have understood what I was saying and that would have been fatal.

"Let me know if you can't hear me, Foster, because this is important to both of us."

"Loud and clear at the moment."

"I assume you know your little lot's just ganged up on me, do you?"

"We thought it best, considering."

"You couldn't be more wrong. You know what I'm doing out here."

"Do I?"

"I'm nosing around the Czyn situation to see what's in it for John Bollocks."

"More than that," he said, "I think." The line crackled like someone frying. "What about the diplomatic support that's expected from the U.K. if—"

"Oh, for Christ's sake, if I'm going to save us both a lot of trouble you'll bloody well have to talk sense like I am." He only wanted to find out how much I knew. "It was Merrick spreading that guff around and you know it, you gave him the orders. Now listen to me a minute. I've been in direct contact with London since you chose to start blocking my signals through Merrick, and my orders are to drop everything and try to make sure there isn't a revolution here next Wednesday. In other words the reports we've been sending in have given them a nasty turn and they're frightened the talks are going to come unstuck. This means in effect that you and I are now on the same side and although quite frankly I'd rather work with a dead rat I've not got any option."

We were the only people in here now. The men and women and the kid with the red plastic guitar had cleared out as soon as they'd seen what was happening. The woman who'd brought our soup was behind the counter again, washing up; her face was gentle and motherly, reminding me of Mrs. Khrushchev's; I think she was quietly praying there wouldn't be any shooting because the place had just been redecorated.

"Any questions?" I asked him.

The silence went on for a bit and I let it. My impression of him in the Moskwicz saloon had been that he was a civilised person with a soft core of morality that wasn't giving him any peace: he'd be sensitive for a long time, perhaps all his life, about how the English thought of him, and at this moment he was probably taking his time to swallow my last remark. That was all right because I'd made it deliberately to persuade him I was in a position of strength and we could talk on equal terms.

But I didn't like it, the silence on the line. I had to sell him cold in the next couple of minutes or lose the whole thing: a compromise wasn't possible because the setup I'd worked out would still function and the timing was a bit near the hairspring.

"You'd better come and see me," he said.

"There's no time."

"Pity about that."

"You're not being very bright, you know. I'll give it to you straight: call your people off and let me go on doing my thing and as soon as I can I'll hand you the lot. Those are my new orders from London. Or you can shove me in a cell and three days from now you'll find out you've been losing your grip and you won't like that, a bloke with your reputation in Moscow. Incidentally you'll cost the lives of quite a few of your own people and that won't go down so well either."

The line sizzled again and I began sweating badly: it'd be damned silly if I lost the mission just because the Polish telephone system had got dry rot in the selector units. My left eyelid had begun flickering to a rogue nerve: I must be getting old.

"Perhaps you'd just give me a clue, old boy."

"Would you, in my place? Think straight. I've got too much on and bloody little time to do it in, so for Christ's sake get off my neck."

"You're being," he said slowly, "a wee bit proud."

"All right, I'm rotten with it. At least it's something you can understand. I represent an intelligence service whose present interests happen to line up with yours and if you want me to cooperate it's got to be level pegging and if you think I'm going to start by licking your boots you've got another think coming."

He kept me waiting again. Then on the line I heard a faint sound that brought his face suddenly into my mind, the puffy eyes in the crumpled tissue-paper skin, the long thin mouth with its hint of private irony. He was using his flask.

In a moment he said: "What's your field?"

"Czyn."

"Same old thing."

"I told you, didn't I? London wants me to do what I can to help keep the peace for the talks. You've been clearing the streets as quick as you can, but there'll still be a nasty lot of TNT going up on Wednesday because there are one or two units left intact and you won't ever find them." When I'd counted up to five I said: "I know where they are."

Something snapped, near where I was standing. The woman had broken the handle off a cup she was drying, her nerves in her fingers, making them clumsy. She put the handle onto the zinc draining board; it looked like a bit out of a puzzle picture.

"Oh, we'll find them all right."

I'd expected him to say that. He couldn't have said anything else. I'd laid my ace and he'd trumped it.

"And the best of luck."

"Of course," he said reasonably, "that doesn't mean we wouldn't be able to do it quicker, with your help."

"I'm not helping you, Foster, so get it straight. I don't trade with your type. Our interests are parallel, that's all, so you're in luck." The line went fuzzy and the sweat came again; this thread was so thin and it was all I had. "Listen, you can do something practical as a kickoff. Ten days ago the U.B. pulled in someone from Czyn and we're going to want him." I gave him the name. "He's got a head full of essential info that you won't get out of him: they grilled him and drew blank. But he'll tell me."

"What sort of info, old boy?" Tone rather lazy.

"Don't be bloody silly. Put it this way: we're trying to open a safe and he knows the combination."

"If they got him ten days ago he'll be across the frontier by now."

"Of course. Get him back."

"I know it sounds easy, but he's just one of—"

"Find him and fly him in, use a snow-patrol chopper, I don't care how you do it, that's your headache. Hold him for me till I'm ready."

It was all I could do now but I believed he was hooked.

"Sorry, old boy, but it won't work. It's all so awfully vague, you see. If you could just give me the odd pointer."

The wooden boards under my feet started vibrating and the whistle came from the distance, a muted shriek. It would be small at first but it was coming fast and would grow gigantic, a black mountain on the move towards me.

"I'm ringing off now, Foster. You've had your chance."

"Just the odd pointer."

The thunder gathered, beating at the windows; a glass on the shelf tinkled against another. An express from the north, from Olsztyn, running through to Warsaw Central.

"Where's your pride?" I had to shout a bit above the noise. "You're asking an intelligence officer in the other camp to give you clues and pointers, you know that? Christ, you're far gone, no wonder you got yourself blown!"

He was saying something but I couldn't hear properly, something about surveillance.

"What?"

"We'd have to keep you under surveillance."

I let my eyes close. I wanted to sleep.

The train went through and smoke billowed against the windows, dimming the light as my eyes came open.

"As long as they don't get in my way. Tell them that. Tell them to keep their distance, and no tricks. For your own sake, you get that?"

I handed the receiver to the thin man.

The sound faded. The floorboards were still again.

"Yes," he said. "Yes," he kept saying. "Yes, Comrade Colonel."

They were all standing to some kind of attention because they knew who was at the other end.

An honorary rank. He must have hated that, to have his brand of subtle and specialised intelligence brought by implication to the level of the bovine military mind; but they'd thought it was a compliment and his courtesy wouldn't have let him refuse. A private Englishman, Colonel of the Red Army. His own bloody fault.

"Yes," the thin man said. Then he put down the telephone and turned away from me, speaking to the others. Two of them left, by the door to the street. The rest didn't move.

I went out to the platform and noticed Merrick on a bench, sitting alone and crouched over his gloved hands, staring at the ground; he didn't look up; he may not have heard me. I walked past the dark-windowed saloon and came to the open street.

The first pair were already ahead of me, looking back sometimes; the other two had taken up station behind me. It was a box tag and we don't often meet with it, especially towards the end of a mission, because when the heat's on there's no time for either side to formulate rules; but this was a specific situation and the rule was that if I didn't try any tricks, they'd leave me alone except for overt surveillance.

I led them to the Hotel Kuznia, thus blowing my new cover. I wouldn't need it again. By the time I'd reached Room 54 they were checking the register at the desk and getting the passport number of the *anglik* who'd just taken his key, very well, the West German, yes, Karl Dollinger, this one. By the time my shoes were off and I was propped on the bed they were passing my cover to Foster. That was all right: he had to feel reassured until I was ready to start the thing moving. It would have to be tomorrow and I didn't care for that but it was too fragile to handle roughly; it would break.

Thought began streaming. I couldn't signal Egerton that

the untrained novice he'd sent me to look after was a double agent for the KGB because my only communications were through the Embassy and through Merrick himself. There was nothing wrong with the cypher-room staff: when Foster had bottled me up he hadn't left the cork out. The cork was Merrick. They would have been content to sit back and wait for me to spring the trap, but when I'd asked Merrick to get me three people from Czyn as a back-up team, he'd passed it on and Foster had decided not to risk anything: he'd been afraid I'd got some kind of coup lined up, fancy him thinking a thing like that.

Merrick himself hadn't known they were going to pick me up or he wouldn't have bothered to give me the signal from London.

My hand moved and I stopped it, have to do better than that. The phone wouldn't be bugged: they'd just put a man in the switchboard room and leave him there. I'd have to do it from outside in forty minutes from now at 1600.

She was there and all I said was that I'd phone her again tomorrow on the hour or the half-hour. She sounded edgy about something.

"You all right?" I asked her.

They watched me from the corner by the state super-market. The others were across the road.

"Yes. But the police came here."

"When?"

"Not long ago. An hour ago."

"Your papers were all right."

Nothing could have happened because she was still there, but I had to relax my hand on the receiver, do it consciously.

"Yes." She'd been unnerved, that was all. "Yes, they looked at them, and went away."

"They come to see you, or was it just a routine check?"

"They checked all of us."

"Fine. You won't see them again. You know it's all right now, you can rely on your karta."

They stood like penguins, their arms hanging by their sides and their heads raised slightly. They were damned good, I knew that; on the way to the phone kiosk I'd thrown a feint, doubling and using a street-repair gang for cover, nothing too patent because it didn't have to look like a test, and they'd closed in very fast and revealed a third pair on the flank across the road: it was a six-box and it wasn't going to be easy when the time came.

She said good night. For me to take care, and good night.

On the way back to the Kuznia I slipped on a patch of packed snow, just in front of a parked taxi, and the driver got out to see if I was hurt.

"Where do they go?"

"To the Hotel Cracow."

"Nowhere else?"

"Always to the Hotel Cracow."

I hit the dirty snow from my coat. "I won't need you again." After I'd gone a dozen paces I heard the loose thrust of the starter.

The forecast had been right: snow began falling on the city before midnight, the wind bringing it from the forest lands in the north.

Wtorek. Tuesday.

The streets had become altered, the new whiteness covering the soot and making the sky seem lighter. During the morning, I went out twice and made a show of telephoning, talking with the contact down and using the chance of thinking aloud, going over the major points and looking for trips, not finding any. I couldn't give it much longer now and the nerves were playing up because once I'd hit the switch the pace was going to be fierce and there wouldn't be time to rethink. I'd give it till noon.

The time factor didn't balance. I had to go slow to keep him happy, letting them observe and report, letting him see that I was ostensibly in contact with Czyn; and I had to go fast, bringing the deadline back as far as I dared: to noon. The waiting was unpleasant and I sensed being caught up in the feverishness that today had come to Warsaw, showing in people's eyes, in the sudden movement of their heads when they believed someone was near them, in small accidents as the snow thickened and the traffic tried to keep up speed, impatient with the conditions, in the increasing efforts of the police to search out the last of the suspected hostile elements: a man in the Hotel Kuznia itself, going with them peaceably through the lobby and then making a bid at the doors, glass smashing and shouts and a shoe wrenched off and slithering across the pavement and under the wheel of a bus as they crowded him and threw him limp into the back of the saloon.

The fever had a name: Sroda.

At 1040 I was in my room and used the phone to book a call to London, so that the man in the switchboard room could confirm what I'd told Foster: that I was in direct contact. The delay was estimated at two hours and that was well across the deadline so I made it the Foreign Office,

Governmental Communications Headquarters, and told them to give me what priority they could.

At 1100 I blanked off mentally and let the subconscious review the whole setup without disturbance while I thought of irrelevant subjects: they'd probably done it with photographs and I'd have to deal with that; it had been a light brown shoe with arrowhead indentations on the sole for better grip, still lying there when they'd driven away, would they find a pair his size? Foster hadn't telephoned me although he knew my room number: I'd half expected him to get through, how are things going, old boy, to remind me that I was entirely in his hands, but perhaps he'd found a bit of pride at last, didn't want me to think he'd started panicking, afraid of losing me.

At 1145 I rang the switchboard and asked if they were giving my London call priority. They said there was nothing they could do: there were many visitors here for the coming conference and the pressure on the lines was heavy. I asked for a precise time check and rang off and set my watch.

No point in packing anything: washing tackle could stay where it was on the shelf over the basin, a chance, a thin chance, of coming here again. Check shoelaces and make double knots. Couple of glucose tablets. All.

Sweating a lot. Stress reaction developing, hypothalamic stimulation, pituitary and adrenal cortex, secretion of cortin, pulse rising, the organism responding to the brain's warning of danger to come. Normal therefore reassuring.

At noon I left the room and took the stairs and handed the key in at the desk and went through the doors and down the steps into the street and began walking.

15

BREAKOUT

They came with me, two ahead and two behind, keeping their distance. I checked the flank and saw two more and it threw me a fraction because they wouldn't have left the rear of the hotel uncovered. It was an eight-box. He really didn't want me to do anything that he didn't know about.

The snow fell from an iron-grey sky and in a lot of the windows the lights were on. I took the yellow Trabant at the head of the rank and told him the Dworce Warszawa Glowna and as we pulled out I saw a black 220 making a U turn across the station gates. It tucked in and waited and I leaned forward with my arms on the front squab so that I could square up with the mirror. It was an eight-box with mobility. We passed two of them walking back to the Kuznia to cover the point of departure, routine and predictable. Two others were using an M.O. telephone point to report movement.

You can't plan anything specific when you have to flush an overt surveillance complex but you can't rely on luck either: the compromise is to watch for breaks and take them and play them as they develop. The difficulty is built-in: with a covert-tagging operation the assumption is that you don't know they're onto you and if you sense and start flushing they won't risk showing themselves, but in an overt situation they'll close in and block your run the minute you start anything fancy because they've nothing to lose: you already know they're working on you. So it has to be done very fast and the danger is that when you choose a break it's got to be the right one because it's going to be the only one you'll get.

In this case there'd been a gentleman's agreement between a rat and a ferret and when I broke the rules and made my run they'd go for an immediate snatch. Those were their orders because Foster was taking a chance and he knew it. My offer was quite a big one or he wouldn't have listened: they knew that even if they decimated the population of Warsaw by midnight tonight, there'd still be a few isolated Czyn groups ready to shed their blood across the barricades and I'd told him I knew where they were. But he didn't trust me: he wasn't a fool. The risk he'd taken was calculated and he'd imposed a break-off point: the point where I went out for a flush.

The Slasko-Dabrowski was a mess. A five-tonner was spreading sand and clinker dust along the north side and the traffic was being diverted, a man with a flag at each end of the bridge. Someone had spun a Mercedes and put the tail through a gap in the balustrade and a crowd was there, but it had happened some time ago because a small boy had lost interest and was throwing snowballs, lobbing them high so they'd burst on the roof of the car. A crash truck was crawling through the diversion lane with its heavy-duty chains throwing out clods of broken ice and we had to wait and my driver said it was very *malowniczy*, the snow in Warsaw, very picturesque, did I not find it so? The public services had been briefed by Orbis and tomorrow when visitors were running for cover they'd be told how exciting the city was, how very animated, did they not agree?

First-class chance of a break here with the five-tonner available for cover and the crash truck turning through ninety degrees across our bows and if it had been the boy with the quick eyes in the beaten-up Wolga I'd have told him to get traction and beat the gap and keep going, but this was the Trabant and I'd have to do it on foot and we were standing halfway across the bridge so there'd only be one direction I could use, no go.

The 220 had closed right up, not chancing anything. In the mirror I saw their faces and they could see part of mine and we looked at each other.

"It would be quicker for you to walk, I think."

"Perhaps."

It was tempting.

"What time does the train go?"

"In twenty minutes."

Let him go through the gap when the crash truck had pulled over and get out and walk and use it for cover, a fair chance, a respectable chance.

"You could walk there in twenty minutes."

"I'm not sure of the way. I'll stay with you."

Because a fair chance wasn't good enough: it had to be as close to a certainty as I could make it. This was only the first step in the operation I'd spent twenty-four hours working out and the setup was so flexible that even the Merrick thing had only called for a bit of tinkering and if I made a mistake as early as this I'd blow the whole lot.

Get out here on a bridge in daylight and I'd be a rat in a rut.

"We can go now."

"There's no hurry."

At the end of the bridge I saw an M.O. patrol car coming away from the kerb along Wybrzeze Gdanksie and going through the amber in front of us, pulling in again while we stood idling at the red. They'd used a radio somewhere, probably at the Commissariat three blocks from the station: *Yellow Trabant taxi registration 00–00–00 moving west across Slasko-Dabrowski survey and contain.* You couldn't say he wasn't the cautious type.

It was going to be difficult.

"Have you got some paper, an old envelope or something?"

He rummaged in the glove pocket.

"Will this do?"

We cleared the lights.

The M.O. patrol was three cars ahead of us and the 220 immediately behind. It was a year-old leaflet, *Jazz Gala at the Andrzej Kurylowicz Wine-cellar*, but the back was plain. Writing wasn't easy because we were meeting with cross ruts at the intersections but he wouldn't be fussy. When I'd finished I folded it twice.

Dworce Warszawa Glowna.

"You only have five minutes."

"There's time."

"Get your ticket at the other end. It is permitted."

Warsaw Central was busier than Wilenska and I began

watching the breaks as soon as I was in the main hall, aware of conflicting needs: the need to make a quick flush because time was running out and the need to protect the overall operation from the risk of a precipitate move.

Two main entrances and three gates towards the platform area, upwards of a hundred people and a lot of them in groups of three or more, bookstall, Orbis kiosk, island cafeteria, static and mobile cover, say 75 per cent in normal conditions but he was being so bloody windy, wouldn't give me a chance.

There was another factor now coming into play: my movements were surveyed and they didn't have to be aimless. Take a taxi to a station but I couldn't just loaf around and walk away again; they wouldn't like that. On the other hand I didn't have anywhere to go except to the unknown place where in a minute from now or an hour from now I'd try for the break.

Purpose-tremor was setting up in the muscles, normal but hazardous: my feet felt light and I breathed as if I'd been running. Check and decide and in deciding remember that the whole of the mission hangs on this and that he's up there rubbing his bloody chilblains waiting for the phone to ring so for Christ's sake don't go and muck it just because the nerves are overtuned.

Two at each main entrance, two splitting up and bracketing the cafeteria blind spot, two going down to the ticket barriers at three and nine o'clock from centre, all minor exits covered. This wasn't a box. It was a net. These were élite Muscovites, trained till they ticked like a clock; they may have been in force to this extent round the Hotel Kuznia or held back in reserve until the movement report had gone in. The thing was that within ten paces of the entrance where I'd come in they'd deprived me of visual cover. Their specialised field overlapped a neighbouring discipline: the observation of VIPs in public places; the two jobs had various factors in common and the chief of these was geometry: they moved to their stations as if instructed by the computed findings of compass and protractor; they knew the distance I'd have to go before the island cafeteria obscured me from points A and B, the angle subtended by the view of C and D, the sector through which I could move under observation from E, F and G before the A and B zones picked me up again.

They didn't see the cafeteria or the bookstall or the ticket gates; they saw vectors, diagonals, tangents. It amounted to this: if each man were a spotlight I would have no shadow.

All I needed to do was get where *just for ten seconds* they couldn't see me and they knew it and they weren't going to let me, so I crossed to the bookstall and bought a noon edition of *Zycie Warsawy* and gave the woman the leaflet I'd folded in four.

"Would you be kind enough to keep this for a moment? A friend of mine will ask you for it."

I offered ten zlotys but she shook her head, putting the message in the inside pocket of her lamb's-wool coat.

"Will he give his name?"

"No, but he's a Russian gentleman; you'll know him by his accent."

I didn't look back until I'd reached the cafeteria towards the far side of the hall. One of them was already there at the bookstall.

"*Kawa, proszę.*"

The girl pulled a waxed-paper cup from the column.

They hadn't necessarily seen me pass it but they'd seen me talking to the woman and a station bookstall is one of the classic letter drops.

I estimated that he'd get it within ten minutes.

Two birds: my movements were surveyed and mustn't be aimless and this was what I could have come here for; and it would keep him happy for a few more hours.

"*Dziękuje.*"

I stirred it.

All going well. You'll be glad you cooperated. I shall see you this evening either at the Praga Commissariat or the Hotel Cracow, in time for you to take all necessary action.

They wouldn't know it was for Foster but that was where they'd send it, immediate attention. He was crossing over to the row of telephone kiosks now and one of his team was shifting obliquely to cover his p.o.v. I sipped my coffee.

Most of the time would be taken up in spelling the thing out and if it had been something I'd wanted to hurry I'd have written it in Russian but there was no hurry needed and I was damned if an ex-scholar of the Basingstoke Elementary was going to write a note to an Old Etonian in Slavonic hieroglyphs, the English are born snobs.

Something was trying to come in and I gave it attention. I shouldn't be drinking coffee but that was what I was in fact doing and there must be a reason. An old ferret, long in the tooth and scarred from the years among the warrens, knows better than to add caffeine to the stimulants already flowing from the glands in a stress situation with a delay factor present. There was another thing I was aware of: place-feel. The instinctive feeling that a given place was the *right* place, a positive satisfaction in being there, a negative reluctance to leave it. The fighting bull's *querencia*.

The antennae of the organism had been waving sensitively around while I'd been watching the bookstall and the primitive animal brain had worked out an answer, the sixth-sense solution to the forebrain problem that had been presented since noon, since noon precisely. And there was an obvious link between caffeine and the delay factor. If there weren't any question of delay, of having to move through the city inside the moving net until a break came and I took it, the caffeine would be perfectly acceptable, an ultimate priming dose at the threshold of action. And there was a link between the idea of throwing out the delay factor and the sensation of place-feel: the first meant *now* and the second meant *here*.

I would go with that. Modern man, arrogantly conscious of his sophistication, is in trouble if he ignores the dictates of the primitive brain because he's not long out of the jungle by the evolutionary clock and jungle laws obtain; there were trains here and telephones but the mechanism controlling my situation was infinitely more complex and whether in the next few minutes I got clear or got caught or lived or died depended on an exchange of neural impulses reciprocating at the speed of a hundred yards per second in a data-analysis-decision motor system responding to the signal that for longer than four thousand million years has ensured the continuance of life on earth: *survive*.

Check. Analyse the data, make the decision, act.

No go. He was coming out of the phone box but he wasn't resuming station and the pattern had changed. I hadn't expected that. Absorb new data. He was a short man with a

small head and a sloping walk and his shoes were quiet as
he came and he came looking at no one, looking everywhere
but at no one, not at me.

Panic tried getting in but I took a slow breath: the
answer to panic is *prana*. Immediate construction: I'd mis-
judged the conditions. Foster had decided that I was leaving it too late—I'd said 'this evening'—and that he'd settle
for the info I'd collected since he'd let me run, without
waiting for the rest. He was edgy about the H-hour for
Sroda; they all were; they'd pulled in enough Czyn people to
know that Sroda would begin at midnight plus one, eleven
hours and thirty-one minutes from now. *We have stockpiles
strategically dispersed, sub-guns, grenades, land mines, you
name it. Wednesday morning, 0001 hours, the three main
generating stations hit the sky. Will you be here? Don't be
here Wednesday, pal.* The station at Tamka wouldn't go
up because they'd wiped out the unit there but in other
places, other buildings, there'd be radio-controlled detonators still set up and the U.B. knew it. The U.B., the KGB
and Foster. His problem was simple and it was acute: he'd
got to balance the risk that I was working against him with
the hope that I was working for him, and as the time ran
out he'd be driven to a compromise.

The man with the sloping walk looked at me now as he
came. I heard the faint squeezed sound from his crêpe-
rubber soles. He stopped.

"Do you speak Russian?"

"Yes."

He pulled a cheap plastic-covered notebook out of his
black leather coat, finding the page. His breath smelt of
czosnek.

"Listen, please. 'Good of you to get in touch but you're leaving it too late. We'll have to meet earlier than this evening. The orders are to immobilise you at four o'clock, so do what you can before then.'" His small head lifted. "Do you understand?"

"Yes."

"Do you wish to send a reply?"

"No."

"Very well."

I watched him go back to his station.

Seven minutes. Call it half that for the field-to-base transmission including his walk to the bookstall and from there to the telephone: it was good communication. On the move in a capital city with a travel pattern that could take me five or six miles from receiver base I could hand in a signal to anyone, bookseller, roadsweeper, barman, or just drop it on the ground, and within an average of three and a half minutes Foster would be reading it.

He was as close to me as that.

Time was 1231 and I made it an overt movement, checking my watch with the station clock as I walked from the cafeteria to the ticket-gate area. Of course it was logical: blind instinct is a contradiction in terms. There was more chance of a break, of *making* a break, in a mainline station than in the streets; a fair percentage of the place-feel had reached the brain through the feet: this was one of the few extensive areas in the city where a running man wouldn't slip on snow. The rest had been visual and deductive: the sight of blind spots, obstacles, ticket barriers, the awareness that patterns would change and provide opportunities as groups of people moved and the trains came in and went out. The trains particularly: in half a minute they'd throw a wall across the scene and in half a minute knock it down again; a street was static and its confines predictable.

Four of them had moved, pacing along the two flanks, turning when I turned, going back. The express for Rzeszow was scheduled at No. 5 ticket gate: 1245. People were moving up. Visual cover story for the tags was that I was here to meet someone and they'd be coming in from Bydgoszcz in the northwest.

It was important to show that I was here to meet a train and not to catch one and this was made easier because Foster had sent his reply in Russian, not English. He'd accept that any agent sent to this side of the Curtain would understand Russian and he'd used it for two reasons: to save time by using normal speech instead of having to spell out, and to let his operator commit the situation to memory as he wrote it down in his own language. The operator thus knew that I was to be immobilised in approximately three and a half hours and would assume I was agreeable to this: 'Good of you' and 'We'll have to meet' were phrases indicating a certain amount of accord between Foster and me. I therefore wouldn't be expected to leave Warsaw on a train with a first stop two hundred and fifty kilometres away. Also it had been seen that I hadn't bought a ticket, though there'd been plenty of time.

Paradox: the barrier was my best exit.

The first representatives of the Bonn Government began arriving in Warsaw this morning. Among them were the protocol secretariat and the personal aides of Herr Otto Reintz, the State Secretariat for Foreign Affairs (who will be leading the delegation), and Herr Siegfried Meyer, the

204

*West German Coordinator for the Talks. They were greeted
in English on their arrival at the Polish Foreign Ministry. In
a brief formal discussion they confirmed that the recognition of the Oder-Neisse frontier will be placed high on the
agenda.*

1235.

*Wieslaw Waniolka, the young student of the College of
Fine Arts who a fortnight ago forced the pilot of a LOT
Antonov 24B aircraft to alter course for Vienna, has been
charged on three counts of extortion, restricting personal
liberty and contravening the Austrian Firearms Law.*

1236.

*It has now been established that although avowed Right-
ist groups were responsible for inciting disorder in the city
during the past month, demonstrations were mainly staged
by students dissatisfied with educational conditions, which
are now receiving attention with a view to revision. Calm
has returned to the capital, thanks to the courageous efforts
of all police departments.*

1237.

I dropped it into the litter basket by the Orbis Information kiosk and turned back to the barrier.

"Will it be on time?"

"Perhaps a few minutes late. It's the local lines that suffer
most. You have your ticket?"

"No, I'm meeting a friend from Bydgoszcz."

"Ah. He'll have had a pleasant journey; the forests are
very beautiful under the snow."

The gates were double, thin wrought iron and flat-topped,
head-high, both locked back by ball-weighted tumbling lev-
ers. He was the only official guarding them, fifty to fifty-

five, twelve stone, five-nine, slow moving, the muscles unused to sudden demands.

I checked my watch and paced to the centre of the hall, trebling the distance and taking an interest in the schedules board. When I turned back I saw one of them at the barrier.

What did the foreigner say to you?

He asked if the train would be late.

Which train?

The train from Bydgoszcz. His friend is coming from there.

What friend?

He didn't say.

The visual cover story had now come alive and been put into the spoken word and it was important to establish *meet* as distinct from *catch* because it would keep them on *this* side of the barrier.

He crossed to the man with the small head and spoke to him and resumed station. None of the others moved: there'd been no signal to move, because they believed in *meet*.

1243.

'A few minutes': say three, four. But he could be wrong; an official was moving some people away from the edge of Platform No. 3 and in the far distance a whistle sounded, its thin note drifting on the wind and funneling into the arched mouth of the station. Fifteen seconds or so later I saw signal wires jerk on their pulleys.

1244 but chronometric time was no longer useful: a train was on its run in and it was probably the express. It was now a matter of sighting it and adapting my movements to its approach so that I would be nearing the barrier as it drew in, nearing the barrier without changing my pace. It would be perfectly normal to turn sooner, hearing the train, or to quicken my steps a little, impatient to meet my friend; but I preferred to keep the pattern unchanged because I'd now made them familiar with it.

Similarly any train would do for my purposes since what I needed were the attendant confusion and the erection of the sliding wall: it didn't have to be the express; but the pattern had been established to focus on No. 3 barrier and I didn't want to use a new one, a different one, because even the most experienced tags are human and therefore fallible, mentally predicting the actions of the target *and basing their own on his*. The consequent lulling effect produces a subsequent shock when the actions become inconsistent with their prediction: in the Höcherl reaction test the electroencephalograph will shift critically when the conditioned subject sees the pointer change its motion after a mere twenty-five beats, and this is always confirmed in verbal questioning: 'I thought it moved to the left again and I saw a kind of phantom image for a fraction of a second.'

The pattern was going to be changed on the *other* side of the barrier and the visual plus psychological shock would produce a time gain of much more than a fraction of a second. I might never need it but that kind of reasoning is sloppy and can be fatal: preparation for *any* important action has got to be 100 per cent and the instructors at Norfolk have a word for it—'A bull at a gate's never yet got out of the field.'

From here the snow looked grey, a mottled and slanting veil covering the mouth of the station, and through it came the outline, its size increasing, dark grey on light. Other people were moving towards the barrier, their voices rising, and I made a final turn and came back, noting the group's disposition, the narrow gap between the two men on the left and the people in the middle, the wider gap towards right centre. Distance now closing, obstacles registered: big suitcase near the women on the right, unattended baggage trolley halfway between the two men and the gates, ticket collector's stool close against barrier, all.

Train slowing, coasting to a crawl, conrods lazy, snow caked on the front of the locomotive and thick along the carriage roofs—someone moved at the edge of the vision field and I looked back at the clock and down again, porter, not one of them, not one of Foster's men. Three more paces and I stopped, filling the gap, the wider gap towards right centre, the one I would use.

Of course they might have put someone into the platform area and it was a risk but a calculated risk, so discount. Discount and wait.

And don't muck it.

Wait for the first door, the first one, not till then.

When it swung open I moved.

16

FOXHOLE

He shouted at me but that was anticipated and there was nothing he could do because he couldn't leave his post at the barrier and within the first ten seconds I was behind reliable cover as the passengers began filling the platform between the train and the ticket-gate area and then I heard him again, but the nearest official was two carriages away on the forward end and by now I was walking, taking my time, keeping to cover but nearing the mid-section carriage where most of the passengers had got out.

"She'll be here. She said she would meet us."

A woman wept, a fat woman buried in her thick coat, the tears bright on her face, no, she won't be here, it said in the paper, you saw the paper.

"I tell you she couldn't telephone because the lines were down at Inowroclaw and besides they don't arrest the students, they know there's no harm in them."

Snow on the wet platform where boots had dislodged it from the footboard. I climbed and turned left, away from the head of the train, edging along the corridor with my back to the windows, then a clear run for the length of half a carriage, then people again, and baggage.

"But it was in the brown one, I remember putting it in there."

"I haven't got the brown one."

"Then you've left it in the compartment."

"We'll have to go back."

They were so slow, so slow, they moved slowly, they had arrived, but I was just starting.

Somewhere behind me a guard was using his whistle.

Assumption: there were ten of them and they'd deploy in open formation with the flank men covering Platforms 2 and 4 and the centre group concentrating on 3 and working the narrow area limited by the train's length and the two adjacent lines. Estimation: I had another ninety seconds and there were two more carriage lengths to go. I would need to hurry now.

"Mind what you're—"

"Sorry, I've left something—"

"There's no need—"

Oh, yes, there was need.

Sweating badly, the limits so very fine, calculated but hazardously fine, the centre group through the barrier by now and working their way along. One or more would check underneath the train and that would slow them a bit but it wasn't a bonus, it was allowed for, part of the ninety seconds, eighty, seventy.

Baggage stacked in the coupling bay, climb over it, not so many here now, one more carriage, stifling, the heat full on and the windows misted, watch for the orange-coloured poster through the misted glass, get a bearing on that.

Bloody well *think*.

Back the way I'd come, five seconds, the top bag from the stack in the coupling bay, a big one with retaining straps, two seconds, forward again with a total loss of twelve seconds but with the advantage of an altered-image component. Orange glow on the window. Fur képi tilted to the back of the head, coat unbuttoned and hanging open, swing the bag down first onto the platform, the breathing heavy and the gait shortened to a fat man's waddle, look directly towards the barrier, nowhere else.

From the main hall the acute-angle perspective had given something like a ten-yard error and although I'd allowed for it I now found that the entrance to the subway was well beyond the orange poster but there was nothing I could do about it. The last of the passengers from this end of the train were giving their tickets in and going down the steps and I waddled after them, puffing a lot, stopping halfway to drop the bag and change it to the other hand, coat flapping open, picking up the bag and going on. Impression of people near, some would-be passengers moving up the platform to this end of the train, destination Rzeszów, one or more would be Foster's men but discount proximity, whole thing depended on the altered image.

It was a single gate, concertina trellis and half open but with enough room to go through at a run. I wasn't going to run.

"I have come from Bydgoszcz. I have no ticket." Heavy Berlin accent. The bag made a thump as I put it down, getting my breath.

"Didn't you have enough time?"

"Please?"

"Were you late for the train?"

"Ah, yes." I found my wallet.

"You are prepared to pay?"

"But, yes, of course."

He nodded, a stocky man with his peaked cap set conservatively straight, a man without imagination but with a sense of responsibility, too old now to be stirred by the rumours of a fight for freedom in tomorrow's streets, a stolid man prepared to weather the strictures of a régime he'd come to accept since middle youth, a man to whom I couldn't say *the police are looking for me, let me through quickly in the cause of Sroda.*

"I must see your papers."

"Here they are."

He opened my passport at the first page, his thumb misshapen by an old accident, the nail split and clogged with the grime of years, of trains.

"How much is the fare?"

"We shall see."

I listened to the footsteps. They had started hurrying: the people who walk all the way to the rear of a train are people who like a compartment to themselves. They hurried past me, behind me.

"You must pay one hundred and thirty zlotys." He stood over his fares schedule, reluctant to close it and put it away, a priest devoted to his Bible. "The single fare is one hundred and twenty zlotys, and there is the obligatory supplement of ten zlotys for failing to purchase a ticket at the—"

"Here are one hundred and forty. Please keep the change."

I lifted the bag.

"I cannot do that. I am an official of the Polish State Railways." He turned towards his booth. "Besides, you will require a receipt."

"I do not wish for one. I am in a hurry."

"Just the same, I have to make out a receipt."

If I pushed past him through the gate he probably wouldn't shout after me because he'd be too surprised. The notes lay on his fares schedule so there was no question of failure to pay, but I'd still be committing a breach of the rules and he would try to stop me, raising his voice. It couldn't be risked. They were behind me now, directly behind or to the right or left, concentrating on the train, searching for a man in hiding. They mustn't be distracted. I put the bag down. He had found his receipt pad.

"Point of departure, Bydgoszcz. That's what you said?"

"Yes."

They would make a thorough search, delaying the train until they were satisfied. They could take their time because they were certain I couldn't leave the station: a call would have gone out not later than a minute after I'd made the break and the station police would have been told to phone for M.O. assistance and a net would already be extending around the area.

"And your reason for not purchasing a ticket was because you had no time?"

"Yes."

It was an oblong form with eight or nine blanks, Point of Departure, Time of Departure, Intended Destination, Particulars of Personal Identification, Amount Paid (Fare),

Amount Paid (Supplement), Total Amount Paid, Remarks.
I watched him write, the ball-point pen sloping at an odd
angle because of his thumb.

"I must see your passport again."

I gave it to him.

They knew I would never get through the net. It would
remain in place until the reinforcements of civil police had
searched the station and questioned everyone in it. They
would be ordered particularly to look for a man who might
try to pass a barrier without a ticket.

"This name here, is it 'Stuttgart'?"

"Yes."

"The writing isn't very clear."

Foster's men wouldn't check the barriers: they'd be de-
ployed in the immediate area of the Bydgoszcz-Warsaw-
Rzeszów express, covering the north end of the station
where I might be expected to run if I left cover. The M.O.
contingents would see to the barriers and one of their men
would be on his way here now. He would question the
ticket collector, who would report a passenger without a
ticket, and from that moment the search would focus on the
subway area.

These were the limits I'd have to work in and I'd known
that, but the time factor was tightening and I began noting
the aural character of the footsteps to the left side of the
barrier: the patrol would approach from that direction, from
the main hall. It was difficult because they'd started getting
some of the baggage off the train and there was the rattling
of trolley wheels.

"One hundred and forty." He counted the notes and
opened his cash box. "So the change will be ten zlotys."

A sound rhythm was coming in, gradually dominating the background. It was to the left and there were two of them, two men walking in step, their heels metal-tipped.

"Ten zlotys."

"Thank you."

I picked up the bag.

"Wait a minute." He tore the form at the perforation. "You'll want your receipt."

Close now, walking in step.

"Thank you."

I took the receipt.

"Enjoy your stay in Warsaw."

"Yes, I will."

I didn't think there was time but it had to be tried and I went through the gate and one of them called out when I was on the fourth or fifth stair down, so I swung the bag forward and back and let go and heard the shout break to a grunt as the bag struck, and then I dived with my weight taking me clear across the rest of the stairs and sending me onto the subway floor in a feet-first slide that was stopped by the wall, with one shoulder taking the shock and my shoes finding a grip again and pitching me forward into a very fast run.

Police whistles.

The coat was a nuisance, flapping.

From the main hall I'd seen that the subway had five double staircases giving access to the eight platforms and that the one blind spot was made by a central waiting room shared by Platforms 4 and 5, but now that I was actually working the area it didn't seem safe to rely on the blind spot because at this stage I didn't know the observation vectors on this side of the train: the train gave me high-wall cover from only three of the platforms so that the blind-spot value of the waiting room was nil except for a five-yard stretch of the train itself.

I would have to stay below ground.

This had been allowed for: the *Toaleta* signs had been visible from the hall and their arrows pointed downwards. That was why I had turned to the right. There were two smaller signs just beyond the centre staircases and the wash-room had a wide entrance with no doors, the line of hand-basins facing it below mirrors. There was a key on the outside of the cleaner's cupboard and I took it in with me and locked the door.

They were young or sketchily trained or too used to work-ing in pairs because they both came into the subway instead of splitting up, one following me and the other staying on the platform to watch the subway exits. Or they thought I might be difficult. Their boots were ringing and making echoes along the glazed-ceramic walls so that it sounded as if more than two were there. Soon there would actually be more than two because of the whistles.

The cupboard was very small and I was standing on one end of a broomhead, gripping the handle to make sure it didn't tap the wall or the door if I shifted my position. Acrid fumes of carbolic and hypochlorite and the smell of a damp rag.

They were splitting up now: both had checked the stair-cases I'd passed just before the *Toaleta* signs but one of them had been quicker and he was here now, clattering about and kicking open the cubicle doors. Then the handle within a few inches of my sleeve was rattled but he didn't persist because he knew I couldn't have got through a locked door.

He went away, joining his partner, and the echoes grew faint. I unlocked the door and went to the line of hand-basins, drinking from my cupped hands and splashing my face. Time was 1253, eight minutes from when I'd made the break. It wasn't possible to know how long they'd keep up the search but the moment would come when the officer in charge would call it off, leaving a skeleton cadre manning key points while he extended the hunt city-wide.

I buttoned my coat: running would be easier and the image was no longer useful. There would be slight confusion when the reports went in because Foster's KGB men were looking for someone with normal build and no luggage and the M.O. section had gone after a fat man with a bag he'd thrown at them, but they'd check and find Karl Dollinger on the carbon copy of the receipt at the ticket barrier and that was the name they'd found in the register at the Hotel Kuznia, Room 54.

I tore up the receipt and dropped it into a pan and flushed it and waited and flushed it again because one of the pieces was still floating. Principle: don't carry items of identification even if they tally with your passport. As a mental exercise I could have worked out more than one situation involving a search of the person in circumstances where it would be acceptable to be Karl Dollinger but not to be someone who'd passed through Warsaw Central between noon and one o'clock today.

The mirror showed the eyes still flickering a bit from the reaction, otherwise fresh. The fur képi had come off when I'd cleared the stairs and they would have found it and reported the new image. I'd have to get another one because on this day in this city there wouldn't be a single man bareheaded.

The ballcock was shutting off and there was quiet here. The train hadn't moved: I would have heard it rumbling. I would give them an hour, an hour and a half at the most; then I'd have to get clear because there was a lot of work to do before I called on Foster this evening.

A freighter went through at 1320 on the line directly overhead and the vibration set up noise from the handle of the metal bucket. Two other trains had come in and when the passengers had filled the subway I went into a cubicle and shut the door and waited until there was quiet again. The risk pattern was formal: the cleaner must arrive and it could happen at any time and if he found the cupboard locked and the key gone from the outside of the door he would report it at once, knowing the police were looking for someone. Therefore I had to be in a cubicle, not the cupboard, when he came. But the second wave of the search must also arrive and similarly it could happen at any time and I would have to be in the cupboard with the door locked and the key on the inside, because they would search the cubicles.

But I couldn't distinguish between the footsteps of the cleaner and the footsteps of a single police patrol and a decision would have to be made: cubicle or cupboard. There was nothing to be done about this until the time came. The low-risk periods were when a train arrived and the passengers came through the subway: the police wouldn't make a search for one man with the field confused.

I had spent a fair amount of thought on Merrick. Some of

it was constructive: at a convenient moment, before the
normal life of the city was disturbed by action in the streets,
I would have to deal with him. Some of it was retrospective,
the hindsight clarification of points that had foxed me before I'd known what he was; but despite the attitudes I'd
learned and come to recognise as valid I couldn't think
about him impersonally as just another component of the
East-West intelligence machine: his face kept coming in
front of me, pale, nervy, vulnerable, his eyes incapable of
hiding the misery that was breaking him down.

Double agents don't last long: the strain is killing. The
exceptions are people like Sorge, Foster, Obermann, but
the strain on them is no less killing: it's just that they're
harder to kill. For a boy like Merrick to go double was simply an elaborate attempt at suicide.

It was irrelevant that he'd tried to take me with him.

Other thoughts: intensive attempt to work out how to get
the maximum amount of information into Egerton's hands
before the possibility of my non-survival. Foster wanted me
alive but captive and the risk lay in the actions I'd have to
take to remain free. Intensive thinking on this too. Intervals
of free-ranging images, disjointed, unimportant.

Cannot locate reference in mission report to actual train
journey Bydgoszcz-Warsaw therefore question amount of
130 zlotys paid at Dworce Warszawa Glowna 1250 hours
Tuesday 19. Silly bitch.

I heard them coming.

At first one man, and I listened for clues: the cleaner
might be a woman, her steps lighter, but this was a man; the
cleaner would be older, possibly, than an M.O. officer, thus

might shuffle, could detect no shuffle. Then suddenly there were the others and within a minute the confines were sharp with echoes: they came from all directions, down the double staircases and from each end of the subway in a blanket operation designed to remove the risk inherent in a simple wave motion; a wave coverage moving from one end of the subway to the other could drive the quarry in front of it and allow him a chance of finding an exit.

All the exits were simultaneously blocked.

They were civil police in uniform, their boots metalled and their pace regular. None of them spoke. Their sound filled the passage.

I had to be quick getting into the cupboard because some of them were coming down the twin staircases close to the washroom and they would be here in a few seconds. The metal bucket was a hazard, its sound alien to the background, and I was careful. The locking of the door gave no trouble since the tumblers came within the same aural range as footsteps on stonework.

The earlier patrol had smashed the hinges of three cubicle doors in kicking them open but I'd left the other five closed so that these people would find something to do that would take their attention from the cupboard. The mind of one policeman becomes much like another's: they're trained to work as a group and their imagination is corporate. The earlier patrol had gone for the obvious—the cubicles—and had given the cupboard only token attention. It was possible that these would do the same.

Two of them came into the washroom. The others went past.

One began on the cubicles, his boot crashing at the doors.

He would be standing back as he kicked, his gun out of its holster and prepared to shoot and to shoot first. The aim would be low: Foster would have given orders that I was to be taken alive. The other had noticed the cupboard.

He wrenched three times at the handle. I felt its movement against my sleeve. Then he crossed to the cubicles and used his boot. The noise of the doors crashing open was very loud, overwhelming the sounds coming from the subway. The smell of the cleansing fluid had become stronger because my sense of sight was frustrated and the others were compensating, stimulated by a crisis situation.

They finished with the cubicles and turned and came past the cupboard on their way out.

"What about that?"

"I've tried it."

"Is it locked?"

"Yes."

The handle moved again.

"We'll have to make sure."

The explosion made me think he was firing at the lock but it was his boot against the panels.

"That's no good, it opens outwards, look."

"Have to force it, then."

"What with?"

"We'll have to find something."

"Shoot round it?"

"Round what?"

"The lock."

"We'd bring the others."

"What about it?"

"They'll think we've got him. Finish up looking silly."

"How can anyone be in there if the door's locked?"

"We've got to make sure. You know what the Captain said, turn every stone."

"Ask someone where the key is, then."

"Take all day. You stay here and I'll fetch an axe or something."

The sound of his boots faded.

So there was only one of them but the conditions were zero because the instant I turned the key he'd hear it and get ready and I'd run into close-range shots.

He crossed to the far side and urinated at the stalls.

The main groups were leaving the subway and when the last of the echoes died they left total silence. He moved again, passing the cupboard, his feet idling, going through the entrance and then halting, looking along the subway.

I had already raised my hand, palm upwards and with the fingertips leading, and touched nothing. Now I felt for the damp rag and found it and folded it into an oblong and draped it across the end of the broom handle and began raising it by degrees. The risk was high because there was so little room to work in: I'd removed the key after locking the door but the handle and the metal bucket remained dangerous; in total darkness I had to steer the broomhead past them both and touch neither, keeping my elbow clear of the door handle as the arm was extended.

I had to work quickly and it was impossible, discount need for speed and concentrate on need for silence.

Sweat had begun creeping close to my eyes. Heartbeat audible, the pulse fast. Another inch, raise it another inch.

The end of the rag brushed across my face, clammy and smelling of mould. Another inch.

He kicked at something, perhaps a cigarette end, flicking it with the toe of his boot, taking a pace, stopping.

The broomhead passed my face. I lifted it higher.

The sound was loud and came from below me and I froze all movement and stood with the nerves reacting. It was certain that he'd heard and would turn and come back into the washroom and stand listening but he didn't do that and it took a full second for the forebrain to bring logic to bear. The rag was half-saturated and the moisture had started draining towards the ends and the first drip had hit the bucket and the sound was magnified by the funnel acoustics and to my ears it had been startling, but to his it had been a strictly normal sound associated with plumbing and cisterns.

Raising the broom I tilted it, bringing the rag directly over my head, because any sound, however closely associated with the environs, would increase his alertness. Silence, lacking aural stimulus, is an overall sense-depressant in non-crisis conditions. For him there was no crisis.

He moved again, coming back into the washroom and pacing there, turning, halting. Possibly he was looking at himself in the mirror as sometimes we do when we are alone, seeking a reaffirmation of our identity. He had begun whistling through his teeth.

The broom was as high as I could raise it.

I began bringing it down.

The second drip fell, hitting my shoulder.

It would take time, lowering the broom: it would take as long as it had taken to raise it because the hazards were the same. I had made progress: was nearer, by a broom's length, to completing the mission; but that didn't allow me to hurry. I couldn't know how many more minutes I had left. Three or with luck five but not more than that because they'd be as quick about this as they could: their group sense would be disturbing them since the others had gone ahead and left them isolated.

I didn't think I could do it in three minutes but I thought I could do it in five.

Footsteps.

No go.

"Have you got something?"

It would take thirty seconds with a crowbar, sixty with an axe. That wasn't enough.

"No."

"Then what the hell have you—"

"There's a ganger on his way here with something. He's fetching it from the tool store."

"Christ, we'll be all day."

"He won't be long."

Down an inch, another inch.

The rag dripped, this time onto my head.

The thick coat was a hazard, deadening the nerves of the skin: there'd be no warning before the folds at the elbow caught the door handle.

Lower. Smell of the rag stronger.

"See anything of the others up there?"

"They're working towards the end of the platforms."

Stop.

A soft sound had begun near my feet and when I stopped

moving the sound stopped too. I moved the broom again, downwards, a quarter of an inch, and the sound came back. It was the bristles, touching the rim of the bucket. I didn't know it was so close, so dangerous. Down an inch, keep it clear.

The nerves were reacting and suddenly anger came, anger with him, with what he'd say, told me they found you in the station lav, old boy, sorry about that, they've got no sense of privacy, those chaps.

He'd enjoy saying that. My break would have frightened him and he'd want to take it out on me.

Sweat inside my hands because of the anger.

The head of the broom touched the floor.

"Beats me, you know."

"Eh?"

"First we get orders to take things quiet so as not to alarm the visitors, next thing there's half a brigade of us turnin' Warsaw Central upside down."

It would be easier with the coat off but I couldn't take it off without knocking against the door handle. I stood the broom against the back wall.

"Who's that?"

"The ganger."

I heard the footsteps coming.

Do it now or stand here like a bloody fool because you think there isn't time, sorry about that, old boy, don't let him say it, *do it now.*

"Come on then, we're in a hurry!"

"Been quick as I could."

"Let's have it then."

Sweat on the palms wipe it off.

The cupboard was small but not small enough for me to use a foot on each of the side walls and I had to brace them both against the wall in front of me with my back pressed to the one behind but the chimneying action would be just as efficient and I began when they put the end of the crowbar into the jamb and started prising with it.

Sound factor to my advantage, their greater noise covering mine. Splinters were coming away. Unknown datum was the exact height of the ceiling but I knew it was at least thirteen feet, shoulder height plus arms' length plus handle of broom and therefore six feet higher than the top of the door.

Press. Slide. Press.

"It's coming."

"Give me a bit of room, then."

The door was shaking but the sound was below me now, a crackle of splitting timber.

Back muscles signalling strain, ignore, the body will do what you mean it to do when it senses you won't take refusal. Press. Press harder.

"This time."

Shoulders on fire, nerve lights flashing under the lids. Harder. Higher. Press.

Explosion of sound as the lock went, the door banging back.

Stop.

Flood of light below but here I was in gloom.

"All right."

"Wasted our time."

"No, we had to make sure."

I listened to their boots, to the echoes fading.

When it was silent I came down.

I gave them one hour.

The cadre left in place at key points would probably comprise special M.O. patrols with a handful of *Policia Ubespieczenia* manning the public exits, civilian dress.

I must go but the hazard was critical: they knew my image, knew that I was now bareheaded.

A train had been through and some people had come into the washroom and it wouldn't have been difficult to talk one of them into selling me his képi but that would have been fatal. They'd have stopped him at the exit, where is your hat, I sold it to a man in the *Toaleta*. Fatal.

But I had to go now and take the hazard with me.

It was quiet here. Distant sounds: shunting in the freight area, voice on the PA system, background of street traffic.

I went into the subway and turned left for the nearest staircase and we met face to face at the corner because the sound of his footsteps had been covered by my own.

17
COMBAT

He was one of Foster's men.

It worried me because he ought not to be down here in the subway: an hour had been quite long enough for half a brigade to deal with the station area and the main search should have been called off by now, leaving only the exits under observation. He shouldn't be so close to the centre as this and I didn't like it. I couldn't see where I'd made the mistake.

Then I got the answer and it was very simple: he was in fact manning one of the peripheral points but had needed to come down to the lavatory. It was reassuring to know I hadn't made a mistake.

I knew he was one of Foster's men because his face showed immediate recognition: my image was the known image and he was responding by reflex. His actual features didn't mean anything to me but he had a brown leather coat on and I'd seen that two of them had been wearing coats that colour.

He was going very fast for his gun but I had to wait because if I engaged right away the thing would have to stay where it was and he'd be able to get at it later if I got into an awkward position and I didn't want that to happen.

He had the eyes of an Alsatian in the instant of attack, wide open and with the pupils dark and enlarged, the gold irises glittering; his teeth were bared and this too gave him the look of a trained killer-dog. Even so he appeared to need his gun and I had to wait several fractions of a second before it was in his hand.

At close quarters a gun is highly dangerous. The danger is present before it leaves the holster, since it gives a feeling of power, of superiority, thus leading to false confidence and the impression that no serious effort has to be made, that the conflict has already been won. The danger increases tenfold once the gun is in the hand because only one hand is left free for useful work; at the same time the psychological danger remains present: it is felt that the mere sight of the gun will intimidate the opponent to the extent of rendering him powerless, quite incapable of movement. If, at this stage, the opponent decides to move, the danger becomes so great that it dominates the situation and can no longer be averted. The simple act of moving confounds the strongly held belief that no movement will in fact be made, and the surprise has the proportions of severe psychological shock.

Kimura's first rule is grilled into new trainees until they're sick of it but later it saves their lives: when threatened by an armed man, do nothing *until he comes into close quarters.*

It's usually easy enough because he likes to frisk you and then you can go to work. In this case I was lucky because we'd walked into each other and the distance was perfect. The gun was in his hand but that was all: his index hadn't settled inside the trigger guard and he was nowhere near horizontal aim. In another tenth of a second I would have had to use the routine deflection drill designed to get the body clear of the bullet but I didn't wait for that because the noise would alert the nearest patrols.

I chopped obliquely upwards against the wrist nerve and the force swung him partly round as the gun span high and hit the glazed tiles of the ceiling and that was all right but he was already hooking for a kite blow and I knew I'd been wrong: he hadn't been relying a 100 per cent on his gun—he'd just thought it might be the most convenient way.

I went down first and he dropped and tried for the throat, so I used the knee, and he rolled but corrected and I thought it was probably *kaminari*, a bastardised form of *kung fu*, because he got very busy and couldn't relax the tensions, so it was easy until the speed of the blows began foxing me and I had to go for a straight classic hand edge for the shoulder, hoping to numb and not succeeding the first time and not getting the chance to do it again because he was on to it and pulling clear and coming in again with a series of horribly fast kites that burned at the muscles while I hooked at what I could reach: windpipe, groin, plexus, trying for blows and then for locks and not getting them as I should.

Specialised disciplines are effective within their range but none of them are flexible enough: their patterns are too formalised. Pure *karate* can stop any amateur attack because it has the answer to every move in the book but there are one or two others and some of the *kaminari* blows have never been fully understood in the West, so that an element of the unknown enters the conflict, and there's no time to rethink on the established techniques because this form of attack is tense and fast and accumulative: the aim is to break down the opponent before he's had time to work for any kind of finalising strike or lock.

That's why karate has never been taught at Norfolk. They teach something different there.

I still couldn't use it. His energy was appalling and the blows came chopping wickedly fast for the vulnerable points and I knew that if I left only one of them unprotected for a half-second he'd be in there and finish me. His attack was animal: I couldn't believe that this creature could ever, short of killing it, be tamed; or that, once tamed, it could speak or write with a pen in a human hand. His breathing was like a wolf's, his frenzy producing grunts through the teeth and nostrils, a bestial snuffling, and somewhere in my mind there was surprise that these weren't claws ripping at me, that I touched no fur. Yet his blows were infinitely disciplined.

And suddenly I knew that if I didn't do something quickly he'd break me down and I'd have to be taken to Foster in an ambulance. My arms were losing strength and their muscles burned. I couldn't shift his weight from across my legs.

For a long time, for two or three seconds, I let myself relax, bringing the strikes closer to give him confidence, then twisted and freed an elbow and drove it hard enough to disturb his rhythm and he shifted his weight and I went for a yoshida and brought it off but couldn't hold the full lock because he slipped it enough to sap the leverage and come in again with neck strikes, so that I had to roll back and parry them. Light had begun flashing in my head.

A *hokku* and it threw him and I followed with the second stage of the lock but wasn't fast enough and his weight came back and I had to protect again because if only one of his strikes got through it would leave me paralysed. My head throbbed, pulsing to the rhythm of the flashing light, and breathing was difficult now. He fluttered above me, a vague dark shape whose weight increased and bore down and smothered my movements, and its snuffling became excited as the strikes hammered at the crossed shield of my arms and shifted their aim and hammered again and found the target protected but only clumsily now as I lost strength, and worse, lost science. Time was going, no more time. I needed time.

Sorry about that, old boy, but you shouldn't have chanced your arm, these chaps won't put up with it.

Relax and bring him closer. Get the breathing right or it's no go. Relax.

But I was a torch, a body burning, my own light blinding. His blows poured pain into me and the flames burst brighter. There was no time. Then let it be done without time. Now.

Twist. But he was ready and I had to try again and it didn't work but his aim was shifted and I moved the other way and felt purchase available as we rolled with my knee rising hard but not hard enough: it baulked his strikes but he went for a neck lock and I had to stop it because it was a *musubi* and we are frightened of that one, all of us. Lock and counterlock and we lay still, the muscles alone engaged, contraction without kinetics, the hiss of our breathing the only sign of life. Then I felt purchase again: my foot had come into contact with the wall of the subway and when I used it he was surprised and the lock went slack and I had time and forced him over and we lay still again, but the position was changed and I saw that there was a blow I could use if I worked very quickly.

But I hesitated. Morality came into this and the awareness of what I was going to do was holding me back. This was the jungle but even in the jungle there are laws: a male wolf, in combat with another and sensing mortal defeat, will pause and expose its neck and the jugular vein, tokening submission; and the victor will leave it.

Here the law didn't apply: a vulnerable point had been exposed by chance and morality was out of place because the organism was shouting it down, squealing for survival, and I put the last of my strength into the blow. It wasn't very hard because I was weakened now, but it was effective because it struck the point that Kimura has told us about.

Then I got up and leaned with my back to the wall, dragging air into my lungs while the nerve light went on flashing in my head. A sound was somewhere, a rumbling, and I remembered where I was, in the railway station of a modern city where men could speak, and write with pens. It seemed a long time since I was here before: an act so primitive had brought a time shift and the past few minutes had been measured in millennia.

The rumbling became thunder overhead and its rhythm slowed: a train was stopping. I would have liked to rest but there'd soon be people here.

In the washroom I took his coat and képi, putting them on. He was Pietr Rashidov, attached to the 4th Division of the Polish State Information Services on temporary duty, and his credentials carried the facsimile of the Communist Party seal. I sat him in the end cubicle where the hinges were still intact, locking the door and climbing over the partition, dropping and checking that his feet looked as they should.

Then I bathed my face, turning away from the mirror when I dried it. There's always the feeling of personal failure because it's an easy thing to do, and even when there's no choice it still has the look of a cheap trick.

There were more than I'd expected.

The train had pulled out and no one was on the middle platforms except for station staff and the M.O. patrols. Two of them were posted at the north end and that was the way I had to go because there were no ticket barriers.

I walked steadily in the brown leather coat and képi. My legs were all right: the punishment had been taken by the arms because his technique had forced me to shield. Head still throbbing and the throat raw though I'd drunk some water at the basin.

I looked at my watch. The glass was smashed and the dial twisted and the hands torn away and when I took it off there was its shape imprinted on my wrist, a purple weal. The clock over the main hall barriers showed 1420 and it was no longer a question of hurrying but of cutting down the whole schedule and running it closer and hoping not to wreck it.

The two M.O. patrols weren't moving. They stood facing towards me, dark figures against the screen of drifting snow at the station's mouth. They were fifty feet away and there was no one between us along this stretch of the platform. The snow looked easeful, whirling on the wind, and I felt a longing to walk in it and be lost in it. This place was a trap.

They'd want a report at the Bureau, was it necessary, what were the possible alternatives, was the person armed, so forth, and the sweat came on me again because they wanted too bloody much; they wanted you to go in and do the job and come out with your tie straight and your hair brushed and your hands clean, it was rather embarrassing for them, this kind of thing, and you had to be careful not to shout at them, yes I had to do it because I was losing consciousness and it was the last chance I'd get and it was his bad luck that the point he'd exposed was that one, not my fault, can happen to the best of us, what do you think things are like when a couple of ferrets go at it tooth and claw in a tunnel under the ground? Quite put them off their tea.

I was walking faster because of the anger and the distance had closed to thirty feet and when I'd gone another five I began calling out to them in Russian, pointing behind me—"Who's meant to be manning the barriers down there, is it you?"

They didn't bloody well understand, so I said it again in Polish, keeping the vowels flat and rounding the r's, and one of them came towards me with his paces circumspect.

"The two barriers this side of the hall—you think you can survey them at this distance without a pair of binoculars?"

He stood with his bright eyes hating me but all he could legitimately do was ask for identification, showing that just for a moment he had the upper hand by virtue of his uniform. I would even expect it of him: it was said that Dabrowska himself couldn't enter his own official residence without showing his papers.

"I must ask to see your credentials."

Pietr Rashidov. The red seal was sufficient and I didn't give him time to study the photograph.

"Answer my question."

"Our orders are to guard this end of the platform."

"And leave the barriers uncontrolled? Who is your officer?"

"There is a patrol on the other side of the barriers."

"We shall see."

I turned my back to him and began walking again the way I had come, looking to my left and to my right, watching for signs of inefficiency among the uniformed patrols at the flank exits.

My shoulders were stiffening and the glare of the lamps went through my eyes and ached inside my head. Walking in this direction, back into the trap and away from the healing and liberating snow, was retrogressive and irked me and to an increasing extent worried me because he'd be expected back at his post or back in the area he was controlling, say in five minutes, ten at the most.

Two station officials on the far side of the barriers, an M.O. patrol and a man in plain clothes: I stared at them and turned away and stood with my back to them, looking to the left and to the right, swinging again on my heel and pacing to the north end of the platform.

"And what patrols are there beyond this point?"

"You would have to ask my Captain."

"There should be patrols out there. Or is it that you're afraid of the cold?"

The Muscovite élite is not afraid of the cold and I moved past them and down the slope to the drifts that in the last hour had covered the tarred pebbles. The rails made dark skeins through the snow. I came back.

"You have another hour here. Don't relax your vigilance. Pay particular attention when a train comes in."

I paced away from them, slowly now, turning my head to demonstrate that the demands of efficient observation are unremitting: one must never be still, one must look here, look there, one's eyes must be everywhere. I stopped half-way to the barriers and stood sideways on, my head still turning, my gaze sweeping along the flank areas.

Thirst was increasing because the combat had dehydrated the system and there hadn't been time for more than a few gulps in the washroom. Blood from burst capillaries was filling the lacerated tissue along the forearms, and the muscles were still half-numbed. I didn't know if there was facial bruising because I hadn't looked at the mirror but I would need to check on that.

Movement left.

I looked along the platform and saw someone on this side of the barriers, a man in plain clothes, one of the Policia Ubespieczenia patrols I'd stared at just now when I'd gone down there. He stood facing towards me. He would want to know who I was or he believed I was Rashidov in the brown leather coat but wanted to know what I was doing here when recently I'd been in a different area, so I signalled him, a brief movement of my hand, yes, I am Rashidov, and turned away without seeing if he acknowledged.

The pulse, quickening, made the throbbing worse in my head. Instant availability of adrenalin but I had no use for it, I couldn't run. In ten seconds I turned my back to him, finding something under the sole of my shoe and fretting at it, chewing gum, rubbing my shoe across the edge of the platform to scrape it away, walking back towards the north end of the platform, deep breaths, deep regular breathing, *prana* the answer to most ills, the answer to panic.

The two M.O. patrols were watching me. They had been standing, the whole time, with their backs to the snow. They would have seen the man down there by the barriers. When I was within a dozen feet of them I turned again and saw that he was still there, standing quite still, facing in this direction.

I signalled again, more emphatically, jabbing a finger towards one of the flank exits. He turned his head but could see nothing of interest, and looked back at me, not making any sign. I shrugged, he didn't understand, he was a fool.

They declined to look at me when I turned and walked slowly past them. They looked pointedly away from me, in detestation.

The slope was gentle under my feet and I walked as far as the end, where the drifts had begun covering the tarred pebbles. The snow whirled from the open sky mesmerically, some of the flakes touching my face as I lifted it.

I would hear them if they moved and they hadn't moved. Then I walked on through the deeper drifts, slowly at first and then making my way more quickly over the rough terrain when I knew that the screen had thickened behind me and I was obliterated. It was *malowniczy*, the snow in Warsaw, very picturesque, did I not find it so?

18

CRACOW

It smelt of mothballs.

From where I stood I could see the door and I didn't look away from it.

"When?"

"In an hour."

"All right."

"Do it by phone. I don't want you to go out."

She said it might be dangerous to use the phone.

"Less dangerous than going into the streets."

I felt surprised that it worried me so much but I suppose it was because the whole thing was entering its final stages and it'd be a shame if they caught her as late as this. Once they'd thrown her into a train she'd be lost for years among the camps but if she stayed in the city until after Sroda she'd have a chance: a general amnesty was certain because of the talks, as witness to the bountiful mercy of the Mother State.

It was black astrakhan, a hat to match and a cheap wristwatch, seventy zlotys plus the brown leather one plus the hat, the last of Pietr Rashidov hanging flat on a hook in the corner with the macs and duffle jackets near the door where cooking smells came. Because when they found him they'd know who it was who'd walked out into the snow.

"Don't leave where you are. Give me your word."

"Very well."

"You can tell when a line's bugged?"

"Yes."

"Then there's no risk."

Before I hung up she asked if she were going to see me again and I said yes and this time it wasn't a lie.

The rendezvous was for 1630 a hundred yards north of the Slasko-Dabrowski Bridge along the west bank, three Czyn people, if possible trained in unarmed combat. This time I'd get them because this time I wasn't asking Merrick.

But they didn't turn up.

I waited thirty minutes and by that time my scalp was creeping because it had been bloody Merrick who'd exposed every one of my moves and I hadn't known it and now I knew it and he couldn't do it any more. Neither he nor Foster could possibly know the moves I was making now: every patrol of every branch of the civil and secret police was in the hunt and if they found me they'd slam me straight into a cell. There was *no* chance that Foster was giving me rope again, letting me run.

And the line hadn't been bugged. When you make an rdv in a city where there's a dragnet out you take damned good care of that.

At 1715 I went into the bar at the corner of Mostowa and got through again.

"They weren't there."

"Are you sure?"

I was listening to her voice, the tone of her voice, because I was right in the middle of a red sector and pushing my luck and it was just about as safe as taking the pin out and hoping it wouldn't go off.

"Quite sure."

"I don't know what happened."

Her tone was quiet with worry.

"They got picked up."

She said: "It must be that."

A black Moskwicz was pulling up outside, with big M.O. letters on it. I watched it through the window.

"Get me three more."

The receiver was beginning to feel slippery.

"Yes."

"Tell them to take care."

The hours were running towards midnight and anyone could be picked up, they were busting whole units.

"I'll tell them."

No one was getting out. There were four of them and they sat with their heads turned, watching the bar.

"In half an hour. The same place."

I trusted her because it was logical. They would have caught me there, otherwise, at 1630 on the west bank.

"All right."

The Moskwicz was moving off and I remembered there were traffic lights at the corner. They'd stopped for the lights. I'd forgotten they were there. I mustn't forget things.

"Will it be long enough? Half an hour?"

The coffee machine roared and I lost what she said.

"What was that?"

"I will do all I can. Remember that, please."

The thought came after I'd paid for the call. You grow sensitive at this stage of a mission. She'd said it with slow emphasis and it could have carried the undertone of a classic alert-phrase: all I *can,* am under duress.

Stomach-think. Discount.

This time they should be there.

They didn't come.

An hour ago the wind from the north had changed and it had stopped snowing. Beyond the balustrade the Vistula was a desert of white, untouched by the soot that would later darken it. Along the Wybrzeze Gdanskie the traffic was still running, its sound deadened by the new fall. Ashen light flowed from the lamps above my head, triplicating my shadow.

I had asked Merrick for them and he'd blocked me. Now I had asked Alinka. *All I can.*

Patrol car and I went down the steps again into shadow. The steps were a hundred yards from the bridge and that was why I'd made the rendezvous here. There was no time now to phone and make another one. This was where time ran out.

There was no usable alternative project: this was already the alternative to the one that had been blown up when they'd doubled the guards on the Praga Commissariat. I could switch and go in alone and do damage but it wouldn't be enough and the risk was prohibitive: not only to me but to the Bureau. The risk to myself was acceptable because of professional vanity: we know that one day there'll be a mission we shan't complete and that the chances are that we shall go in ignominy, a slack shape spread-eagled below the window of an empty room, something afloat in a river, and that it will have been for nothing; and sometimes we think of how it could be otherwise, of how we might play the odds and go out winning and be remembered for it, be granted at least an epitaph: *Hunter? He was Bucharest, '65. Went down with the ship but Christ, what an operation.* We all remembered Hunter.

Discount considerations of stinking pride: there'd be a risk to the Bureau, to the Sacred Bull.

The chains crumped rhythmically through the snow and from the city centre came the moan of trams.

If it had been a deliberate alert-phrase meaning she was under duress I would have to go along there and do something about it, at least do that.

I expected him to go past but he stopped and stood with his back to me, to the steps, looking both ways, taking a pace and coming back, watching the traffic.

Decoy.

You get too sensitive. I was behind him before he heard me and when I spoke he swung round with his hands whipping into the guard posture.

"Where are the other two?"

He relaxed.

"With the car."

"Where?"

"Along there. We didn't want to—"

"Come on, we're late."

The Hotel Cracow was busier than yesterday because there'd been a couple of flights in and the foyer was crowded: most of the atmosphere-coverage journalists were hemming in the dip. Corps people, free vodkas, and I recognised Maitland of the *Sunday Post*, one of the brightest of the I-Was-There boys.

I showed my credentials at the desk and they said they hoped there was to be no trouble and I said none at all, I just wanted to visit one of their guests, and they gave me the number of the suite.

"Don't announce me."

It was on the first floor and I pressed the buzzer. There were voices somewhere, speaking in English.

He was a short square man with his jacket pulled permanently out of shape by the holster. I told him my name and he came back in less than five seconds and opened the door wider for me.

This was the sitting room and there were four people here.

With typical courtesy he left his armchair and came towards me. "Hello, old boy, come along in."

19

KICK

Foster went across to a trolley.

"I hope you'll have a drink?"

"There isn't time."

"There's always time, old boy." His laugh wasn't quite in key but he was doing pretty well because he must have been upset when they told him I'd slipped their surveillance: I was his personal responsibility.

"London wants a report."

"Yes?"

"They'll be lucky to get it. Don't they know we've enough to do? Don't worry about the Czyn people I asked for."

There was a clinking sound: perhaps the woman washing a cup.

"I can try—"

"Won't you ever bloody well listen? I said don't worry about it. They were to give me support while I tried to break out of Warsaw but there's no need now."

"I see."

Foster turned round with a drink in his hand.

"Switch that thing off, there's a good chap."

Merrick reached for the tape recorder and the voices stopped. He wouldn't look at me: he sat hunched in the armchair, just as he'd sat on the bench at the station. I felt sorry for him: he thought I was only just finding out that he'd used audio-surveillance in the buffet while we'd sat with our bowls of soup.

That was all right: it was what I wanted them to think.

"You put a mike across me, did you?"

He didn't answer.

"You know how it is, old boy." Foster tilted his glass and drank. "We like to have things on record."

He'd been much more than upset when they'd told him I'd slipped them. It wasn't coincidence that the tape had been playing when I got here: he must have run it a dozen times since he'd got the bad news from Warsaw Central, listening for clues as to what kind of op I'd got lined up, clues to where I'd gone.

"Well, I hope it was worth listening to."

"So-so."

Most of the tape could be dangerous but it was too late to worry about that. It was safe—even valuable to me—from the point where Merrick had exposed himself, because from then onwards I'd suspected a mike and used it for my own purposes. It was the point where he'd given me the signal he said was from London.

In that instant he was blown.

There'd been three things wrong. 1) The code was fourth series with first-digit dupes. 2) PKL was instructed to furnish a fully detailed interim report. 3) These instructions were sent during the final phase of the mission.

Fourth series was Merrick's code, not mine, and London would have used my own code or if for any reason they'd changed it to a different series they'd have put a prefix to indicate express intention and there wasn't a prefix.

They would have sent the signal to KD for Karl Dollinger and not to PKL for P. K. Longstreet because Longstreet had ceased to exist when they'd given me the new cover.

They wouldn't have asked for a fully detailed report during the final phase of the mission because they know that at this stage of a mission you're lucky if you can hit the Telex or the short wave, let alone draft a ten-page coverage with itemised refs and carbons. They knew I was in the final phase because Sroda was the deadline for all of us.

Merrick had been given the signal by Foster's group because they too knew the deadline was close and they wanted all available info from me before Sroda broke and the confusion gave me a chance of getting out of Warsaw. So the poor little tick had blown himself but my immediate decision was not to scare him by telling him I knew. Maybe I could have tried saving him, at that moment, by breathing on the bit of compassion he'd managed to find in me, giving it warmth: tell him to get out and hole up and pray. But I could use him now, and anyway I think he would have walked out of the buffet and across the platform and under the next train.

He'd been usable because of the mike. Foster knew I'd asked for three Czyn people because Merrick had told him, so I'd let Foster know why I wanted them, direct on the tape. I told him two important things: that they were to help me leave Warsaw, *and that I no longer needed them.*

These were things he could accept. The first gave him a

plausible reason for my asking Czyn for support: to get me out of the city, *not to mount an offensive operation.* The second gave strength to what I knew I'd be telling him later, here in this room: that I no longer needed them because I'd been in direct touch with London and had orders to work with Foster and not against him and would therefore expect him to let me out of Warsaw as a temporary ally.

It wouldn't have mattered if there'd been no mike: the gist of it would have been passed on to Foster as routine info; but the tape gave it substance. I wasn't in fact sure there was a mike: it was just that Merrick had been sitting unnaturally still at the table and I'd put it down to chest pains, the asthma, until he gave me the duff signal. Then I knew it could be because he was trying not to fuzz up a mike with background noise, the friction of his clothes when he moved.

He could never do anything right, tripping on things and dropping things, cocking things up. Even when he used a mike on me it kicked back and he didn't know.

"I believe you've already met Voskarev."

The man in the other chair got up.

"Yes."

He was the man with pale hands and thyroid eyes who'd directed my interrogation at the Ochota precinct after they'd ordered Merrick to have me pulled in. He lowered his head in a token bow but his eyes stayed on me, round and staring, the eyes of a fish. He didn't sit down again but turned slightly away and stood gazing into the middle distance as if listening for something.

But I wasn't ready yet. I had to wait for Foster. I needed a cue from him and it had to be the right one because it depended on his next words whether I had to kill off the whole operation or kick it into gear.

"How's London?"

Kick it.

"I've just had my orders confirmed."

London was the key. He believed what I'd told him on the phone, or believed some of it, enough of it to test me for slips. Otherwise he wouldn't have been replaying the tape, wouldn't have been interested, would have told the man at the door here to put me in a cell and make damned sure this time I didn't get out.

"That's good." His tone was sleepy. "Been onto them direct?"

"Yes."

"Not from the Hotel Kuznia." His tone hadn't changed.

"There was too much delay."

"Oh, yes, of course, they told me." He took a sip of scotch. "So you're still on our side, that it?"

"What's it look like, Foster? You think I'd have come here under my own steam, otherwise?"

I had to work up some anger. The whole thing had to sound exactly right and a show of anger would do that.

"I suppose not. On the other hand you gave those chaps a lot of trouble, not very sporting. I mean if you're meant to be on our side—"

"*Christ*, haven't you got the picture yet? I told you I'd got a lot to do before I could come here and hand you the full works and I couldn't do it with a bunch of thick-eared clods treading all over my heels the whole time. You put them there because you were shit-scared I'd go off on some lunatic suicide mission and do some damage, right? I don't expect you to trust me but I expect you to trust your own judgement and see the sense in what I was telling you on the phone. Does this man understand English? If not I'll say it again in Russian because I want the whole of your outfit to know that if you start blocking me again you'll cost your-selves a good deal of valuable help and God knows you need it." I looked at Voskarev but he was staring at the wall. "Bet-ter still, tell him yourself, your Russian's a bit more fluent than mine, part of your contract."

Foster was looking into his tumbler. In a moment he said idly: "They found a man this afternoon. In a lavatory." He looked at me and I saw that a certain shine had come to his eyes under their puffy lids. He didn't like what I'd said about his contract and he didn't like his people being found like that. My anger was counterfeit but his was the real thing and I was going to keep working on it because in anger the judgement suffers.

"That was your own fault—I told you not to let them get in my way. You're slipping, you know that? What are you by this time, a bottle-a-day man? They all go like that once they're blown." I went close to him and he didn't look away. "The trouble with you Slavs is that you can't stand back far enough to get a world view. The Bonn proposals have opened up the chance of an East-West détente that could wipe out a lot of the mutual fear that's keeping both camps with one hand on the hot-line telephone and the other on the nuclear trigger and all you can worry about is a thug found dead in a lavatory."

I could hear movement behind me. Voskarev, getting rest-less. It was a fair bet he understood English and didn't like what he heard because Comrade Colonel Foster was their blue-eyed boy and I didn't sound too impressed.

They can't stand heresy.

Foster was perfect. Give him that. He took a sip of whisky and savoured it and said mildly: "All I mean is, old boy, that you must have been rather keen to go off on your own, which makes it difficult for us to believe you've nothing to hide from us. Why did you have to—"

"Listen, Foster." I turned away and moved about so that I could keep them all in sight: it wasn't the time for anyone to do something silly. "I told you there are one or two Czyn units still intact and I had to go and talk to them and I didn't intend exposing them to your people so that you could give orders to have them wiped out. They trust me and that might be a new idea to a man like you but it's a fact of life. If you've any more stupid bloody questions I don't want to hear them now because Warsaw's going to blow up if we don't do something to stop it and we haven't got long."

I went over to the trolley and found some soda and hit the tit and drank a glassful. It was very quiet in the room.

"You'd better be more specific."

"Now you're talking." I turned back to him. "Did you bring in Ludwiczak for me?"

"He's on his way."

"But I told you to fly him in and that was thirty hours ago!"

"It's not really the problem of transport. There are always formalities."

"How long's he going to be kept hanging around while they're filling in forms? He's our key man and we can't do much without him. Can't you phone someone?"

He spoke to Voskarev in Russian and he stopped staring at

the wall and picked up the telephone. Merrick had left his chair and stood with his back to us and I heard the atomiser pumping. The guard was still by the door.

I had to do it now and the sweat was coming out because if it didn't work first time it wouldn't ever work at all, and I watched Voskarev at the phone as if it was important that Ludwiczak was here.

He spoke to Foster, not to me.

"They are bringing him through the airport."

Foster nodded and looked at me to see if I understood.

"We can't wait for him," I said. "You'd better leave orders that he's to be brought here and kept under close guard till we get back."

The pain in my head was starting again and the bruises along my arms felt like muscular fever.

"We're not," Foster said gently, "going anywhere."

I shrugged, looking at my watch.

"Do it your way, I'm easy, but the Praga Commissariat's due to go up in an hour from now. I make it 2105 hours, that about right?"

"To go up?"

His tone was extra sleepy and that was all right: he was absorbing reaction.

"It's detonated for 2000 hours."

He glanced at the gilt sunburst clock.

"Oh, is it?"

I saw Voskarev transferring his stare to Foster. He understood English all right.

Foster drained his tumbler and took it across to the trolley, his steps short and with a slight spring to them. He nodded as Voskarev went to the telephone, then turned back to me.

"What sort of detonators are they?"

"Ludwiczak could tell us that. I'd imagine they're radio-controlled like the ones at the Tamka power station. I suppose the police found that stuff there, did they?"

"They did, yes."

He watched me attentively, no smile now, the eyes less sleepy.

"Fair enough. Tamka was for midnight."

He nodded. "Yes, they told us. Nobody told us about the Commissariat."

"Then you're lucky."

Voskarev was speaking in Polish, quite fast and with a lot of authority. When he'd put the phone down he got his coat and the heavy black briefcase that had been resting against the chair.

Foster hesitated and I knew why. The Praga Commissariat was his base and he'd got to get in there and out again while the walls were still standing.

Then he got his coat.

"I want you to come with us. I want to talk to you on the way."

"I thought maybe you would."

The courtyard was cobbled and the big saloon drifted a bit on the snow in spite of its chains.

Foster took the occasional seat and sat hanging on to the looped strap as we turned east towards Praga. He spoke more quickly than usual and his eyes were alert.

"You weren't actually sent from London to take any kind of action against Czyn?"

"I told you what had come up."

"Yes, but keep on filling me in, will you?"

"There's nothing new except that my people have started panicking at the last minute because the F.O.'s putting pressure on them. First they told me to explore and report on the Czyn situation and then they began chucking fully urgent signals for me to assist and advise the U.B. and now I'm apparently expected to keep the lid on Warsaw single-handed, their usual bloody style. I opted to cooperate with you off my own bat, why should I skin my nose on the grindstone while you sit on your arse?"

He gave a brief smile but the nerves still showed through it. "I've hardly been doing that, I think. We've quite a big problem here, and I don't expect you to understand its proportions. These urgent signals," he said with polite interest, "didn't reach you through the British Embassy, I suppose?"

"Oh, Christ," I said and we both laughed.

It was a private joke: we were two seasoned professionals and shared the understanding of our trade and our trade was deception so I knew what he was doing: he was testing his own agent, Merrick. "Of course they didn't. He would have passed you the dupes."

"I just wondered."

"Give the little bastard his due: he did a first-class op. for you and if London hadn't sent me new orders it would have been chop-chop and no flowers, you know that. Surely that's worth at least a lance-corporalship in the Red Army?"

He laughed again but it didn't have quite the same sound because he knew I was guying his colonelcy.

I wiped the steam off the window and looked out at the people along the pavements. The reaction was starting to set in, the delayed shock of what had happened in the station buffet. One minute I was watching Merrick and feeling glad that he'd soon be back in London and safety and the next minute I was trying to absorb the realisation that his job in Warsaw had been to cut me down and trap me for the KGB.

I hadn't thought about it since it had happened because there hadn't been time: it had floated in my head like a nightmare you can't remember in detail but can remember having had. I was thinking of Egerton now, rather than Merrick. Egerton with his chilblains and his prim confidence in what he was doing: *he's been fully screened, of course, I've no intention of saddling you with a potential risk.*

If I had the luck to see London again I'd have Egerton out on his neck: the least we expect of Control is that they don't recruit an agent already recruited by Moscow and then tell us to hold his hand.

I couldn't do it by signals. My only communications were through Merrick and the Embassy because direct contact had been banned since Coleman had used a phone in Amsterdam and didn't hear the bugs.

The saloon gave a lurch and Foster hung on to his strap: a fire-service vehicle had been klaxoning for gangway and its amber rotating lamp went past as we tucked in to let it through. I think we hit the kerb with a rear wheel before we pulled straight again, the kerb or a drift of packed ice.

Foster was looking at me rather sharply.

"We'd have heard it," I said, "from this distance."

"Are you sure?"

"The basement's crammed with the stuff."

He looked away.

Nervous and physical courage don't always come in the same package. For twenty years this man had run the most sensitive type of operation known to the trade, watching his words and weighing them whenever he spoke, wherever he was, cold sober in his Whitehall office or half-drunk in a woman's flat, fabricating his lies and testing them, detecting flaws and repairing them and listening all the time for a false note in the speech of others that would tell him of danger, carrying for twenty years a bomb that ticked in his pocket.

But he'd no stomach for the real thing, for trinitrotoluene.

"There are other places?"

"According to the Czyn people I spoke to."

"Which places?"

"You're not thinking straight, Foster. If I knew which places I'd tell you. The only one I'm certain about is the Praga Commissariat and I told you as soon as I could. My orders are to help you keep the peace in this fair city, try getting it into your head."

"The Records Office," he said reflectively, "would be another place."

"I'd say so. What price an amnesty when you can blow up the evidence?" The Records Office stocked secret information on every single citizen. "It's your own fault there's not much time left: you've wiped out most of Czyn and the die-hard survivors are going to make sure there's some action before they join the rest. Praga was rigged for midnight originally, the same as Tamka. You'd have had more time."

He shut up for a bit. I think he was working out the odds: he was still a top-line professional and he had a big operation running and he could only save it by going into his

base and pulling the documentation out in time. On the
other hand he didn't like thinking about his skin plastered
all over what was left of the ceiling.

Voskarev hadn't spoken since we'd got into the car. I
watched his reflection on the glass of the division between
the dark shapes of the driver and escort.

In a moment Foster said: "If they find the explosive and
defuse it we'd better have Ludwiczak brought along to talk
to us."

"He'll talk to me. He won't talk to you."

Gently: "The same thing, surely, since your instructions
are to help me prevent disorder?"

"I just mean don't scare him off."

"We don't want to scare anybody, old boy. The thing is
that we'll need to put some calls out as soon as we know
which are the other places. Evacuate the night staffs and
so on."

"You're not worried about the night staffs. You don't want
one and a half million dossiers to go up in smoke because
you can't run a slave state without Big Brother."

There was another lurch and he steadied himself on the
tip-up seat. Through the clear patch he'd made on the window I could see the arc of lamps in the distance, the Slasko-
Dabrowski Bridge.

Then we began a nasty wobble and I could see the wheel
jerking in the driver's hands. Foster held on to his strap. The
wobble got worse and we slowed, pulling alongside the
kerb.

"What's happening?"

"It looks like a flat."

The car stopped and the driver got out and tapped at the

window, calling something we couldn't hear. Voskarev opened the door, asking in Polish what the matter was.

"I regret that we have a puncture."

"You must get us a taxi," Foster told him quickly.

The driver pulled the door wide open and chopped for Voskarev's wrist to paralyse it in case there was a gun. Apparently there was, because the left hand went for the pocket of the coat, but the driver got there first so it was all right.

I told Foster: "Don't do anything silly." I didn't bother to look for a gun on him, he wasn't the type to carry one, the only thing you could say for the bloody man.

▶•◀▬•◀▬•◀▬•◀▬•◀▬•◀▬•◀▬•◀▬•◀

20

DOCUMENT

I told Voskarev I wanted his keys and his papers.

He stared around him as if looking for a street number through the clouded glass, as if lost in a place he'd thought familiar. I said:

"I'll get them, otherwise. Don't embarrass yourself."

He opened his astrakhan coat, fumbling like an old man.

"Fast," I said, "very fast indeed."

The driver said he'd get them for me and I told him to shut up. The driver wanted to kill him, I knew that.

Six, all cylinder-type, two on a separate ring, series numbers in sequence.

"Papers."

The engine was still running. Exhaust gas came through the open door. Yellow light flooded the snow and went out.

"Oh, come on," I said.

Sweat was on his white face, glazing it like a toffee apple.

Foster spoke to him quietly in Russian telling him not to worry, he would retrieve the situation. Such a windy phrase, that.

N. K. N. Voskarev. Deputy Chief Controller, Coordinated Information Services Foreign Division, seals and frankings U.B. liaison, all facilities requested up to ministerial-privilege level.

Big fish.

I kept the passport and gave the identity card to the driver. "There's a man under escort arriving at the Cracow within the next half an hour. Show this to his guards and tell them you're taking him over, Voskarev's orders. Get him to base."

"Understood."

A red card had dropped out of the folder and I picked it up and looked at it.

"Where's your insulin?"

"Here." Voskarev tapped his case.

"Get it."

The air came in, freezing against our legs. The driver stood impatiently, his breath clouding. The escort had shifted behind the wheel in case we had to take off suddenly.

"Look, you want that insulin? Give you five seconds."

Stuff was flashing us, no parking here, only wanted a patrol. Red, very red sector. I looked at the driver.

"Right."

The briefcase was still open and Voskarev was trying to zip it. He clutched the hypodermic kit in one hand.

"The case stays here."

He tried to take it with him and the driver did the wrist thing and papers hit the floor. Then he was pulled out.

"Bloody well calm down will you? He can keep the insulin and use it when he wants to, he's no good to us in a coma. You beat him up and I'll have you kicked into the camps, I can do that, now get moving."

I dragged the door shut.

The man at the wheel got into gear and I slapped the division and told him to wait.

"It doesn't," Foster said, "look too well organised."

"Best you can do with hired labour."

I wound the division down. The handle was loose and took a bit more off the veneered panel.

Foster sat with his hand still in the looped strap. His eyes were almost closed, two slits glinting in the baggy flesh.

"You're making it worse for yourself," he said.

Police klaxons were piping a seesaw note somewhere on the far side of the river.

Doors slammed much closer, behind us.

"Don't do that."

I had to kick upwards before he could reach the handle. He'd seen it done on the telly or somewhere: this wasn't his type of field at all; he was political-intellectual, the big moves made over a glass of bubbly.

Then a man came past from the other car and got into the front and shut the door and I said hurry but don't crash.

Foster showed his expertise, the top off one-handed, still straphanging.

"Calm the nerves?"

Trick after trick down the drain: he should have smashed it into my face. Not his field.

"Information: they're Poles and proud of it and Voskarev's been responsible for filling the trains with their own brothers and they know that. I'm going to phone them in fifteen minutes, failing which they're going to kill him.

They're hoping I won't be able to phone. Don't make it easy for them will you?"

I got the loose papers and stuffed them into the briefcase and zipped it and sat back and watched Foster. He screwed the top on and put it away.

"If you think about it," he said earnestly, "you really haven't the ghost of a chance, right in the middle of Warsaw. I do wish you'd try to be reasonable."

I didn't feel like answering: I was fed-up because he was probably right.

The two in front were talking but we couldn't hear much, something about Sroda. They sounded pleased with themselves, thought we'd captured the city between us.

"What happened to the other chaps?" Foster asked me.

"What other chaps?" I was trying to think ahead, about the photographs and things.

"My driver and his mate."

"Were they Russian or Polish?"

"Russian, I think. I didn't really know them."

"Then you're too late now."

They were no use as hostages and I hadn't given any specific instructions about what should be done with them afterwards, happened in the courtyard, you've got a flat tyre, and they'd got out to look. A night for flats but we were still running all right, making good time.

"I can get you a reduced sentence, you know. I've quite a lot of influence."

"Oh, balls."

The bridge was clear, stuff crawling in both directions, a hole in the balustrade where the Mercedes had spun, the gravel making dirty-brown streaks on the late snow. Foster said something, ought to be sure what I was doing, something like that, but I wasn't listening because there was so much to think about and I didn't want to make a mistake although with a setup this sensitive a mistake was almost guaranteed and it wouldn't have to be a big one, just a slip and she'd blow.

There were some police cars when we reached the Commissariat and the steps were cordoned off. Just before we pulled up I said:

"Don't forget the situation, will you?" He didn't answer but sat there squinting at me and I got a bit worried that he'd do something awkward simply because this wasn't his kind of terrain: for instance you can't stop a charging bull by pointing a gun at it because it doesn't know what the thing is. "You've got to look after Voskarev and the only way you can do it is to look after me."

He leaned forward, the alcohol on his breath. "There are so many aspects you haven't considered. They make it all so dangerous for you. So impossible."

"Just be careful. For his sake." I opened the door and he followed me out. "Get these bods out of here. Tell them it was a false alarm."

He stood perfectly still.

"Was it?"

"Of course."

He looked so relieved that I think he would have done whatever I asked just from gratitude. One of them came up to us, captain's insignia, and Foster showed him his card, absolute assurance incorrectly informed, no explosives, personal responsibility, so forth. Then we passed through the cordon and went into the building and the contusions started throbbing again because the very acute fear that he might chance it and hand me over had dominated physical pain.

When we were going up in the lift I heard the bomb-disposal team in the basement being told to pull out. Foster stood idly watching the wall sliding downwards on the other side of the gates. His breathing had become heavy, the only sign that he was disturbed. There was a city-wide search going on and he'd just passed me through a cordon and he hadn't liked that.

It was the big double-windowed room at the end of the third floor and he used his key and I told him to go in first, then I followed.

Define, infiltrate, destroy. I had defined and was now infiltrating.

I picked up the phone and told them the situation was in hand and that I'd be phoning at fifteen-minute intervals.

Foster got his keys out but I took them from him: there could be a gun in a drawer and I was going to be too busy to stop him playing about.

"We really ought to discuss the position you're in, old boy. You'd thank me, later."

"Take that chair over there and sit on it."

Three reasons for utmost haste: Given enough time I knew that Foster could outthink me. The sector was still bright red until I could get him to my own base. Merrick or the guard at the Hotel Cracow might telephone the Commissariat to ask if things were all right and if I answered their call they'd want to speak to Foster and I'd have to let them or they'd know things weren't all right and he'd use an alert-phrase and I wouldn't be able to stop him.

The safe came open with the two keys on the separate ring of Voskarev's bunch and I began with the top metal drawer because it was logical to file recent and current material highest.

Most of the stuff was in Russian but none of it encoded and I went for main headings and serial-numbered collations and found one specific document summarising the whole of the operation under sections *Preliminary Evidence—Prima Facie—Integration of Testimonies—Dossier of Accused—Summary of Charges*. The name of N. K. N. Voskarev appeared throughout with the title of *Chief of Enquiry* and the name of Colonel A. S. Foster began appearing on the reports dated later than January 16 which was the day he'd flown in from Moscow. Two other names were featured.

My senses were atrophying to a slight degree: the sound of the traffic seemed muffled and the light in here was keyed lower. Quite normal, the effect of sudden concentration as the typed symbols jumped and the mind span, incapable of containing this scale of significance.

Movement and my eyes flicked but he was only crossing his legs. In reflex I said softly:

"Sit still."

I looked again at the document.

So here it was: the programme I'd sensed was running in the silence and in the dark, smooth and massive and perfectly engineered, designed to protect the East-West talks from abortive collapse in the event of insurgence by the people of Poland and subsequent control of the capital by armed force under the provisions of the Warsaw Pact.

Précis: a special tribunal to be convened in Moscow for the immediate trial of a Western agent sent into Warsaw for the express purpose of activating the interests of an international imperialist conspiracy. Indictment: inciting dissension and revolt, providing clandestine liaison with Western factions, conveying assurances of diplomatic support from capitalist powers. The trial to be attended by international correspondents with all facilities required to make manifest the guilt of the accused and the gravity of his acts.

A show trial on the Garry Powers scale with a scapegoat dragged into the limelight and butchered on the block of political expedience. A man with two names.

P. K. Longstreet, alias Karl Dollinger.

"There's nothing," I heard Foster saying, "you can do about it. Because you can't leave Poland."

I went through the rest of the drawers.

He was standing behind me.

"Get over there and sit down, damn you."

Angry because I'd let him move without my seeing him. Postpone all thoughts about the document until the sector was green, otherwise highly dangerous.

"I'm not going to do anything, old boy." But he couldn't get his tone right. "We're alone here, and there might not be another chance like this. We can talk the whole thing over and do a deal on the quiet. I'll accept your word and you can accept mine. Give me a brief confession and I can arrange that you won't get more than three years, good conduct, special remission, you know the drift. Otherwise it's for life. Now do be sensible."

I tugged at the last drawer but it was locked and I had to open it with one of Voskarev's keys. Then they were in

my hand: 35-mm. strip of negs and a set of prints. I'd always
thought it was how they'd done it, with photographs.

The streets looked different but not because of the new
snowfall: there weren't so many people about and the traffic
was thinning; between Praga and the city centre there was
a darkened car standing at almost every intersection. Those
who didn't want to be involved were keeping indoors and
those who were waiting for midnight were lying low.

No one stopped us: the Moskwicz carried police plates.

There'd been a briefcase in the office and I'd cleared it
out and refilled it with the stuff I wanted and it was on the
carpeted floor with Voskarev's. The main document was on
my lap and I leafed through it because there might be a
chance to summarise the key facts in signals before I had a
go at breaking a frontier. That would be when they'd get
me, if I reached that far. Voskarev was working satisfactorily
as a hostage but there was a deadline on that: he and Foster
weren't officially involved in the counterinsurgent operations but they were in liaison with the police divisions and
they'd be reported as missing, any time now.

"After all, we only need to prove our point that the uprising was incited by the West. We've nothing against you
personally." His smile had great charm in it and his tone
was patient. "Once you've been convicted you'll be of no
further use to us—sorry to put it that way but I'm sure you
understand—so there'll be no point in taking it out on you
afterwards. We're not spiteful, you know."

He was on the tip-up seat: he seemed to like it there. I
remembered something about back trouble, a slipped disc
or something: at parties he always chose an upright chair.

"You couldn't have used Merrick, didn't you know that?" On the relevant pages of the document Merrick's name had been crossed out and *Longstreet* written above it by hand. "He's got diplomatic immunity. The most you could have done was kick him out of the country."

"Generally speaking, yes, but we'd have made sure he'd elect to go on trial. That's why we chose him, instead of a known agent like Browning of MI6—he's piddling about at the Embassy. I expect you're aware of that."

"I never know anything about MI6."

He gave a soft laugh. "Same old thing, the departments in London don't hit it off, do they, never have. But young Merrick was just the job, you see: we wanted to *create* an inexperienced man and groom him for stardom. Someone we could rely on to say all the right things at the trial. Then *you* turned up."

"Supposing you can ever get me inside a tribunal, you think I'll say all the right things?"

"*You* don't need to. You've been incriminating yourself since the day you flew in, and it's all down there in the reports sent in by Merrick. It won't really matter what *you* say."

Lights reflected in the glass division and I watched them and they steadied and followed for two blocks through the central area past Ogród Saski Park and I began sweating because the minute they were reported missing the Moskwicz would become a trap.

"I don't think it's a police car, old boy. But it will be, sooner or later." He leaned towards me and said with absolute sincerity: "You'll have to accept my little offer, so you ought to do it now, because don't you see you're only

adding to the charges, playing right into their hands? I'll try
telling them I went with you to the Commissariat of my
own free will, but old Vosky's going to bleat out the whole
story. You must see you're making things difficult for me."

Basic brainwash technique: the operator allies himself
with the subject without any pretence of switching loyalties: 'their' hands. Friendly attitude: 'old Vosky,' not such
a bad chap if you treat him right.

"What d'you think the chances are, Foster?"

He wouldn't tell the truth unless it suited him but it'd
give me an idea of what else he wanted to sell me.

The puffy lids opened wider in surprise. "They're 100 per
cent. I give you my word that the maximum will be three
years, providing you—"

"The chances of Moscow sending tanks in."

He looked away. I hadn't done it deliberately but for a
moment he'd thought I was hooked.

"It depends how far things go."

That could be the truth. For the past three days there'd
been careful announcements about tank regiments carrying
out winter manoeuvres ten miles outside the city, 'to test
the efficacy of mobile armoured units in snow conditions.'

"How far d'you think things'll go?"

He spread his hands in appeal. "We've done all we can,
as you know, to weed out the rowdy elements. If those re-
maining decide to make a nuisance of themselves then we'll
just have to keep order. Surely that's reasonable? We had to
do it in Prague."

Page 9 paragraph 3: *The proven guilt of the accused will
not only make it clear that incitement to disturbance was
wholly motivated by foreign capitalist powers, but also that*

similar motivation led to similar events in Czechoslovakia,
a fact that hitherto other nations have shown the most ob-
durate reluctance to accept.

"It was different there. In Prague there weren't any talks
set up. It'll make you think twice this time."

"Actually, no." His eyes had gone sleepy again. "In Prague
we lacked evidence of foreign conspiracy. Any necessity to
keep order in Warsaw tomorrow will be seen to be fully
justified. As a matter of fact—unofficially of course—we'll be
rather in your debt."

The Hotel Alzacka was in a side street of the station district and a commissar-style saloon would attract attention
there, but we couldn't get out and walk the last hundred
yards because the M.O. patrols were stopping everyone
and checking papers and we could be past the deadline by
now: they might be looking for Foster as well as for me.

"Take it east of the river and leave it in the dark and
make your way back separately."

I got Foster across the pavement and inside.

He recognised me, the man with the Bismarck head and
the weathered face. He said they were upstairs.

It was a billiard room on the first floor and the guns came
out when they heard us and I told them to put the bloody
things away. Strain was setting in and I tended to sweat too
easily and resented it because there wasn't time for the
nerves to start playing up.

Voskarev was on the floor with his back to a leg of the
billiard table. A thin boy with a torn coat and a shocked
face was huddled in a leather armchair and Alinka was
crouched near him, rubbing his blue hands to warm them.

The three Czyn people stayed near the door after we'd come in: one of them was the driver who'd brought Voskarev here. Voskarev looked numbed, his face waxy in the flat hard light from the lamps over the table. He was clutching his handkerchief in a stained ball.

"Who hit him?"

"I did."

Medium weight, gymnastic type, the small eyes close together, the head lowered a fraction as he came across to me, typical boxer's pose for the local sports page. His hands came up much too late and he span once and smashed into the rack of cues and sent a chair over and hit the wall and slid down it and didn't move any more.

The other two looked at him.

"I told you to leave that man alone. The same thing goes for this one. God help you if you forget again. Throw some water on him."

A lot of noise came and the shaded lamps began swinging. Through train.

Alinka moved across to me, stopping halfway, her feet together, her dark eyes quiet. She looked younger. From behind her, Jan Ludwiczak watched me, not sure of me, not sure of anyone after the bright lights and the rubber coshes and the blind-windowed train to the east.

"Why was he brought back?" she asked me.

"He was the only one with a name I knew."

I went over and looked at the man on the floor in case it was anything serious but there was only a scalp lesion: the cues had taken the initial impact.

"Come on, where's that water? And put Voskarev in a chair, get him a drink, ask the patron for some vodka up here." They had to help him and I went across. "Did they take the insulin away?"

"No."

"Can you do it yourself?"

"Yes."

"You'll need food afterwards."

He stared up at me.

"I wish to speak with Colonel Foster."

"I can't allow that."

Typical police thinking: show them a shred of humanity and they think you're a bloody fool.

There was a tap running. I had to know the meaning of all sounds. This one was all right: a Pole had gone into the next room for water. I told the other to watch the brief-cases and see that Voskarev and Foster didn't talk. Then I went downstairs to the reception desk.

He asked straightaway where I was.

I listened for bugs and said: "I'm still with Foster and Voskarev and everything's under control. Is the guard there?"

"Yes."

His tone was bleak. This was the first time he'd spoken to me since he'd said he was sorry.

"Tell him we want you to meet us at the Praga Commis-sariat immediately. Is that clear?"

"Yes. But what—"

"The bomb has been located and it's all right now. Listen carefully. Tell the guard you're going to the Commissariat, but go to the British Embassy instead. To the Chancery, not the Residence. Get the cypher-room staff back on duty as soon as you arrive. Tell the Embassy guard to expect me in half an hour: my papers are in the name of Karl Dollinger and I'll speak to him in German. I shall ask to see you. Have you got that?"

For a moment he didn't answer and I knew why. He was being crucified. Then his voice came faintly: "Yes, but I can't—"

"Listen, Merrick. Stay in the Embassy and don't contact anyone except for the signals crew. You'll be safe there."

The silence drew out again.

"No, I won't. They'll only—" but he couldn't finish. In those words I heard all human desolation.

"They can't do anything more to you now. I've got the photographs."

Silence.

"Merrick. Did you hear what I said?"

In a moment:

"Yes."

He began sobbing and I rang off.

21

ASHES

At 2306 hours I crossed into British territory.

It had seemed a long way from the hotel to the Embassy though it was only a couple of miles. I'd brought the Mercedes 220, the car they'd used to switch Voskarev from the Commissariat saloon. It had seemed a long way because the coordinated police divisions had been searching the city for me since I'd made my break from Warsaw Central and by now the hunt would have become intensified: I hadn't asked Merrick if he'd tried to contact Foster at the Commissariat but he would have done that when Ludwiczak was taken over at the Hotel Cracow. It would have worried him.

Dangerous not to assume that both Foster and Voskarev were now reported missing, last seen in company of Dollinger.

I left the Mercedes in the yard, parked broadside-on to the main entrance as a point of routine. The plates would have been noted by the police observation post in the street outside but might not have gone on record. No one else could see them now unless they came right into the yard.

Only two of the windows showed light.

Merrick was in a small room on the first floor.

There was a change in him. He looked much the same but the tension was gone. He reminded me of a man I'd seen just pulling out of a killing trip on one of the amphetamines: physically weak, deathly pale, the hand movements uncertain but the eyes calm, perfectly calm.

He said:

"This is Webster."

"Signals?"

"Yes."

Small alert cheerful man, knitted tie and Rotarian badge, breast pocket stuffed with pens. "He's okay now." He looked at Merrick again. "Okay now?"

"Yes."

I asked what had happened.

"Eh? He saw someone run over. Turns you up."

Merrick went and stood at the window, his back to us.

"Is that the cypher room?" An inner door was ajar.

"That's right." With his pert gaze he tried to see who I was, what I was, a red-eyed man with stubble and a German name and no trace of accent, something urgent to send.

"Open up transmission."

"Okay." He'd put a pad ready for me on the desk. "You got a pen?"

"I'm giving it to you direct."

"I'll have to have it written. It's rules."

"Just open it up, d'you mind?"

I dumped the briefcases onto a chair and got one open and took out the envelope and dropped it flat on the desk so that Merrick could hear it. "They're yours."

I pulled the door open. Webster had half-closed it behind him: a cypher room is sacred ground.

"You can't come in here."

I heard Merrick in the other room, opening the envelope.

"Do they ever jam you?" I sat on the nearest stool. "I mean by accident on purpose?"

"Not often."

"Get Crowborough's acknowledgement on a word count for each sending, what code've you got?"

"Standard." He just meant bugger off.

"Don't send standard." The cowled lamps threw a lot of back glare and I could feel needles in my eyes. It wasn't exactly fatigue: the organism had started panicking because some of the brain-think had filtered through and it was squealing to know what I intended to do about its survival and there wasn't an answer. "Send priority." It didn't want to stay trapped in this dark winter city where people would try to kill it.

Webster wasn't touching the knobs. I'd been vouched for by a second secretary but it wasn't enough.

"I'll want some kind of authority."

By approximate reckoning it'd take five minutes to give it in fifth series and another five minutes for him to re-encode. It wouldn't matter if anyone was tuned in: I was destroying their operation and they couldn't stop me. They could only stop me if I gave them enough time.

"These are to BL-565 Extension 9. No copies and no repeats. You ready for me? First: *KGB operation mounted to stage rigged show-trial as proof that—*"

"Hold on a minute." He'd found BL-565 E-9 on his list. For the Curtain embassies it approximates to the hot line and I suppose he'd never had to use it before. He threw a couple of switches and dialled for pips and got them and said: "Okay."

"*KGB operation mounted to stage rigged show-trial as evidence of—*"

"Evidence or proof?"

"Proof." I let my eyes close against the glare. "*Proof of Western conspiracy to incite Polish uprising.*" He was on automatic encode but I didn't want to rush this so I gave him time. "*Justification thus established in event of subjugation by Warsaw Pact forces. Primary aim protection of imminent East-West talks.*" I heard him making an interval reception-check. "*This operation now defused since candidate for trial no longer available but suggest all Western agencies Warsaw receive immediate warning to retrench in case effort made to provide substitute.*"

My foot slipped off the rung of the stool and I sat up and opened my eyes. Bloody little organism trying to flake out and forget its problems.

"*Relevant documents by QM next run. Dollinger.*"

I found him in a room at the end of the passage, putting the lid back on the cast-iron stove. Even though he knew I'd come in he stood for a minute listening to the dying away of the flames. Then he looked at me. I don't know exactly how he saw me, exactly what I represented for him: I'd become a composite creature, the subject of his hate for my having seen the photographs, gratitude for having vouchsafed him their destruction, guilt for what he had done to me and fear for what I might now do to him.

"How did you find them?"

"I knew where to look."

He went to the door and shut it: the building was quiet and Webster was still in the cypher room waiting for an answer to my second signal.

"There won't be any others, will there?"

"No."

The negs had been the middle ten in a roll of thirty-six and the rest were blank: automatic exposure with a dummy run and timed cut-off, the prints tallying.

He stood uncertainly, his raw hands hanging from his sleeves and his feet neither together nor astride. The calm that had come to his eyes was also in his voice: he could speak abstractly about things that had been for him, so recently, a crucifixion.

"It was horrible of them, to do that."

"Just routine. They do it to anyone they can get hold of, embassy staffs, businessmen, didn't you know? It's the classic hello-dearie." I didn't want to ask but I had to because someone else might be glad to know he was off the hook. "Who was the boy friend?"

His eyes squeezed shut behind the spectacles and he couldn't say anything for a second or two, then it was over.

"Someone I met in a bar. I didn't see him again."

"Because if it was anyone here in the Embassy we'd have to fix things."

"No."

The door clicked open: there was a draught somewhere and the catch hadn't quite sprung home when he'd shut it. He could never do anything properly. He pressed it harder this time.

"They told you they'd send those to your father?"

"Yes. And to a Sunday paper."

Sir Walford Merrick, K.C.M.G., O.B.E., Equerry to the Queen's Household. An initialled spoon beside the silver eggcup, the paper knife arranged beside the mail and in the mail a letter with a Polish stamp and in the newspaper the headline.

"First thing you did was throw yourself under that tram?"

"Yes."

Never anything properly.

I hooked a chair from the desk and sat on it and the organism woke up and squealed that we'd got no shelter here because there wasn't any diplomatic immunity, British territory or not, and no hope of a plane and no frontier that didn't border a Russian-controlled state, but there were some things I needed to know and only Merrick could tell me.

"They asked you to give them information on Czyn. What else?"

Suddenly he said: "Why did they choose me?"

"You were in Prague in August '68 so they were going to pin that one on you too. You'd already got friends in Czyn, so you could develop your access to information on their programme. You've got personal tendencies, so they could take pictures to entrap you. Your father's position was their guarantee that you'd obey orders and it also gave you great value as an exchange-monkey if there was no uprising and therefore no invasion and therefore no trial."

He was only taking some of it in: the first time he'd known he was being groomed as a star turn in the Moscow circus was a few minutes ago when he'd heard my signal through the open doorway of the cypher room, and he was having to look back over the recent past and see it in this new light.

I was thinking suddenly of Egerton again, sitting up there rubbing the bloody ointment in while both Merrick and I were headed for perdition. It was a case of murderous incompetence and I'd have him roasted for it. The worst hazard of them all is a mission formulated on false concepts and in this case it was his belief that Merrick was just another second secretary willing to do a little bit on the side for the U.K. secret services. *He's been fully screened, of course.*

I had to stop thinking about it. The man was done for anyway: the document included references to Merrick's recruitment by the KGB prior to his sick leave in London.

"What are you going to do with me?"

His eyes watched me, vulnerable, submissive.

"Send you home."

He nodded. "How—how long will they give me?"

"What's that mean?"

"For what I've done."

"You think you've done anything that matters?"

"I worked for them. For Moscow."

"Don't get any illusions of grandeur. You made a mess and I've cleared it up, that's all." The poor little bastard was trying to get rid of some of the guilt by picturing a stretch in the Scrubs. "You'll be declared *persona non grata* for having engaged in inadmissible activities and put on a plane. They might try fixing you up with a bad smash on the way to the airport because you've been witness to their operation but I'm going to stop that one." Then suddenly I saw what he meant. "Listen, Merrick. Once you're in London the whole thing's over for you. In a case like this there won't be any muckraking because it won't suit anyone's book; we've bust their project wide open and the press handouts are going to be strictly propagandist. Even the F.O. won't know the full story and it won't ask any questions because they'll all be too busy putting the flags out. You'll leave the Diplomatic Service and go into some other ministry with first-class recommendations and that'll be that, so if you're thinking of trying another trick with a tram you can forget it." Slowly I said: "Your father will know absolutely nothing. Nothing about the photographs, nothing about your involvement with the KGB. Nothing."

His face was perfectly blank. I couldn't tell if it had got through to him. Then I knew it had.

"I'm just going to be let off."

"Christ, haven't you paid enough? Stop thinking about crime and bloody punishment, will you, it's old hat. You got caught in the works, you're not the only one. And you've been lucky, so settle for that." I was fed-up with his chocolate-box morality, with his inability to know that in the intelligence services you've got to wrench your sense of values round till they face the other way. "Look, I want to know some things: what were they after, specifically, when they told you to volunteer for a U.K. espionage job while you were on sick leave in London?"

"I'm sorry, I don't quite—"

"Oh, come on, Merrick." He was still lost in his dreams of atonement. "The KGB recruited you and you tried to ditch the perch and it didn't come off, so you went on leave and while you were in London they told you to fish around for a job in one of the hush services and I'm asking you why they did it."

Because I couldn't make it fit. They'd picked him for the show trial, not for infiltrating the opposition.

"It wasn't their idea."

My head seemed to freeze and thought went cold. After a bit I said:

"Whose was it?"

"Mine."

"You'd better tell me."

Then he had to get the bloody thing out and pump it.

"Excuse me."

"Get a chair."

"Yes."

"Right."

"When I was on leave I told Mr. Frazer about—"

"Who's he?"

"Head of Personnel at the Foreign Office. We all like him, because he takes a lot of real interest in us and—"

"All right, Dutch uncle, well?"

"I told him about the photographs, and asked him what I could do. He was very worried—"

"Oh, my God."

The whole picture began coming up: the one I hadn't been able to see when I'd stood at the window scratching the ice away with my nails. At that time I didn't have the facts. I had one now.

Egerton had known.

"What's the matter?"

"He was worried. What did he do?"

"He said he'd get someone's advice."

Frazer could have gone to someone he knew in MI6 or the O.I.B. or the Security Service but it had happened to be Egerton. Frazer was in a bad spot because the press wouldn't have any mercy on him if it came out that yet another homosexual had been posted to a Curtain embassy, a high-security risk because of his susceptibility to being compromised. Since the Vassall case the public had lost patience and this time there were added dangers: the person of Sir Walford Merrick increased the menace of the photographs and at the same time brought the risk of explosive scandal close to the Throne.

"He didn't say whose advice he was going to get?"

"No. He just said it was someone who knew about things like that."

"Then the bastards did a deal."

"I'm not sure—"

"Never mind."

Cosily, over a glass of sherry. Well, what d'you expect me to do about it? I don't know, but I'd be grateful for any advice. Think he'd be willing to do a bit of work for us? I'd imagine so—he's in a pretty awful state about those damned snapshots. All right then, send him along and we'll find a little job for him, then you can both stop worrying.

The time had been right. Things looked like getting rough in the Polish Republic and the U.K. was interested in what

the chances were of revolt and subsequent invasion and
what the effect would be on the East-West talks. Merrick
could keep his ear to the ground and at the same time pass
back info on the KGB: their orders to him would be analysed
in London to provide an insight into the way Moscow was
thinking.

A bargain's a bargain, however foul: a word in the ear of
Sir Walford across the coffee table or in the calidarium or
on the eighteenth green: if he should hear anything, or receive any kind of evidence, to the detriment of his son, he
should discount it totally, since certain duties of high value
to his country might expose him to false accusations.

It was horrible of them, to do that.

And those bastards in London no better.

"I suppose you told them you doubted your capabilities,
no experience in hush operations, so forth?"

He watched me from above his hands. His hands were
cupped against his face, as if he were trying to hide. He'd
get over that, given time, given peace.

"Yes, I did. But they said I'd be among friends at the Embassy, and they'd send someone out here to look after me."

"Who directed you?"

He'd only met Egerton once, and I'd been there.

"I never knew his name."

There was a question he wanted to ask, but he knew it
might sound naïf and make him look silly. He'd had enough
humiliation. I did it for him:

"He said I wasn't to be told you'd been entrapped by the
KGB. I wasn't to know."

He nodded, his hands sliding away from his face.

Because Egerton had seen the risk: that Merrick was doubling for Moscow and his cover story was the photographs and his job was to infiltrate the Bureau. And he'd wanted me to find out.

If a Control director knows his executive in the field, knows his style and potential, he can do things with him that would otherwise be impossible. The director-executive relationship is peculiar to the trade and has immense value for both parties but especially for Control. Egerton had selected me for a mission that I didn't even know was being given me—*a little trip abroad, only a few days*—and he'd sent me in blind, knowing that if I worked to form I'd find the target for myself, sniffing out the directions and scratching away at the earth like a good little ferret until I reached what he knew must be there, somewhere east of the Oder, and made my kill.

He had known, essentially, that most of us would have refused to take on a job as diffuse as this with no local control, no communications except through the Embassy and no positive lead-in data to work on; and he'd selected me because he knew I'd want to go in deeper the minute I sensed the field, simply because I like being left alone when I've found something to play with. It had been the only way to rope me in.

The mission had been to make contact with the KGB, discover their project and inactivate it. *Define, infiltrate and destroy.* That was now accomplished. *This operation now defused.*

The risk hadn't been high: he'd known I wouldn't go nearer Merrick than I'd go to a rabid dog until I'd got the scent of the field and located its hazards.

And if I tripped a snare he'd expect me to cut loose.

"You were told not to expose me to the KGB, that right?"

His hands went to his face again and he didn't answer and I got up and kicked the chair clear and said, "For Christ's sake, give yourself a break will you? London knew there was the risk but I don't blame them and I don't blame you—I'm still here aren't I and I'm in bloody sight better shape than you are, so stop picking your nits about it. All I'm after is plain information. Exposed me by accident, did you?"

He nodded into his hand.

"Well, I'm not surprised. When you're doubling there comes a point when you don't know which way you're facing. That was on Friday, was it? Come on I'm pushed for time."

"Yes." He got up and tried to face me and couldn't and just stood there with his head down and I turned away and looked at the picture on the wall, donkeys in Clovelly, far cry from here.

Friday. The bar. The rendezvous at the Roxana. That's why he'd been worse than usual, ill with nerves: he knew he'd blown me. There'd been no tags or I'd have seen them or sensed them: they'd wanted to pull me in without my suspecting Merrick, or I'd never contact him again. So they'd used window surveillance in relay and passed me from street to street till I was more than a mile from the Roxana and then they'd rigged the pickup with ordinary patrols just asking for papers, for dokumenty. Then they'd sent for Foster.

Have a look at me and let me go, see where I'd run.

That was when they did the switch and started preparing me for the tribunal instead of Merrick.

"I tried not to give you away. I did try."

"Civil of you."

"You don't believe that."

"Oh yes." But he'd had no chance. Driven by both sides till he broke. "Didn't you trust their word, in London?"

"At first." He knew what I meant: he was straight onto it because for weeks he'd lived in terror. "Then when I was out here again they began reminding me, asking me again for my father's correct address, you know what they're—"

"Yes."

"So that's all I kept thinking about. My father actually looking at them, even though he'd been told not to take any notice." I heard him using the thing and then he said: "I wanted to warn you, but I thought you might leave Warsaw if I did, and then they'd have known they couldn't trust me any more, so they'd have sent the—"

"Get it out of your mind." I turned back to him and it was all right now, he wasn't looking so bloody abject. There was only one more thing I wanted to know. "Our last rendezvous in the station buffet. Did you know they were going to come for me there?"

"Yes." I only just heard it.

"Then what made them tell you to pass on that fake signal? What did they want a full interim report for, when I was booked for grilling?"

His face went loose and he lost contact completely because these things had stopped meaning anything to him.

I said: "It's important, Merrick."

He nodded and made an effort and I waited.

"I was meant to give it to you earlier. But I forgot."

I think he saved himself, then, from any grudge I might ever have held against him.

Webster was getting something through when I went along to the cypher room.

There was a phone in the annexe and I picked it up. He came through the doorway while I was trying the buttons.

"How does this bloody thing work?"

"Want an outside line?"

He pressed the one with the worn Sellotape tag and I dialled for the Hotel Cracow.

We looked up.

"What's that?"

"Sounds like a chopper."

He'd put the signal slip on the desk in front of me.

Hamilton. Quay 4. End crane.

"Did you do word-count check?"

"That's right." He was trying to clip another pen into his breast pocket but there wasn't room.

"*Hotele Kraków?*"

"*Tak jest.*"

I asked for Maitland.

The helicopter was still nosing about and a flush of light passed across the window.

"Anything to send?" asked Webster.

"No."

He went to shut down the console.

"Maitland?"

"Who's that?"

"Listen. Tomorrow morning there's a second secretary leaving the Embassy for London and the U.B. might arrange an accident on the route to the airport, so why don't you turn up and follow the Embassy car? Let everyone know you're the press, take plenty of Rollies, you get the drift."

"Well, well."

"You'll need some kind of excuse."

"Human angle: while the pin-stripe élite of the dip. set come flocking into the flashlights here goes one unassuming second sec. on his lone way home, so let's give him a cheer lads. A natural for the mums."

"Don't leave him till he gets on the plane."

"Roger. Thing is, I can beat the Street with a nice faked smash that'll only happen if I'm not there to cover it. What d'you do in the coffee break, make up crosswords?"

The light flooded the rooftops again, slanting off the snow. I asked him if he could hear a chopper.

"What? Yes. They're getting fidgety. Midnight curfew for all Polish nationals, leave cancelled for the police and the army, foreign residents prone to a slight loosening of the bowels, what shall I do with my poor Fido, they won't let him on a plane and I'm not going to leave him behind. Who are you anyway, the Ambassador?"

"Word in your ear: you never had this call."

"Didn't I?"

"We're being bugged, didn't you hear the click?"

"I thought it was your teeth."

He rang off smartly. There was nothing they could do: if they wanted to fake a crump they'd have to do it in front of a Western camera.

Someone was talking in Russian, then a lot of splurge came. I went into the cypher room.

"What station's that?"

"Voice of America." Webster cut the treble and the whole range sank into the porridge.

"They often jam it?"

"They've not done it since Prague." He changed the wave length and there was more porridge. "Radio Free Europe." Then he flicked the band and got a girl in slow emphatic Polish. "One of the Warsaw stations hidden up somewhere."

. . . Been to the point if Minister Podhal had explained the presence tonight of more than five hundred medium tanks and one quarter million motorised troops standing by along Motor route E8 within twelve kilometres of the capital. If we are to conclude that these forces are—

"More?"

"No."

"Think they'll come in?"

"No."

Because they'd lost their licence to occupy the city: the document in the other room.

"Well, I can't see who's going to stop them."

"Do some things for me, will you?" He followed me through the doorway. "Put those two briefcases into the dip. bag and seal it."

"I can't do that—"

"Can Merrick?"

"Not officially, till the morning."

I shut my eyes again because of the light, because of having to think of small important details, because of the worry about what I had to do next, the bloody little organism snivelling for what it knew we couldn't get: a quick plane home.

"Look, phone H.E., get him along here and give him the pitch."

"The what?"

"Oh, Christ, the picture. Ask Merrick. He knows. He's got to leave Warsaw by the next plane, waive all formalities, he's not safe here. And that bag's got to reach London, highest priority: tell the Queen's Messenger what's on, you've got a rough idea." Very far away an emergency klaxon sounded and then the buildings muted it. I bent over the briefcases to check the zips and a muscular spasm gripped my chest and I had to wait till it passed. "Listen, I want you to stay with Merrick. Don't take him to the Residence: keep him here."

"Okay. Fetch the Doc along shall I?"

"Can do. And don't let him go near windows, watch him for aspirins, he's depressed."

"You okay yourself, are you?"

"Yes. Just look after him for me."

"I savvy. Book that call, did you?"

"Call?"

"The local. Rules, see, they're red hot on expenses. I'll take care of it, don't worry." He unclipped one of his pens.

I went along the passage and past the room with the cast-iron stove and its red curling ashes, then down the stairs and into the bitter night air.

It was a clear run back to the Hotel Alzacka. The streets were deserted: the curfew was for thirty minutes from now and people didn't want to be caught out because their watch had stopped. A few taxis: they'd be journalists covering the scene.

The hotel was halfway along the street and they came in from the far end while I was switching the engine off, a dark-coloured mobile patrol slowing on sidelights, and a couple of seconds later my mirror went bright. I knew the Mercedes was all right so it was the hotel itself they were closing on. I threw the door shut and crossed the brittle snow on the pavement and went inside.

22

SRODA

The staircase curved and I caught at the banister rail, pulling myself up. One of them was guarding the door and I told him to get inside.

A tin tray on the billiard table, dirty bowls and spoons and the smell of *czesnik*, the Ludwiczak boy asleep, nothing else different.

"Alinka."

It couldn't be said in front of Foster because there was a last chance: he might not see the vulnerable point that could finish me.

As she came quickly, the slamming of metal doors sounded from below and in the half-lit passage her eyes glittered.

"Police?"

"Listen, I'm taking the Englishman and not coming back. Get control of them if you can, tell them Voskarev's no good as a hostage if they kill him, make them see sense for your own sakes."

The door below came open and we heard their boots. She

turned her head to listen, contempt on her shadowed mouth, then looked up at me.

"Thank you for my brother."

They watched me as I went back through the doorway and Foster was standing up and on his face I saw fear and knew it was for Voskarev.

A man tried to get past me with his rifle and I pushed him back. "Stay here and keep quiet. Foster, I want you."

He looked once at the Russian and may have said something to him. Then he followed me out and I shut the door. Through the banisters I could see the cap of the man guarding the main entrance while the search spread through the ground floor.

"They'll kill him," I said, "you know that."

He looked at me without enmity, his mind too disciplined for abstraction. "I'm not sure," he said, "that I can do it."

"You'll bloody well have to."

We went down the stairs together. A lieutenant was at the desk throwing questions at the *patron* and swung round when he saw us. Foster showed him his credentials and I heard him trying to get authority into his tone: what were they doing here?

The commissar saloon had been reported as having been seen outside this hotel.

Yes, it had brought us here. What was the trouble?

The Comrade Colonel and the Deputy Chief Controller were said to be missing.

"Some fool," Foster told him with a flash of impatience, "is spreading confusion. Comrade Deputy Chief Voskarev has gone to the *Najwyzsza Izba Kontroli*. Now get your men out of here."

I turned to the patron and apologised formally for the disturbance as the orders were shouted along the passage. The tramp of boots gathered at the entrance and an engine started up outside. The lieutenant's salute to Foster was perfunctory: the Polish M.O. branch was at present under control of the Coordinated Information Services Foreign Division and the position was one of sufferance.

Foster was standing perfectly still. I think he was waiting for the sound of a shot from the billiard room: in hostage situations the death rate is highest when a search comes close.

The rhythm of snow chains passed the building and then it was quiet.

"All right." I took his arm because he was turning towards the stairs.

The street smelt of exhaust gas.

"Where are we going?"

The ignition and oil-pressure lights dimmed out and I turned by gunning up and bouncing the rear off the kerb because there wasn't room for the lock. I didn't answer him. He sat without a word until we were into Zawiszy Square and it occurred to me that he knew what I was going to do with him.

Sidelights came into the mirror and I noted them. The Square was heavily patrolled and the white beam of a lamp swung from somewhere above us, a rooftop command post. A long way off I heard the chopping of rotors again. Then there was firing of some kind, nearer to us, and I checked my watch. It was midnight minus one: a minute to Sroda.

Will you be here? Don't be here Wednesday, pal.

The shape was still in the mirror. I don't know if Foster had caught a reflection or heard the chains but he looked round and then sat facing forward again.

"You're going to have a crack at getting out, then."

"I'm taking you to London."

He didn't say anything immediately but I heard him suck his breath in. His fear was in the car, like a smell. He didn't want to go to London; there were people there who'd believed they were his friends and he had something in common with all shabby men: He couldn't face his creditors.

"Throw me to the pack, eh?"

"No. Formal trial." I brought the speed up another few kph. "And no faked evidence." I was taking the odd chance with the unpredictable surface but they didn't drop back. One of my eyelids had started flickering because he'd had time to think about things and there was the vulnerable point that could finish me and I no longer believed he'd miss it.

"Revenge is sweet, that old lark."

"Oh, balls, you don't mean anything more to me than something on a doorstep and it's mutual." There was a soft area in him that I hadn't suspected: an inability not to emote. It felt sticky. "A full-scale trial's going to tell us a lot more about you and your network. I'm just taking some goods home, it's my trade."

We crossed Jerozolimskie and headed north and heard firing again.

"Then you've had it, old boy. Without you in control of those nervy idiots, your hostage is as good as finished."

I felt my scalp go tight.

"Not necessarily."

Suddenly his discipline broke and his voice became very bright. "If there's another police raid they'll shoot him before they're taken. Otherwise they'll shoot him in any case when he's no more use. He was a good man, you know that? He was my one friend, the only man who ever understood."

"Bloody shame, what chance did you give the others to understand?"

He made me sick.

The street lamps flickered and steadied again. I took the next set of lights on the red and the shape closed right in, filling the mirror.

When he spoke again he'd got the control back.

"That's a patrol car behind, as I suppose you know. They weren't satisfied, that'd be it, wouldn't it? They're checking to see where we go. Better pull in, you know the score now."

They began flashing and I tipped the mirror.

When the trap closes you shake at the bars, it's a reflex, all animals do it. Their klaxon started up and I took an intersection and hit piled snow and got her back and swung left and saw I'd blown it because there were barriers across the street and the lights flickered again and went right out, one of the power stations gone up, no help to me, dark figures moving among lamps, the shadows alive and something waving, red-and-white stripes, then flashes poppling the dark and I span the wheel and felt the front end go, Foster calling something, the bodywork taking a shock and then another one, rapid rifle fire.

Still spinning and then the rear hit a kerb and we bounced and some feel came back into the steering and I used it, sudden brilliance striking across my eyes, the patrol car coming at us with the heads full on and then glass smashed behind me and I sat low and found a gear and got traction again as the patrol glanced off and the scene went black in contrast, coming up again as I hit the heads on and kicked the switch to full, a repeater starting a rat-tat from the barricade, a side window going and my arm jerking to the force, pain flaring, then some stability as the chains bit and we closed on the intersection, the sound of the engine taking over from the noise back there, the fusillade fading as I drifted the right angle and sped up, settling along the street's perspective.

Check gauge: tank strike possible.

The slipstream rushed, back pressure flowing through the smashed rear glass, the frozen air from the side window setting up turbulence. The dead street lamps hung above us.

Foster was leaning against me and I gave him a nudge but he didn't sit up straight.

A few kilometres out of the city I passed through the humped shapes of tanks harboured in line at the roadside. Their engines were silent and the troops standing about looked idle, some of them smoking a cigarette. A lamp flashed but that was all: they weren't interested in normal traffic.

I dropped him off soon afterwards. It was only a ditch where the wind had scooped a shallow in the lee of thorn, but better, from his point of view, than London.

On my way back to the car I saw a jewel lying on the snows southward, blue-green and as brilliant in the winter night as Sirius above me. From here it had lost the look of a city, of anywhere I'd ever been, but when later my lights rushed north, the fragments of memory came and went, like a far lamp winking out: a curl of hair, a shadowed mouth, who are you please.

The *Hamilton* had steam up but I wasn't overdue: my signal had allowed for ice conditions and I'd avoided towns, taking my time so as to reach Danzig by dark. I ran the Mercedes into the truck park on Quay 4 and walked to the crane at the end. I wasn't there long: it was in sight of the starboard lookout and a boat came slopping through the flotsam and took me on.

There was ice on the deck and I nearly did a pratfall but they grabbed me and I shook them off, small thanks: I was fed-up because one arm wouldn't work any more and with the two windows smashed the cold had been paralysing.

"I've sent for the ship's doctor," first thing he said.

"Oh, Christ, what are you doing here?" I wasn't in the mood to talk and he'd want me to do that.

"We were worried about you."

I couldn't get him into focus, things looked dim here, touch of snow blindness all that way behind the shifting lights. He said: "I thought I'd come along."

"Well, it won't do your chilblains any good."

"Is he all right?" someone asked, gold braid, I supposed this was his cabin.

"I'm bloody tired, don't you ever get tired?" They were trying to pull the glove off but it was stuck. "Listen, what happened?" The only stations I could find on the car thing had been jammed.

"We're waiting for news ourselves. It's all rather confused, still, but we know the tanks didn't go in."

"Well, they couldn't, could they? Whole idea, wasn't it?" Someone said we'll have to cut it away, I could smell ether, sleeve as well, they said, very dim in here, lying on something now. "Back, right?"

"I didn't quite catch that," leaning over me.

Effort, come on, I want to know.

"Did Merrick get back all right?"

"Ah, yes indeed, we met the plane. You looked after him splendidly, I'm really most grateful. Most grateful."